A gentlewoman should
freedom wi

THE RULES (AC

Some rules should be broken.

TWEEDIE'S RESPONSE

"My reputation?" Dara repeated. She lifted her pert nose. "My reputation is fine. No one saw me leave the ballroom."

"Said many a young woman who found herself ruined."

Dara did not like being contradicted, especially with common sense. She made a dismissive sound. "Am I in danger from you, sir? Are you going to kiss me?"

There was that word *kiss* again.

And suddenly, it seemed like something Michael might wish to do. Just for curiosity's sake, he told himself—except, that wasn't true. Dara fascinated him. She had from the moment she'd confronted him in the Supper Room. She was bold, unabashedly loyal, and vibrantly engaged in life with her schemes and her dreams. She was the Lanscarr he looked forward to seeing when he called.

The one he'd enjoy in his bed.

Also by Cathy Maxwell

The Logical Man's Guide to Dangerous Women

His Lessons on Love
Her First Desire
His Secret Mistress

The Spinster Heiresses

The Duke That I Marry
A Match Made in Bed
If Ever I Should Love You

Marrying the Duke

A Date at the Altar
The Fairest of Them All
The Match of the Century

The Brides of Wishmore

The Groom Says Yes
The Bride Says Maybe
The Bride Says No

The Chattan Curse

The Devil's Heart
The Scottish Witch
Lyon's Bride

The Seduction of Scandal
His Christmas Pleasure
The Marriage Ring
The Earl Claims His Wife
A Seduction at Christmas
In the Highlander's Bed
Bedding the Heiress
In the Bed of a Duke
The Price of Indiscretion
Temptation of a Proper Governess
The Seduction of an English Lady
Adventures of a Scottish Heiress
The Lady Is Tempted
The Wedding Wager
The Marriage Contract
A Scandalous Marriage
Married in Haste
Because of You
When Dreams Come True
Falling in Love Again
You and No Other
Treasured Vows
All Things Beautiful

A Kiss in the Moonlight

A Gambler's Daughters Novel

CATHY MAXWELL

AVONBOOKS

An Imprint of HarperCollins*Publishers*

This is a work of fiction. Names, characters, places, and incidents are products of the author's imagination or are used fictitiously and are not to be construed as real. Any resemblance to actual events, locales, organizations, or persons, living or dead, is entirely coincidental.

First Avon Books mass market printing: March 2023

Print Edition ISBN: 978-0-06-324117-6
Digital Edition ISBN: 978-0-06-324118-3

Cover design by Amy Halperin
Cover illustration by Juliana Kolesova

FIRST EDITION

23 24 25 26 27 BVGM 10 9 8 7 6 5 4 3 2 1

To the best strategist I know—Cheryl Etchison
I am wealthy in my friends

A Kiss in the Moonlight

CHAPTER ONE

Refuse an offer of marriage with grace and great delicacy.

THE RULES (ACCORDING TO DARA)

Because even boorish men are fragile creatures.

TWEEDIE'S INTERPRETATION

1817

"Hurry, hurry, *hurry,*" Dara Lanscarr chided as she scrambled her way up the wooded hill, trampling bluebells in her mad dash to reach Wiltham House.

"I'm caught!" her sister Elise shouted. Elise was a year younger than Dara's one-and-twenty. It had been years since either of them had run this hard.

Dara turned to see Elise trying to unsnag her hem from the dead wood of a fallen limb. "Tear it," she ordered. "We will repair it later. We have to stop Squire Davies."

"I'm trying," Elise snapped back.

Huffing her impatience, Dara stumbled back down toward her sister, her own skirts in danger of tangling. She deftly unsnagged Elise's hem before grabbing her hand. *"Run."*

Together, the women charged toward the crest of the hill, before stopping to catch their breaths. Below them, the white walls of Wiltham, their family home, shone bright against the dark green of the forest—and their fears had not been unfounded. Squire Davies's bony chestnut was being walked by a stable hand.

"We're too late," Elise said.

"We can't think that way," Dara snapped. "We are going to save Gwendolyn." On that vow, she grabbed her skirts up with one hand and practically dragged her sister down the slope toward the house with the other.

Now she understood why her cousin Richard's wife, Caroline, had insisted she and Elise walk a huge hamper to the crofters on the other side of the property. Richard and Caroline had not shown any interest in the crofters since they moved into Wiltham almost a year ago, when they'd claimed the property for themselves.

Of course, all of this was their father's fault. Captain Sir John Lanscarr had left his three daughters in the care of their grandmother while he traveled with the military and later as a gambler. His vices were well-known to his daughters. They had enjoyed growing up with Gram at Wiltham and had lived for those moments when their father would "pop in," as he liked to call it. He would shower them with attention, make them feel special, and then leave again . . . only he had stopped returning. Or sending letters. Or money.

Upon Gram's death, and learning that it had been close to two years since anyone had heard from Captain Sir John, Richard Lanscarr had gleefully moved his family into Wiltham. He claimed their father must be deceased, and the authorities had agreed. Why else had no one heard from him? And though Dara and her sisters protested, they found themselves living in their childhood home as the guests of their cousin.

Yes, there had been the admonishment that Richard should see to the well-being of Sir John's three daughters, but pigs would fly before their cousin thought of anyone other than himself.

Nor was this hamper gambit his first subterfuge.

The ever-astute Dara had been wary of him from the beginning. She might be the middle sister, but she was her sisters' defender, their strategist. She had promised Gram on her deathbed that she would do all she could for her sisters, and she'd meant those words. She was not afraid to butt heads with Richard. It was her responsibility to do so. Nor would she support his plans to marry Gwendolyn off to some belligerent, barrel-shaped squire with six children. Gwendolyn was made for better things than the likes of Davies, and so Dara had told Richard.

In fact, Dara had a better plan for herself and her sisters, and she didn't want Gwendolyn to accept Squire Davies's proposal before hearing her idea. Oh, no, she did *not*.

Reaching the house's front step, she dropped her skirt, shooting a scowl at the ogling stable hand holding the squire's horse, and charged into the house, Elise at her heels. They were both out of breath, but Dara's anger and determination were enough to carry them forward.

Their butler, Herald, practically jumped at the door being thrown open. "Where are they?" Dara asked in a furious whisper.

Herald had been with the family for close to three decades. He was tall and lean with a head of white hair and a face like a fox. He pointed down the hall to one of Wiltham's many sitting rooms. This one was called the Green Room because of its wall color and was the most formal. Richard and Caroline eavesdropped by the door. They were so intent in their task, they hadn't realized the sisters had returned.

Dara relished the moment. She shot a glance to Elise, who nodded. The Lanscarr sisters *always* stood together. They might have just run almost a mile and have twigs and leaves in their hair, but they had come to save Gwendolyn, and so they would.

They marched down the hall, not bothering to tread lightly. They let Richard know they were here *and* they were angry at his attempt at deception.

Caroline heard them first and gave her husband a wide-eyed nudge. Richard looked up. "No," he said, moving forward, followed by his mousy wife. "You will not destroy this. Davies is a good match."

"For a fishwife," Dara flashed back.

"He's respected—" Richard started.

"By whom?" Dara interrupted. She never hesitated to be forthright, and she knew how to throw her cousins into a tizzy, which was what she was doing now . . . so that Elise could sneak around them, open the Green Room door, and walk right in.

"Gwendolyn," Elise called sunnily in greeting. "Oh, Squire Davies, I didn't know you were here. Am I interrupting anything?"

Richard was the one who answered. He stormed to the door, his arms flung wide in fury. "You certainly are interrupting. Out of here—"

Dara slipped under his outstretched arm and into the room, even as she felt the wind stir as he reached to stop her.

She quickly summed up the situation. Squire Davies was proposing, as they had suspected. Gwendolyn leaned back as far as she could on a threadbare settee while the squire held her hand in that limp manner of his. "I requested privacy," he complained to Richard. "I haven't asked her for the honor of—"

"*No one* told us you were calling today, sir," Dara cut in with loud cheerfulness, pretending to be *delighted* to see him. "We would *all* have been waiting for you if we'd known."

"R-Richard knew—" he stuttered and then shot a frown at their cousin.

"Did he? He didn't mention it." Dara marched to the settee and squeezed herself between the squire and Gwendolyn, forcing him to let go of her hand. Gwendolyn's expression was a mixture of relief and . . . what? Resignation? Fear?

Dara knew Gwendolyn believed she must do something to help their lot. Richard and Caroline were overbearing and thoughtless. They had been doing everything in their power to make the sisters and their great-aunt Tweedie feel unwelcome in their own home. However, becoming Squire Davies's wife was not a solution.

Before the world had believed their father dead and back when Gram was alive, the Lanscarr sisters had been lauded as the Beauties of County Wicklow. That they lived in the stately Wiltham was enough to attract suitors, especially those with the mistaken belief they had huge dowries.

Furthermore, they also had good looks. Gwendolyn's hair was the rich color of a blackbird's wing. Intelligence sparkled in her golden-brown eyes. She had an exquisite figure with enough height to meet most men's gazes. In fact, she had to look down quite a bit at Squire Davies.

Most notable was her delicate, aloof manner, which spoke of excellent breeding. Their father had met Gwendolyn's mother when he served in the Indies. Sir John had never tired of lauding the beauty of his late first wife—and Gwendolyn obviously favored her mother. The marriage had come with a plantation that Sir John had gambled away shortly after his wife's death.

He'd then brought Gwendolyn to Ireland, where he'd met and courted Lydia Walsh, the heiress of Wiltham. Their marriage had given him the manor house and two more daughters, Dara and Elise, but then tragedy struck. Lydia had died of childbed fever. That baby, a boy, had died with her. Sir John had not married again. He claimed he was unlucky in love. Instead, he had supposedly dedicated himself to his military career, and later his enjoyment of gambling, while leaving all three daughters in the care of their beloved Gram, Katherine Walsh.

Gram had doted on all of them, but especially Elise, whom she had claimed took after their mother. Elise was a golden beauty whose shy smile stopped men in their tracks. Even women couldn't help but stare when she passed. Her cheeks were rose-tinted, her skin clear and unblemished. When she turned the full force of her almond-shaped eyes on a person, she usually received whatever she wanted.

Elise was almost as tall as Gwendolyn. "A proud woman like my Lydia," Gram had been fond of saying. Gram had also claimed Elise had Lydia's spirit. "I could never tell that child what to do, and Elise is exactly like her."

Fortunately, Elise was rather oblivious to all the attention she attracted, especially from men. "They are so shallow," she complained on many occasions. She'd rather read than accept callers. She claimed, quite rightly, that reading was vastly more entertaining.

In contrast to her beautiful sisters was . . . Dara.

She was the petite one in the family. The one who always had to stand on a stool to reach things. Her hair was brown, like their father's, with some strands of her mother's gold but not enough to matter. Her figure lacked Gwendolyn's grace or Elise's buxom perfection.

She had blue eyes, but hers lacked any memorable quality. It wasn't that her features weren't pleasant enough. If she were a member of any other family, she would have been considered quite lovely. However, her sisters were spectacular.

What did set Dara apart was her ability to think through a situation. She had guided her sisters ever since Gram died. She was the one who had big dreams for her little family—and she wasn't going to let Gwendolyn sacrifice herself by accepting an offer from the squire.

Not when she had a better idea in mind.

"Elise, Gwendolyn," she said, "please, go find Tweedie." Tweedie was Gram's sister, Dame Eleanor Roberson, who had lived with them at Wiltham for the past decade. "She will enjoy knowing Squire Davies is here."

"I did not wish to call on Dame Eleanor—" the squire started.

"No, you did not," Dara agreed. Her sisters had already escaped the room, using one of the Green Room's many doorways. "So sorry. I should have known. But then, I can't call them back now. They've already gone for her."

"Dara," Richard bit her name out. "You were not invited here. Squire Davies requested a moment alone—"

"Not invited? Here? In my own house?" Dara pulled a face as if Richard was being silly.

"You know what he means," Caroline replied.

"I believe I should leave," a highly insulted squire said.

"No, don't take off," Richard said, even as Dara spoke over him.

"Farewell. Lovely to see you." On those words, without waiting for an answer, Dara turned on her heel and left the room, following the path she knew her sisters had taken. She found them on the second floor, standing in front of Tweedie's room.

"Richard locked her in," Gwendolyn said. "That is why she wasn't down there to help me ward off the squire. We don't have a key to let her out."

"Let me see." Dara pulled a wire pin from her thick hair. She bent over the lock, and in less than a blink, there was a click.

"You need to teach me how you do that," Elise said.

Dara opened the door. "Tweedie?"

Their great-aunt was sitting by the window. She had her blackthorn walking cane beside her. Her expression was one of foreboding. "Is it done? Did Richard force you to marry that lout? We had such an argument, and then he locked me in." For being in her seventies, Tweedie was still spry and had all her mental faculties. She was how Dara imagined a leprechaun to be—feisty and sly. She never held back her opinion, and Dara adored her.

Gwendolyn knelt beside their aunt. "Richard said you were in the Green Room, asking for me. When I went in there, Caroline was waiting with the squire—" Her voice broke off. "I knew why he'd come. And I thought maybe I should marry him. Then you, Dara, and Elise would have a place to live without worrying about Richard's threats to send us to the poorhouse."

"I'd like to see him try," Dara replied.

"The county would be up in arms," Elise predicted.

"But we need a place to live," Gwendolyn said. "One where I know you both will have opportunities to find good husbands. We can't trust Richard. I need to protect you."

"So, you would marry the squire?" Elise asked, doubtful.

"For you two I would," the ever-sweet Gwendolyn answered.

"You do realize that if you marry the squire, you will have to see him naked?" Elise questioned. "I wouldn't want that sight in my mind."

"Exactly," Dara said, adding her own shudder. "It is too much of a sacrifice to ask of you, Gwennie."

"But we must do something," Gwendolyn said. "Caroline and Richard want us gone."

"Wiltham is *our* home," Elise said. "It belonged to our mother's family."

"True, but it became Father's possession once they married. It always will go to the next male in line no matter who lives under its roof," Gwendolyn reminded her. "We have no claim."

"It is not fair," Elise answered. "Women should have the right to own property in spite of a husband."

"And if wishes were horses, beggars would ride," Tweedie answered.

Elise practically growled her frustration, and Dara knew the time had come for her to speak. "I have a suggestion," she announced. "Why don't we go to London for the Season and find ourselves dukes to marry?"

"What?" Gwendolyn said, as if not hearing Dara correctly.

"The Season?" Elise repeated.

"How?" Tweedie wondered.

"We just go." Dara sat on the edge of Tweedie's bed. "I've researched the idea."

"Researched?" Elise asked.

"All of those papers from London I've been collecting?" Dara reminded her. For the last six months, Dara had pleaded with neighbors and acquaintances for any London papers they might have received. "I believe we can let a house, and with Tweedie as our chaperone, we can participate in the Marriage Market."

Her sisters looked at her as if she had lost all good sense. They knew what the Marriage Market was. During the London Social Season, families from all over Britain would bring their eligible daughters to show off at balls and events with the hope of finding an even more eligible husband for them.

"But don't you have to know someone of consequence to be invited?" Gwendolyn asked.

"Or be part of the *ton*?" Elise wondered, using the word for those who were members of the highest ranks of society.

"Oh, please," Dara said, annoyed. "We are young women of consequence. Father was knighted for serving his king brilliantly." She wasn't certain that was true. Their father was a bit of a ne'er-do-well, and many had wondered how he'd managed a knighthood. "Also, our mother was related to the Duke of Marlborough."

"Distantly related," Elise reminded her.

"Related is related," Dara assured her airily. "She was the second cousin to the Marchioness of Blandford, who is the duke's daughter by marriage. There. *Related.*"

"But they don't know us," Gwendolyn said. "What are we going to do? Show up on their doorstep and beg an invitation to their next party?"

"Of course not. That is not how it is done," Dara answered knowledgably. After all, she'd been studying this for some time. She had even been compiling a list of the rules of Society. "We will send them a letter of introduction. Then they will invite us to pay a call. Finally, after we have met them, they will invite us to a ball. It is all so clear and simple."

Elise lifted a skeptical eyebrow. "It is?"

"It is," Dara assured her. "The duke will introduce us to other dukes, and then we marry. Oh, don't make those faces. It has happened before.

Have you not heard of the Gunning sisters?" She knew they hadn't, and it gave her great pleasure to share. "They were poor but genteel young Irish ladies—*like ourselves*. They had nothing but their looks and their wits—*like ourselves*. They went to London and ended up marrying important noblemen and becoming great ladies—*just as we can*."

"Could we meet these sisters?" Gwendolyn asked. "Perhaps they could help us?"

"There were two sisters, and they are no longer alive. However, if they could fly high, even several decades ago, why can't the Lanscarr sisters?"

Elise looked to Tweedie. "Did you know these Gunning sisters when you lived in London?"

"I can't say I did," Tweedie admitted. "But I have heard of them. One of them had just died when Sir Phillip and I moved to London. They married very well."

"See?" Dara said, using Tweedie's verification to support her idea. "Bold women reap rewards. We can capture the hearts of the *ton*. All three of us could marry dukes."

Gwendolyn frowned. "Dara, how would we travel to London, let alone rent a house? That takes money."

"And what of clothes?" Elise wished to know.

Dara took Elise's question first. It was the simplest to answer. "We know how to handle a needle. We have been making our own dresses and refashioning them for different Assemblies for years. We will do it there."

That made sense to Elise.

Gwendolyn's question was more of a challenge.

Money.

Dara folded her hands in her lap. She needed Gwendolyn's support to make her plan work. "I've made an accounting of how much we would need for one Season, which should be ample time for us to find suitable dukes to marry." She drew a deep breath and dropped the concerning news. "We can do it for four hundred pounds. We could even," she hurried to add as she watched Gwendolyn's eyes widen and Elise almost fall off the stool she'd sat on, "manage to be highly respectable for three hundred. That is for the whole Season, including lodging, servants, and whatnots."

"Three *hundred* pounds?" Elise repeated in disbelief.

Gwendolyn shook her head. "Sometimes, Dara, your imagination makes you nonsensical. We only have thirty-four pounds between us. Remember?"

She did. They had taken an accounting last week when Richard had announced he was going to let some of Wiltham's servants go. He might have claimed the estate as their father's heir, but that did not mean he could afford it. He'd imagined there had been coffers of money that would come into his possession. The Lanscarr sisters had laughed and laughed over that one. No gambler of their father's stature let money lie around untended.

Of course, Richard's announcement had sobered them quickly.

The sisters had been determined to do what they could to help their faithful servants. They had fifty pounds because their grandmother had been a great one for hiding money. When Richard and Caroline had first arrived to take over the house, the sisters had gone in search of every shilling they could find. Gwendolyn guarded the money in a carved wooden box with a secret compartment.

The sisters had divvied up some of that for the leaving servants. The balance was thirty-four pounds.

Thirty-four pounds was not a small amount. It could support them in a tidy cottage for a year, maybe two if they were very frugal.

But Dara didn't want to live in a cottage, two years wasn't a lifetime, and she knew their days were numbered under Richard's roof. If Squire Davies couldn't succeed, their cousin would find other men to marry them off to.

So Dara spoke with a confidence she wasn't certain she felt. "I believe we can turn our thirty-four pounds into three hundred pounds." For a second there was a startled silence. Dara nodded, knowing she had their full attention, and then she announced her plan. "Gwendolyn gambles for it."

They all stared at Dara as if they were waiting for more explanation. And then Gwendolyn declared, "You are jesting."

Elise burst out laughing before saying, "This is your plan? Sending Gwen to the gaming tables? And you being such a stickler for manners?"

Dara had also expected them to balk at her solution. They lacked her imagination. Therefore, it was up to her to help them embrace the idea.

"I have thought this out very carefully, I assure you. Father said highborn ladies gamble all the time. Remember?" She looked to her sisters for confirmation. Elise's brows came together in puzzled concern, Gwendolyn was withholding judgment, and Tweedie appeared fascinated.

Dara stood and began pacing as she continued briskly, "He also said that few could match Gwendolyn's luck at games of chance, especially faro. Remember how many twigs she won whenever we played with Father?"

"But twigs are not money," Gwendolyn pointed out.

"Dear sister, have faith in your abilities. Father was a renowned gambler. Remember his coming home with his arms loaded with presents? That happened more than once—"

"Perhaps twice?" Elise observed.

Dara ignored her. "And he *always* praised

your talent, Gwennie. He said you had his own luck. That you 'sensed' the cards. Besides, what else are we going to do?" She paused, meeting her sisters' gazes with a solemn one of her own. "Stay here? Marry Squire Davies? Or Mr. Bellamy, the innkeeper? Or, considering how desperately Richard wishes to be rid of us, Patrick Lynch, the pig farmer? Don't worry. He'll save Lynch for me."

Then she made her plea. "But what if my plan works? What if Gwendolyn *could* use her talent to win three hundred pounds, even six hundred pounds, and we take ourselves off to London? What if we introduce ourselves to Lady Blandford, who supposedly was very fond of Mother and even sent a note of condolence when she died? Gram saved it. That was how important that note—and the connection—was. What if Lady Blandford sponsors us into the highest ranks of society? And we meet dukes who are *young* and *handsome* and *wealthy*?"

She paused to let her questions sink in before adding, "Even if *none* of that happens, we are still better off than being under Richard's thumb. His resentment will make our lives miserable."

Dara looked hopefully at her sisters. "Come with me on this adventure. I don't wish to marry Patrick Lynch. The body sounds he makes even in public, such as at the last Assembly dance, are embarrassing."

Her sisters had gone very quiet.

Dara prayed they were considering her words and realizing they must try or be doomed to—what? Losing their birthrights? Unfortunately, that had already happened the moment Richard had claimed the house. They would have to rebuild someway, somehow.

And then help came from another source.

"I think we should do it," Tweedie announced.

All three sisters gave a start of surprise. Tweedie stood, leaning on her walking stick. "Dara is right. There is nothing for you here. Or for me."

"You will be with us," Dara assured her. "You are our chaperone. Besides, you have been to London, and we haven't."

"Oh, aye, but it was decades ago. But what a wicked city. I had a wonderful time. Then I returned home," Tweedie concluded with a sigh.

"There are so many risks," Gwendolyn said. "Too many."

"There are risks to everything," Tweedie said. "I wonder some days if I will climb out of bed without breaking my neck, but that doesn't mean I stay under my covers."

"We'd be doing this *alone*," Gwendolyn said.

"Yes," Dara agreed. "Just the three of us and Tweedie, which is how it has been since Father and Gram died."

"Do you really believe he is dead?" Elise asked. "I don't. He can't be. Wouldn't we have been informed? Expected to fetch his body or something?"

Dara and Gwendolyn exchanged glances. They'd had this discussion before. Elise really wished to believe he was alive.

Gwendolyn answered, not unkindly, "I think he has been gone for longer than he usually stayed away."

There was a long moment of silence.

Gwendolyn broke it. "There is a club in Dublin that Father frequented, the Devil's Hand. He said the play was good there, and I believe it was one of his favorite haunts. I say we go there."

"You'll do it?" Dara was both stunned and triumphant. Dublin was the next county over. It couldn't be that hard to reach. She'd never visited, but why not now?

"Of course," her older sister answered. "I have to save you from Patrick Lynch and his body noises . . . and myself from Squire Davies and all of those children." But there was no triumph in her voice. Instead, her shoulders slumped, and she whispered, "If we fail, I would never forgive myself if anything happened to you, Elise, or Tweedie."

"My dear," Tweedie said, "what if you *succeed*? Why, the three of you haven't even been to Dublin, let alone London. You have barely traveled across County Wicklow. Isn't it high time you took a risk?"

"Exactly," Dara agreed. "And don't we owe it to ourselves to at least *try* for a better life? Are we not our father's daughters?"

"Richard will want to stop us," Elise warned. Then she added with a sly smile, "We'd best sneak out tonight."

She was right. They needed to act before reason cooled their desire for action. And just like that, Dara's plan was set into motion.

Chapter Two

A lady should always have a care for her reputation.
The Rules (according to Dara)

Until she marries, and then she can be herself.
Tweedie's promise

Dublin

Beckett Steele stooped to enter under the door of the Devil's Hand. He never worried about what he might have to deal with in disreputable establishments such as this. He was big enough and strong enough to solve any situation. Especially unsavory ones.

Unfortunately, he was tired. It had been a long, trying day of travel and walking the streets. He was searching for Bartholomew Tarrant, a wealthy Chester merchant's son who had stolen from his father and then run for Ireland. Tarrant was a gambler, an unlucky one, and his father wanted him returned before all the money was gone.

Young Tarrant obviously believed Dublin was

far away from his father's strict hand. He was wrong. Especially since his father had hired Beck.

Beck always caught his quarry. He took pride in his prowess. No one escaped when he was on the hunt.

The Devil's Hand was like all the others of its kind. It smelled of men and stale ale. Tallow candles sent black smoke toward the ceiling and gave off a hazy yellow light. There was nothing fancy about the place. Men didn't need pictures on the walls, decent furnishings or even a clean floor to have their pockets emptied out.

Beck had been told the play was fast and hard at the Hand. A fortune could be made or lost in an hour. If that wasn't something to attract a foolish merchant's son, Beck didn't know what was.

Well, that wasn't true. There were the brothels. If Beck failed to find the fool here, or the few other gaming hells left, then he'd have to start combing through them. Beck grumbled under his breath. He was becoming too weary for this nonsense, no matter how well it paid.

His plan was to poke his head into the Devil's Hand, look for Tarrant's red hair, and move on to the next—until he came upon a sight that upended his plans.

Hazard was Tarrant's game. But no one gathered around the hazard table. To his surprise, it was empty.

Instead, everyone, including the serving wenches, were crowded at least three deep around another large table on the other side of the room. No one was paying attention to the door or to two drink-bitten men helping themselves to the ale keg. They poured it down their gullets as fast as they could.

Beck frowned, trying to make sense of it all. The crowd around the table shifted, and then thoughts of red-headed Tarrant vanished at the sight of a dark specter of a woman sitting amongst the faro players.

She was dressed all in black from the top of her head to the floor. Even her gloves were black. A mourning veil fell over a velvet hat and to her lap, hiding her face from view . . . and yet there was no doubt that she was young—and possibly beautiful.

Isn't that the way men's imaginations worked? They always assumed beauty. Beck's mind was no different. He moved toward the table, his earlier fatigue forgotten. Instead, he had a new quarry. *Her.*

Best of all, she was no common doxy. Her back was straight, her head held high, her movements graceful.

He watched, mesmerized. Everything about her from the trimness of her figure to the way she tilted her head before placing her coin on the cards spoke of Quality.

Quality.

What the devil was she doing here?

The faro dealer had the look of a weasel. He had a sharp nose, flaring nostrils, and narrow eyes trained on her. Did she realize the danger she was in? How any one of these gents would have her skirts over her head in a blink given the opportunity? And the Weasel would happily lead the way.

Beck watched the next play. Faro was a simple, but fast, game. There were thirteen cards on the table, faceup, ace through king. Players placed their bets on which card they believed the dealer would draw from his deck next. The suits did not matter. The game was about the numbers.

The Weasel drew two cards. The first was the losing card or the "banker's" card. Any wagers placed on that number were immediately claimed by the dealer.

The second card was the winning card. Whoever placed a coin on it had his wager matched by the bank. In this house, there was also a win for the player with a wager on the highest card *above* the banker's card. The odds to make money were good.

Except the woman was not winning.

Beck didn't know how much she had brought to the table, but the stack of coins in front of her was quickly dwindling—especially since the Weasel was cheating. The dealer deck had probably been stacked. The Weasel would let her win one, and then lose the next rounds. Did the other men know what was afoot? Beck pictured them as buzzards, waiting to see what they might pick off in this duel between the Weasel and his unwitting victim. They played but they were waiting for something to happen, and who knew what they might win then? It was obvious they all lusted for the woman in black, their prurient imaginations picturing a host of crude desires.

Beck was not one to ignore an innocent. He knew too well the pain of being deceived. She didn't belong here. She wasn't one of their ilk, and he could only wonder at what desperate or reckless measures had drawn her to this table.

His quest for the merchant's son was pushed aside. She was far more interesting.

Besides, he'd been searching for a woman like her, one who could help him exact vengeance.

Unfortunately, first he must help her.

Beck stood back, waiting for his opportunity.

THE FARO PLAYED at this table was faster than what Gwendolyn had ever enjoyed at home with her father.

The banker was quicker. There was no pausing to count out coins, or, as in her childhood games, twigs. He claimed money and handed it out with hardly a blink, and then the game was on again.

At first, Gwendolyn had believed she was keeping up. She won several hands. But that had apparently been luck, because after rapidly gaining, she was even more rapidly losing. At one point, she'd taken her thirty-four pounds up to at least a hundred. Now she was down to fifteen pounds and in danger of losing it all.

Perhaps her nerves had gotten the better of her. Her mind, which had always been quick to remember the cards, was failing her.

Worse, she was failing her sisters. They waited in an inn some distance away for her return. They had wanted to come with her, but she wouldn't let them. She preferred knowing they were safe with Herald, the family butler, who had decided to join them on their adventure. He had promised Gwendolyn to watch over them and Tweedie.

Besides, she'd reasoned, in even the worst areas of Ireland, a woman dressed in widow's weeds was safe.

Well, except for the Devil's Hand.

Gwendolyn rubbed the coin between her gloved fingers. She was sweating beneath her heavy mourning garb. The disguise had been another of Dara's ideas. Gwendolyn was deeply thankful no one could recognize her. Yes, Father had claimed that genteel ladies gambled, but did they in Dublin?

The men were practically eating her with their eyes. Did her disguise make her more alluring? Or were they like birds of prey, always waiting, always hungry—

"Are you in this round, Mrs. Bunsaway?" the dealer prodded. He spoke politely, and yet she had the sense there was a private jest going on among the men, one in which she was the source of amusement.

She also wished she'd picked a different name than Mrs. Bunsaway.

In truth, she hadn't thought of using a fake name. The need for it hadn't struck her until she'd first walked into the Devil's Hand. The faro dealer, a man they called Darby, had rushed up to her, pulling her in and demanding her name.

Gwendolyn had known better than to say Lanscarr, but she wished she and her sisters hadn't overlooked this detail. She had pulled the name Bunsaway out of the air, and a silly one it was. It had been her first mistake, among others.

"Mrs. Bunsaway?" Darby prodded. "We are waiting."

Gwendolyn lowered her hands to her lap, almost afraid to touch the few coins in front of her. She was treacherously close to losing it all. Her sisters trusted her to be wise. They still needed to pay for their room at the inn.

She cleared her throat. It was hard to speak

around the heaviness of failure growing in her chest. "I will sit this round out."

Actually, she would leave. That is what she wanted to do. She'd run, and perhaps once she was outside where she could take a decent breath, she could get her courage back . . . or not. She'd ruined them, and their only hope was for her to return to Wiltham House and marry Mr. Davies.

Dear God, Elise was right—Gwendolyn did not want to see him naked.

Other players had sat rounds out and Darby had gone on with his business. He didn't this time. He gave her a feral smile. "Come, Mrs. Bunsaway, your luck will change. Trust us to see you through."

As if on command, the men around her seemed to press forward, leaning toward her.

Abruptly, she stood. "I can't . . . play." Dear Lord, she felt as if she might swoon. Lanscarr women never had feminine vapors. They were a robust lot.

But then, no one had ever failed her family the way Gwendolyn had.

She turned, ready to shove her way through the men fawning around her when Darby caught her gloved wrist, his fingers long, white, and meaty. "Don't run. Terms can be worked out. And you will like me. I can make a woman like you happy. *Very* happy."

Gwendolyn wasn't quite certain what he meant, until the guffaws rose around her, then she understood exactly what he was saying.

She attempted to pull her hand away. Darby tried to tighten his hold. She slid her hand out of the glove. Too late, he realized what she was doing and found himself holding the empty glove. Gwendolyn gave a sharp elbow to the man closest to her and grabbed what was left of her money off the table. The man jumped back with a yelp. Holding her veil close to her face, she pushed her way free, not caring if her sturdy walking shoes stomped on toes. In fact, she hoped they did.

And then she was away from the close cluster around the table. She wanted to run from this place, but then stopped.

The terrible image of her sisters back at the inn waiting, all their hopes on her, glued her feet to the floor.

What was she going to say to them? What *could* she say? That she'd failed? That she'd had a change of heart and couldn't wait to be Mr. Davies's wife? That they'd been foolish to let themselves believe Dara's scheme had a chance? It wasn't fair to blame Dara—

"You aren't a bad player," a deep male voice, an *English* voice, said from behind her. "You shouldn't leave."

Gwendolyn glanced over her shoulder, and then almost stumbled back in shock.

The man was the size of a barn. Tall, broad-shouldered . . . and very good-looking under his wide brimmed hat. He wore buff riding breeches, his boots were good but dirty, and any dandy would envy the number of capes to his coat.

How could she not have noticed him earlier? His jaw was lean, although in need of shaving. His nose was straight except for a small bump where it might have been broken. His eyes were like shards of blue glass, and he looked at her as if he noticed every detail.

"If I was a decent player, I would have more money in my hand."

"Yes, but the Weasel was cheating."

The blunt statement broke through her stressed senses. "Cheating?"

She whirled to frown at the dealer. Darby glanced up, caught her looking at him and, with a lecherous grin, curled his finger, begging her to return to the table. He disgusted her. When she turned away, he cackled.

"I'd believed this was a good house," she said, more to herself than the stranger.

He gave a short laugh. "It is a gambling den. Of course they cheat."

"But that is not fair."

"That is why it is called cheating," he replied reasonably.

"I trusted them . . ." She broke off, amazed at her own culpability. Her games with her father had been innocent and fun, but hadn't she caught him cheating a time or two?

A new truth was borne home.

Perhaps her father had let her win? And she had no talent at all?

"Oh, God." Her words were a prayer. What had she and her sisters done?

She needed to leave. Now, while she had enough money to return her little family to Wicklow—

"You could use a benefactor." The stranger's words cut into her fears. "And not," he added quickly, "for a bedding."

Gwendolyn blinked at the word. Yes, of course, that was what Darby wanted. She was just put off by the stranger's bluntness. "I—I don't know what to say."

His sharp gaze assessed her. And then he held out his hand. He wore black gloves. Riding gloves. Worn ones. "I solve problems."

She didn't touch his hand. This was not a drawing room. Dara's rules held no sway here. "What does that mean?"

"It means nothing. I'm stating a fact. It is what I do."

"Like some oracle?"

A dimple appeared at the corner of his mouth as if she'd caught him off guard. "I don't deal in riddles."

"What problem are you solving this evening?"

"I'm hunting for someone."

"Hunting?"

He shrugged. "Searching," he corrected.

"For a price, I assume."

"A man must live."

She narrowed her gaze. "Why are you telling me this?"

"Because you have a problem." He nodded to the coins in Gwendolyn's hand. "This is not the sort of place for a woman like you. You are here for a reason, probably a desperate one."

"Go on," she said, not wishing to confirm or deny his assumptions.

"You are a good player. You know what you are doing. I suppose you track the cards." He didn't wait for an answer. "That's a gift and one that any gaming hell would wish to stop, but it is fair."

That is what she'd thought.

"I propose we return to the table. I will have a word with the Weasel—"

"The who?"

"The dealer."

"Oh, Darby." She had to smile. "'Weasel' is a good name for him."

"I suggest we continue to call him that."

His calm matter-of-factness with its hint of humor eased some of the tightness in her chest. Then she realized she had another problem. "I've lost almost all my money. I need what is left to see myself home."

"I will loan you money."

Her guard went up again. "At what price?"

"Not the one you are thinking."

Gwendolyn didn't believe him. Or trust him. He was too—well, too *everything*. Too handsome. Too certain of himself. Too glib.

"I'm leaving," she said, and would have walked out except he hooked his hand in her elbow, turning her to him. She startled at the jolt of energy in his touch.

He noticed—or perhaps felt it, too? He let go, then raised a palm as if showing that he wasn't playing any tricks. "Don't give up on yourself."

She lifted her chin. "I'm not. I'm also not selling myself."

He shook his head. "I feared you would place the worst notion to my offer. Then again, those other lads were very clear about what they wanted. I'm not like them."

"You aren't?" Gwendolyn didn't hide her doubts.

"Of course not. I want to see you have a fair chance." He paused and then added, "I would also like to teach the Weasel a lesson. I hate seeing the green ones fleeced. You have the talent to teach him manners."

Gwendolyn would like to do that very much. She was tired of being pushed around by callous men like Richard, and even her father, the man who disappeared. So she was tempted . . .

"If I play with your money, what will you expect in return? Especially if I lose?"

"My terms?"

"Every lender has them."

Triumph lit his eyes as if he knew she would swallow the lure. "I'll loan you the money and if you lose it, I'll not demand to be repaid, if that is your fear."

"If I win?"

"It is all yours. However, someday I will ask a favor. A *small* favor and one where your skirts will stay right where they are."

Gwendolyn frowned, and then thought of having another chance. "What is this favor?"

He put his hands in his coat pockets and shook his head. "I don't know—yet. It is only an idea. Perhaps I will not need your help at all. But when and *if* I ask, I expect you to say yes."

This was not something she should agree to, and yet she and her sisters had wagered everything on her success this night. "How much money are you offering?"

He pulled a leather bag from the deep pockets of his coat. "Fifty pounds more or less?" He shrugged as if such a large sum was nothing to him.

Then again, he was a gambler. They were having this discussion in a gaming house. One thing her father had taught her was that men who gambled had very little respect for money. What was lost today could be earned back tomorrow.

And if her father was in her shoes?

He'd take the money and keep playing. Because the other option would be to return to Wicklow.

She glanced over to the table. The Weasel was going about his business, but he had his eye on her. He winked and nodded to her still-empty chair. Several men who were not playing watched her hungrily. They thought she was fair game.

"You can stop him from cheating?" she asked.

"Of course."

Gwendolyn faced him. She'd become accustomed to his extraordinary looks. He no longer dazzled her eyes. Instead, she noticed the rough edges. Life was more complicated for him than he wished the world to know.

"If I don't win," she said, more to herself than to him, "I shouldn't owe you a favor."

"You'll win. Your pride won't let you fail a second time." Then he lowered his voice. "Furthermore, I will be beside you."

"And you are?"

"Steele," he answered, with a slight courtly bow. "Beckett Steele."

The name meant nothing to her, although it fit him.

"And you are?" he asked in return.

"Mrs. Bunsaway," the Weasel hollered from across the room. "Come play." Snickering followed his words.

She wanted to destroy every man at that table who laughed at her. She straightened her back with resolve and replied, "You heard him. I'm Mrs. Bunsaway." This time she didn't cringe about the name. It was her protection. "And I am ready to give the Weasel a lesson he won't forget. We have a bargain, Mr. Steele." She held out her hand to shake.

The hint of a smile softened his lips as he shook her hand, her gloveless hand, and then he placed the purse in it. The soft leather molded to her palm.

This was so much money.

He offered his arm. "Are you ready to reclaim your seat at the table as the Weasel suggests?"

Her answer was to place her hand in the crook of his elbow.

CHAPTER THREE

It is never acceptable for a genteel woman to owe money to a stranger.
THE RULES (ACCORDING TO DARA)

A woman must do what she must to survive.
TWEEDIE'S ADDENDUM

Her father had always claimed Gwendolyn had a talent for cards, and she'd believed him.

"However, you are different from me," he had assured her. "You are lucky, but you also have an uncanny sense of which card will be played. That knowing is a gift."

It hadn't been tonight, and she'd been confused. She'd feared her gift had deserted her. Now that she knew the dealer had been cheating, she wanted redemption.

Approaching the table with a man as commanding as Mr. Steele gave her confidence.

The Weasel—such a good name for Darby—was not pleased to see her with Mr. Steele. He stopped making payouts as he eyed her champion with annoyance. "You could have chosen a better protector, Mrs. Bunsaway. Just because a man is big doesn't mean he is *big*." He grabbed his crotch to show what he meant.

Gwendolyn was thankful her veil hid her blushing. His crudeness made her all the more determined to beat him.

She took the chair that the Weasel had been saving for her. Mr. Steele claimed the seat next to hers by tapping the man in it on the shoulder. When the man looked up, Mr. Steele lifted one brow, and that was all that was needed for the man to scurry away.

With both of them settled, Gwendolyn said, "Mr. Steele has informed me that you have been *cheating*."

"I've never cheated in my life," the Weasel claimed. "Have I, lads?" His question was met with silence. The Weasel didn't need confirmation. He preferred the sound of his own voice. "It sounds to me, Mrs. Bunsaway, as if you are a poor loser."

Before Gwendolyn could react to that outrageous statement, Mr. Steele smoothly injected himself into the conversation. "Then you will gladly change the deck of cards in the box in front of you."

The Weasel tapped the top of the box with the dirty nail of his index finger, but he didn't move to comply. Tension filled the room, and not just from the dealer. Those gathered around the table seemed to be choosing sides. Mr. Steele could no doubt handle himself with a few of them, but all of them? Gwendolyn didn't want to see that happen, especially since she needed to play. She'd promised her sisters at least three hundred pounds.

"Or," she said, "you may let us see the deck in your box. Then we will all know the truth." She'd once heard her father say such a thing in a story he was telling one of his companions. He hadn't realized his daughters were hanging on his every word. Gwendolyn hadn't truly realized what her father had meant until this moment. "I may not be the only one you've attempted to deceive."

The other gamblers at the table turned their scowls on the Weasel as if they were just realizing he could have been cheating them as well.

The Weasel glared at Gwendolyn as if he wished he could make her disappear in a puff of smoke. Then he muttered, "Lass grabs herself a man and has gone saucy." He punctuated the statement with a snort of contempt.

He also reached for another deck.

Before he could put it in the box, one of the other players said, "Perhaps you should spread it out."

The Weasel glared at him. The player leaned back on his chair legs. "What? I've been losing money, too. Come on, Darby. Run a fair table."

"Yes, Darby, run a fair table," Mr. Steele echoed sardonically.

With an angry growl, the Weasel spread the cards out, barely giving anyone a chance to look at them before he swept them up again. Oh, he had good sleight of hand. Only John Lanscarr could have spread the cards that quickly. However, Mr. Steele was satisfied. "Let's play."

"Are you in the game?" Darby challenged him.

"The lady will be playing my hands." There was a beat of silence, and then Mr. Steele said quietly, almost pleasantly, "I hate cheaters."

A few of the men eyed Mr. Steele nervously as if they were glad they weren't in the Weasel's position.

The play began.

Gwendolyn took off her remaining glove. She opened and closed her fingers before deciding where to place her bets. She expected to lose these first few rounds. The deck was fresh. She needed to see how the cards were going.

However, an hour later, she had a sizeable stack of coins in front of her, and this was only a portion of her winnings. Elise had sewn deep pockets in her gown, and Gwendolyn had stealthily been tucking away a few coins into them.

At one point, she'd returned Mr. Steele's fifty pounds to him with an added five as a lender's fee. She'd slid them over in two neat stacks.

He didn't move to take them, but she felt as if

her conscience was clear. She'd paid him back. And that is when she realized there was no longer a need for her to do a "favor" for him, even if it didn't involve her skirts over her head.

In truth, she didn't believe his promise to not touch her. There was something between them. A pull, an interest, an attraction. He might be interested because he couldn't see her face. Men were a curious lot.

Whatever it was, a decent woman would steer clear of a man like Mr. Steele. It wasn't just that he appeared strong as an ox and was sinfully handsome. No, this man had secrets . . . and Gwendolyn did not wish to be a part of them. She sensed danger. Besides, how could he hold her to a "favor" that he refused to explain? She might have promised to help, but that was only because she and her sisters were in a desperate situation. They were doing what they had to do.

But she had paid Mr. Steele back in full. It wasn't fair of him to take advantage of her . . . or so she told herself. Their transaction was finished.

Of course, the trick would be to take her money and leave without him learning her true identity. If he felt cheated by her, let him search for Mrs. Bunsaway.

Gwendolyn would be in London.

For the next twenty minutes, as the play seemed to grow ever faster, it was as if she couldn't lose. Luck was with her. She glanced heavenward, thanking her father, because only he could have helped her with these hands. She needed three hundred pounds. Maybe more. She prayed Elise's pockets were strong enough to hold the money. Her confidence soared. She no longer doubted herself.

Mr. Steele didn't play. He watched. Everything.

But especially her.

Gwendolyn sensed he evaluated her every movement, and not for her card skills. Evading him would be difficult.

A group of drunkenly giddy young men in brightly striped coats and starched collars so high they could not turn their necks joined the game. Their attention immediately went to Gwendolyn's black-shrouded figure at the table, and they began giggling and making randy comments that she didn't bother to overhear. She knew by their tones that she would not like what they were saying. She saved her concentration for the cards—

But then, Mr. Steele leaned forward, his shoulders lifting like a bulldog going on guard.

The group reacted to his implied threat by trying to correct itself, but drunk men always had difficulty reining themselves in, and this lot was looking for trouble. When one of them started whispering what sounded like Shakespeare under his breath, it sent his companions into fits of laughter.

Gwendolyn didn't hear what was said. But Mr. Steele stood, his hands curling into fists. Others around the table joined him. The play stopped as the Weasel raised his hands as if warding off trouble.

He was too late. The dandies looked around in surprised delight, and then one of them threw his drink in the face of a burly gambler to his right.

And Gwendolyn knew that here was her opportunity to escape. There was going to be a fight. She scooped her winnings into her lap as the offended gentleman jumped up, almost upsetting the table. The other men came to their feet, including Mr. Steele. She shoved coins into her pockets as the fops howled with laughter over their own antics. An angry Weasel started shouting at them for interrupting his game. A fist was thrown, and the fight was on. Men jumped on the table and onto each other.

Mr. Steele pulled Gwendolyn out of her chair and placed her behind him. One of the dandies attempted to grab her, but found his skinny puce-striped arms wrapped around Mr. Steele instead. The two began tussling and Gwendolyn found the opening she had needed to leave.

She ducked her head and made a straight brisk line for the door, her skirt heavy with coins. She did not look back. She trusted her luck would hold, and it did. Behind her, the table cracked and crashed. The language grew fouler and the shouting louder. She kept moving.

The street outside was quiet at this late hour. It had to be close to midnight or past. Her new challenge was to see herself back to the inn with her winnings.

Again, her black would help, although Gwendolyn wished she could remove the veil. Not yet, she warned herself. She was too close to the Devil's Hand. She didn't want anyone to have the chance to recognize her in the future.

She took the nearest alley, hurrying as fast as her weighted skirts let her. She stayed in the shadows as she rounded a corner onto a deserted street—

A gloved hand caught her elbow and whirled her around. She hadn't heard a step behind her or even sensed Mr. Steele's presence. He didn't say a word but placed his arm around her and marched them even further away from the Devil's Hand. There was shouting behind them now as if the fight had ended up in the street. Mr. Steele didn't break his stride and, although Gwendolyn was tall for a woman and enjoyed vigorous country walks, she was having a hard time keeping up with his pace, especially when fear had lodged her heart in her throat.

He had her. There was no escaping him.

They turned a corner. He seemed to know where he was going. She grew confused, wondering if she would ever find her way back to the inn.

"Would you please slow down?" she whispered to him, genuinely trying to catch her breath.

He ignored her. He knew she wasn't going to honor their bargain. She couldn't. She wouldn't—and yet her defiant "I paid you back your money" didn't sound reasonable and authoritative. She sounded frightened, and she was. Why, he could stuff her into a barrel and no one would ever find her body.

Of course, this very situation had been why Dara had wanted to accompany her, to provide protection. But her sisters would have been no match for Mr. Steele, and Gwendolyn was relieved they were safe.

They came to a street lined with dim, filmy lamps. Fog drifted along the street, a sign they were close to water.

The night watch holding a lantern and a cudgel seemed to materialize out of the mist. His presence caught her off guard. She opened her mouth to plead for help—

Mr. Steele spoke before she could, yelling to the watch, "Devil's Hand. There's a fight, and they are going to *kill* the man who started it."

The watchman frowned. "Fight?"

Then, from a distance, they could hear shouting and running feet. "They may have already succeeded in *murder*," Mr. Steele declared.

"Murder?" The watch's chest puffed up manfully.

"You need to restore order," Mr. Steele instructed him, letting go of Gwendolyn so that he could turn the watch in the direction of the Devil's Hand. "Do you have a whistle?"

"Whistle?" the man repeated blankly.

"Yes, whistle," Mr. Steele affirmed. "I would start tweeting it. Let them know they can't behave that way. Send them running."

"Send them running?" the man echoed. He maneuvered his cudgel so he could pick up the whistle tied to a cord around his neck.

"Yes, that way. Go." Mr. Steele gave the watch a helpful push and the man left.

Gwendolyn had been so caught up in the nonsense in front of her, she had almost forgotten that she needed the watch to protect her from Mr. Steele. And then she realized Mr. Steele had let go of her arm.

She turned abruptly and practically tripped on her veil, catching it under her shoe. The action jerked her head forward. Meanwhile, her skirts, heavy with coin, threatened to throw her off balance. She pulled at the veil and ribbons holding her mourning bonnet in place. The pins she had used to secure it yanked at her hair. For one tangled second, she felt as if trapped in a spider's web.

"Let me help," Mr. Steele's very masculine voice offered.

"I don't need—"

Her words were too late. He lifted the veil from her bonnet and folded it back from her face, his height allowing him to do so easily, and she was free. It felt good to be able to breathe fresh air.

"This thing is—" he started, and then his tone changed, warmed. "You are lovely."

His surprise startled her, almost as much as his words.

Gwendolyn knew she wasn't unattractive, but this was not her best moment. Her velvet bonnet was askew, loose locks of her hair were tumbling around her face and down her back, and her face felt flushed and angry.

"Truly amazing," he continued, and that's when she realized he wasn't enamored.

No, he was *evaluating* her. And to what purpose?

Fear vanished. "What are you saying?"

He recovered himself. "I mean, I knew you were young and, well, I suspected attractive. It was in your poise, the length of your back."

"My back?"

"You have an elegant back. Perfect posture. You had on the veil, but I could see you were Quality—" He stopped abruptly as if catching himself. "I'm a clod. Telling a woman she is far more attractive than I anticipated is not exactly a compliment."

"You are right," she snapped. She straightened her hat, making her feel a bit less ridiculous.

Gwendolyn didn't trust anything about this man, especially his assumption she was obligated to him. She was not. Standing under this streetlamp, she also felt far too exposed to his gaze. "I paid back what I borrowed *with interest*. I appreciate your confidence in me and that you made the Weasel stop cheating. However, we are acquitted of each other, sir. Thank you and good night."

She would have marched away crisply, except, with surprising swiftness, he took the few steps to place himself in her path. She stopped, annoyed. Then began in a new direction, only to discover that he blocked her there as well.

"Not so quick, Mrs. Bunsaway. The terms of my loan were not interest but that you would grant me a favor."

"I changed my mind. And you may stop hounding me." Gwendolyn again tried to move around him. She didn't care what direction she took as long as it was away from him. She certainly didn't dare approach the inn. She didn't want him to know her real name or learn about her sisters.

What was it Mr. Steele had said when they'd first met? He hunted people.

"I'm not hounding you," he answered in a perfectly reasonable tone, falling into step alongside her. "Perhaps, if I'd known you were so deliciously attractive, I might have. However, we have a bargain. You owe me a favor."

"I paid interest," she reminded him.

"I don't want interest. I didn't even wish my money returned."

"I thought you promised not to pull my skirts over my head."

He surprised her by tilting back his head and laughing with genuine amusement. "Irish women are refreshingly blunt." He shook his head, then added soberly, "I also wish you would stop being fidgety, because the truth is, Mrs. Bunsaway, I'm not certain *what* I will request. Or even if I will. It certainly won't happen now, if that is what you fear. Still, I do need to know your name and how to reach you."

Oh, she was not going to give him that information. Not ever.

Gwendolyn stopped, looked him straight in the eye, and said, "Mrs. Bunsaway from County Cork." There, that should send him off on a fool's chase. She would have marched right past him, but he held his arm out as if exacting a toll.

"You shouldn't lie, Mrs. Bunsaway. It is an unattractive quality."

"I'm not lying." A touch of heat rose to her cheeks. Gwendolyn was a terrible liar. Dara was good and Elise much better, but Gwendolyn always winced at any untruth.

"Of course you are not," he agreed. "However, I trusted your word to be your bond. When I come for you, and I will, because I am very good at finding people whether they want to be found or not, you will grant me that favor."

No, she wouldn't. But let him think what he wished.

"Very well. Good night then," she said. Again, she would have left, but he didn't retract his arm.

With an impatient sound, she frowned up at him. *"What?"*

The streetlamp behind her caught the glint in his eye. He smiled, melting some of Gwendolyn's resistance like a flame to tallow.

"A name?" he whispered, taking the slightest step closer to her. "You owe me that much. Especially as I would never peg you for someone from County Cork. You are far too refined." There was also a hint of laughter behind his words, as if he was enjoying the game between them.

And suddenly, she realized that for all her irritation, she was enjoying it, too. He was tall, bold, confident, darkly handsome, and so unlike any man she'd ever met before—

Something moved behind Mr. Steele and then there was a "whump" as it collided with Mr. Steele's head. His too-knowing eyes widened right before he stiffened, and then those eyes closed as, with a grunt, he fell heavily to the ground at her feet.

Startled, Gwendolyn knelt to the mound of

man before raising her eyes to see her sisters in front of her. Dara held a very hefty piece of wood. "Did you hit him with it?"

"Yes," Dara answered as if it should be obvious. "Is he dead?" She sounded almost pleased with herself.

Gwendolyn placed her hand on Mr. Steele's neck. His hat had fallen off when he fell. He had a thick head of dark hair with a hint of gray at the sides. The gray made him look distinguished, although he could stand a visit to a barber. Thankfully, there was a pulse. She released the breath she held and looked to Dara. "You are so short. How could you reach his head and have the strength to do this to him?"

"I'm *not* that short," Dara answered. "He bent down and I jumped up."

"Dara is surprisingly strong," Elise observed, adding slyly, "for being so short."

"We were anxious," Dara said, ignoring her. "He kept chasing you. Are *you* all right?"

Instead of answering, Gwendolyn rose. "You were supposed to wait for me at the inn."

"We did wait," Elise said. "For hours."

"Then we began to worry," Dara agreed.

"Where are Tweedie and Herald?" Gwendolyn asked, looking around for at least the butler. It had been a relief to all of them to have a male escort, although Herald was almost as old as Tweedie.

"Our aunt is asleep, and I'm certain Herald is as well," Dara answered.

"He said that traveling wore him out," Elise added.

"And you didn't stay with Tweedie because . . . ?" Gwendolyn prodded. "You wished to ignore my explicit instructions to remain with her? You thought it a good idea to walk about Dublin at night?"

"Because we didn't think it was a good idea for you to walk around Dublin at night," Elise answered as if it should be obvious.

"We couldn't let you do this alone," Dara agreed. "You need us."

"Then we come upon you being accosted by this big brute of a man," Elise pointed out.

"We arrived just in time," Dara concluded, then changed the subject. "Did you win the money?"

"The money? You could have killed him," Gwendolyn said.

Elise poked at Mr. Steele with the toe of her shoe. "He seems alive."

Dara didn't act concerned at all. She dropped the wood. "He appears to be alive, but it wouldn't be wise to linger to find out. He will be furious with that lump on his head."

"Yes, right," Gwendolyn said. "Time to leave." She spun on her heel and began walking as fast as she was able away from Mr. Steele's inert form. Her sisters scampered after her.

Dara said, "If you wish to go to the inn, it is this way."

Gwendolyn gave an impatient huff. *Sisters.* "If you know where it is, lead the way."

Elise started walking in a new direction. She and Dara followed.

"Did you win?" Dara asked again.

"I did." Gwendolyn also thought about telling them that she had succeeded because of the man they had just struck down, but really, what good would that do?

Her sisters would feel bad—although they had yet to show remorse—and besides, nothing could be done about batting Mr. Steele over the head now. As their Gram used to say, there was no reason to worry about matters that were already handled.

"Did you win *enough*?" Dara had to ask.

"*More* than enough."

Elise and Dara stopped in their tracks. They exchanged a look as if they feared Gwendolyn might be jesting.

Gwendolyn lifted her heavy skirts to show how the pockets of coin weighed them down.

Dara and Elise burst out into happy laughter, each doing a bit of a jig.

Their celebration was cut short when Gwendolyn grabbed them by the sleeves of their dresses and rushed them along.

"But we want to know what happened," Dara said.

"Yes, you must tell us everything," Elise agreed. "And who was that man accosting you? Dara feared we wouldn't be able to rescue you."

Gwendolyn would never tell them who Mr. Steele was, or about his demand for a favor. Or that he hunted people for a living and would now probably hunt her.

Except she would be in London. As a guest of Lady Blandford. He'd never find her there. The nobility wouldn't let him in the door. She was safe. Her sisters were safe.

She smiled at the mighty Dara, who sometimes had more courage than sense and who rarely ran out of ideas. And now, thanks to her, Gwendolyn and Elise had a chance for a life that was more than rusticating in Wicklow under Richard's thumb. Or her being in some squire's bed to keep a roof over her sisters' heads. A thought struck her. "Do you think Father would be proud of us?"

"After what you did tonight," Dara answered, "I think he would crow to one and all that he taught you everything you know."

He would, and he had.

"I miss him," Elise said.

Gwendolyn nodded agreement. Their father had not been the most doting of parents, but he'd been the one they had. She picked up the pace and didn't stop until they were safely in their room in the inn, where Tweedie was loudly snoring in her bed. Herald had been sleeping on the floor outside their door. He hadn't stirred when they had stepped over him to enter the room.

Before they undressed for bed, Gwendolyn emptied her pockets. Her sisters marveled that she had been able to walk at all carrying so much weight. They let the coins run through their fingers, and then Dara began counting them. Even Gwendolyn was excited to learn there were three hundred forty-eight pounds.

Dara had them divvy the money among their valises. "We are going to London," she announced. "And we are going to each marry a duke and live the very best lives."

On that announcement, the women sought their beds. Despite Tweedie's snoring, both Elise and Dara seemed to fall right to sleep.

However, for Gwendolyn, sleep didn't come easy. All she could remember were Mr. Steele's words—*When I come for you, and I will, because I am very good at finding people whether they want to be found or not, you will grant me that favor.*

She couldn't wait to be away to London.

Chapter Four

Visits of "duty" must never be neglected.
THE RULES (ACCORDING TO DARA)

We seem to be the only ones following these rules?
TWEEDIE'S PUZZLEMENT

London, Three Weeks Later

Their journey to London had been very smooth. They'd arrived three weeks ago and had quickly found a small house on Willow Street, a somewhat genteel neighborhood close to Hyde Park. They had hired a maid, Molly, and a cook. The rooms and furnishings were shabby, but the Lanscarr sisters set to work, and in no time, the house interior appeared very respectable, especially with Herald minding the door. Tweedie and Gwendolyn each had a bedroom while Dara and Elise shared as they always had.

The sisters had plunged into the enjoyments of the city. There were museums, exhibits, and people from every corner of the world walking the streets and going about their business. Dara had never seen the like. Reading about experiences was far different from actually being present, from having the sounds and smells all around her. Dara had a powerful imagination, but it had not been large enough to encompass how magical London was.

Best of all was the shopping. Anything a person could want was readily available. Even a trip to the market revealed unexpected riches like fruits that were out of season in England but had been shipped all the way from Spain.

She and her sisters made almost daily trips to the linen-drapers or to seek out notions for the three dresses each of them owned. They couldn't afford new gowns, but with ribbon and lace, they could easily refashion their old muslin ones. They were certain no one would be the wiser to the limitations of their wardrobes because no one had noticed back in Wicklow. They were very good with their needles. They prayed this held true in London.

The most wonderful gift of all was when Gwendolyn, who was the master of the money, had decreed that a subscription to a lending library was a necessity. They only had to join one of the many libraries in the city. It alone housed more books than they had seen in their lifetimes. They would never be able to read them all, but, as Elise said, they could try.

Of course, ever since they first arrived, Dara had been plotting how she and her sisters would gain admittance into the glittering world of parties and soirees known as the Season. The quickest way was to have a sponsor.

And that is when all her dreams and clever scheming came to a frustrating halt.

Her original plan of ingratiating themselves with the Marchioness of Blandford did not work out . . . because what her study of collected London papers had not told her was that the fourth Duke of Marlborough had sadly passed away in January. She had missed that important tidbit of information.

Granted, the marchioness—who was married to the new fifth duke—was now a duchess, but the family was in mourning. The duchess had left London and retired to the countryside. Dara had also ferreted out the information that, as a rule, the Duchess of Marlborough was not fond of London life. Society rarely saw her, even when she was in town.

Ever hopeful for this connection, and in spite of the odds against them, Dara had insisted they visit the duchess's London residence and leave a letter expressing their condolences, as one should. She reasoned that the servants probably sent the duchess's correspondence to her, wherever she was. That is what Dara would ask if she were a duchess. Perhaps Her Grace would take pity on them. Remind herself how much she had liked her second cousin Lydia and perhaps suggest some friends invite Lydia's daughters to a party? Or two?

Gwendolyn had been horrified. "We should not disturb the duchess's mourning."

Dara had disagreed. "This is the best time to disturb her. She may be looking for a distraction. I would be. One can only mourn so many hours a day. We read everything we could find when we were mourning Gram." The truth of that reminder settled the matter. They sent a letter that had just the right touch of heartfelt, cousinly concern while also letting the duchess know they were alone in London.

There had been no reply from the duchess.

And the sisters found themselves shut out from Society. They knew no one, and therefore, they couldn't be introduced to anyone. Or invited anywhere. They overheard women planning for balls and routs in the stores they visited, but they couldn't gain even a toehold. They could not marry dukes if they didn't have the opportunity to meet any.

Well, they did know someone—a fellow Wicklowian, Lady Byrne, had brought her daughters to London for the Season.

The Lanscarrs and the Byrnes had been rivals back in Wicklow. Helen and Sophie were twins and a year younger than Elise. Lady Byrne had been caught several times speaking ill of the Lanscarr sisters, especially Gwendolyn. She liked to suggest that Gwendolyn's hair was too black, or make a comment about how her mother had not been Irish. Gram had said Lady Byrne was sour because her daughters were not as well favored in face or personalities. When the Lanscarrs arrived at a Wicklow Assembly dance, the lads all lined up for them, ignoring the Byrne sisters.

Good manners should have dictated the Lanscarrs call upon their fellow Wicklowians soon after their arrival in London—something that Gwendolyn and Elise had passionately refused to do. Dara had allowed the lapse in manners because of sisterly loyalty and her belief that they would probably run into Helen and Sophie at some ball. Then they could pay their respects in that false way that satisfied propriety without having any true feeling behind the actions.

Of course, that was back when Dara had been confident she and her sisters *would be* invited to a ball.

Yesterday, desperate to do what she must to help her sisters enter Society, even knowing her sisters would hate the idea, Dara had grabbed their maid, Molly, and secretly left a calling card with the Byrne residence. That's all. She just left a card.

Her stratagem had seemed worthwhile when, a few hours later, the Lanscarrs had received an invitation to call upon the Lady Byrne and her daughters for this afternoon.

Her sisters had not thanked her. Dara had needed to prod them into honoring the invitation. Elise and Helen detested each other. "She is cruel," Elise had declared, and she was right, although Sophie was little kinder.

"Their mother is no friend to me," Gwendolyn had complained, but she had donned her bonnet and accompanied them with their maid, Molly, trailing behind as a chaperone.

Tweedie had refused to go. "Make an excuse for me," she'd said.

In the end, Tweedie was the wise one to not attend. The Lanscarrs had been tricked in the rudest way possible.

The Byrne butler had escorted them to a Receiving Room and left them there. No one came to greet them. There wasn't even an offer of refreshment. Instead, after what seemed an endless wait, the butler had returned to inform them that Lady Byrne and her daughters were so sorry but they couldn't receive the Misses Lanscarr after all. They were no longer "at home."

But they were. Dara could feel their presence.

Then the butler had opened the front door, letting them know they needed to leave.

Inviting guests and then ignoring them by leaving them to cool their heels in the front room as if they were intruders, was beyond rude. The Lanscarrs walked decorously away from the Byrnes' London house, conscious someone might be spying on and giggling over their departure from a window. However, once around the corner, Elise let her true feelings be known.

"I have *no* desire to return to the Byrne household, to speak to a Byrne, or even look at a Byrne *ever* again," Elise declared.

"I'm so sorry," Dara said, conscious that her sisters had been right about the Byrnes. "I was trying to shake the tree, so to speak, to find a way into Society."

"Perhaps you should share your list of the rules with Helen and Sophie?" Elise suggested pointedly.

"Perhaps *we* should *never* trust them," Gwendolyn said. "If they weren't kind in Wicklow, we can't expect them to be so here. They see us as competition."

"Well, they aren't competition for us," Elise countered. "They may play their little tricks, but someday, they will be repaid in kind."

"I just hope we are there when it happens," Gwendolyn said.

"Their behavior was unfortunate," Dara agreed primly. After all, they were still in public—

"Unfortunate?" Gwendolyn lifted a brow. "That is an understatement. Dara, after what they just did, inviting us to call and then making us cool our heels in their sitting room—"

"Where *all* we had to look at was that unremarkable landscape painting," Elise cut in to complain. "Or those silly porcelains of—what were they?"

"Shepherdesses, I believe," Gwendolyn offered.

"They looked like ghouls. I shan't sleep tonight from the memory of them," Elise declared. "How I wish we could have done something more interesting this afternoon like staying in our *own* home and darning our socks." She walked a few steps before saying, "What bothers me is that Helen and Sophie spent a good forty-five minutes upstairs laughing at us."

"And their mother was with them, too," Gwendolyn agreed. "Rude, rude, rude."

She was right, and Dara felt guilty. She had pushed the acquaintance because she had been hopeful that Lady Byrne would be kind to them. Her sisters were right—she should not have been so naive.

"What is best for me right now is a walk in the park," Gwendolyn said. "I wish to put all of this behind me."

"I wish to return to Wicklow," Elise muttered. This was not the first time she had mentioned going home. Of the three sisters, Elise was the only one who missed Ireland.

"We must keep the faith," Dara declared. "We must tell ourselves that we *will* meet dukes. We *will* be a success."

"You speak as if you are trying to convince yourself," Elise said.

"I have to believe we can," Dara answered. "I started this, and I don't wish to fail you."

"Oh, Dara, we all agreed to this venture," Gwendolyn said with sympathy. "It isn't your fault that we are nobody of importance. However, I have been enjoying London. No matter what happens in the future, I'm glad we attempted to do something for ourselves. Now, let's see if Tweedie wishes to enjoy a nice promenade with us, shall we?"

"I believe that is a capital idea. Just think, Helen and Sophie might drive by, and I'll have the opportunity to throw a dirt clod at them," Elise sweetly suggested.

Her sisters laughed. They wouldn't let Elise do it, although Dara rather relished the mental image, and she began to feel better. Whatever happened, she, Gwendolyn, and Elise loved each other.

Tweedie declined their offer to have her join them for their walk. Molly was happy because that meant she was coming with them.

The promenade through Hyde Park had become a daily exercise for the sisters. It was what fashionable people did. From four to five, the park was filled with carriages, riders, and walkers such as themselves, all there to see and be seen.

While Gwendolyn and Elise relished the always entertaining sights, Dara focused on the hard work of trying to search out and identify anyone of importance. As far as she was concerned, this was her primary purpose for being in the park. Some vehicles had coats of arms on their doors, but many did not. She could be walking right next to a duke and not know it. Such was the frustration of her self-assigned task.

The day was a lovely one to be out and about. The paths were more crowded than usual. That didn't mean the Lanscarr sisters weren't noticed. Elise's golden beauty was like a beacon. All eyes, especially male ones, seemed to home in on her . . . and then their gazes would travel to Gwendolyn with her graceful height.

Both Elise and Gwendolyn were oblivious to the stares, ignoring them as proper young women should. It was up to Dara to be very much on guard and frown the rudest of the gentlemen into looking away. She excelled at the task. Her sisters and Tweedie knew they could count on her and her rules to keep them proper and acceptable—

Dara came to a sudden halt, stunned by the sight of the most handsome man she'd ever laid eyes upon. Responsibilities, rules, and worries were wiped from her mind as she did what no one of good breeding should ever do—she gawked at him. She couldn't help herself. He was exactly that amazing.

The gentleman—and he was a gentleman,

judging by the fine cut of his coat and the expensive leather of his boots—was lean and tall, his shoulders broad. He stood as if he understood exactly how important he was in the world. More interesting, the gentlemen accompanying him gathered around as if jockeying for a place in his circle.

Power was an interesting commodity to Dara. She valued its intangible qualities. However, it was his looks that grabbed her attention. There was something about his height, his dark auburn hair and the squareness of his jaw that made the very core of her shaky and weak. He was like no other.

And then he turned to look in Dara's direction while listening to what one of his compatriots was saying. His eyes were a bright, light gray, and when his gaze met hers, she felt miniature bolts of lightning . . . before his interest traveled on as if she was part of the scenery—that is, until those quicksilver eyes landed on Elise, and there they stayed.

Of course.

He was not as obvious about his interest as other gentlemen were. He knew how to be discreet. However, Dara recognized the signs. She'd witnessed them before. Except this time, she experienced a pang of what might be called jealousy. It was all so easy for Elise and Gwendolyn, but she had never begrudged them until now.

And then she chided herself for the uncharitable thought.

She moved to catch up with her sisters when she realized they had stopped to converse with an older, rather horse-faced woman whom Dara recognized immediately—Lady Whitby. She was one of the most important political hostesses in London. She held weekly salons where only heavy subjects were discussed.

Dara could barely stifle her horror. All thoughts of the handsome stranger fled her mind. She and her sisters had met Lady Whitby at their lending library. They had all found her engaging—however, the Park was not the place for the sort of conversation her ladyship enjoyed. It would not serve the Lanscarrs to be seen as bluestockings, the name given to women who had learned tastes. Dara's research had impressed upon her that men looking for wives did not value intelligence. Possible husbands shied away from women with strong opinions, which was the reason debutantes were encouraged to be demure.

It was true that Dara and her sisters did have strong opinions. *Bluestocking* might be a good sobriquet for them. Except, Dara would prefer this not be open knowledge until after they had married their dukes.

With that in mind, she went charging forward to rescue her sisters.

Elise smiled as she approached as if happy to see her. "Dara, you remember Lady Whitby."

"That I do," Dara said, giving a small curtsy. "My lady."

"My pleasure, Miss Lanscarr. I was telling your sisters they should join us at one of my salons."

"We would love to attend," Elise said with enthusiasm.

"You are kind to include us," Gwendolyn echoed.

Dara's smile froze on her face. Attending would be husband-hunting suicide. But how to refuse such an offer?

And then a man with the honeyed tones of Ireland in his voice said from behind Dara, "Good afternoon, Lady Whitby. I pray I'm not interrupting something."

Dara turned, curious, and then almost choked on her shock. *It was him. The gentleman.* And he was so close to her, she caught the warm scent of his shaving soap.

"Mr. Brogan, always good to see you," Lady Whitby said with genuine warmth. "Here, have you made the acquaintance of the Misses Lanscarr? They are your countrywomen. Miss Lanscarr," she addressed Gwendolyn, the oldest, as she should, "I give you Mr. Michael Brogan. He is a member of Parliament for your country."

"Are you now?" Gwendolyn said with smiling interest. "From what county, sir?"

"It is my pleasure to be from Carlow," he said with a bow that was neither foppish nor obsequious. "And you and your sisters, Miss Lanscarr?"

"We're Wicklowians," Elise announced, jumping in with the eagerness of a green colt—a sign she was interested in this gentleman. She beamed a smile at Mr. Brogan, one that had knocked many a man off his game, and he was no exception.

He smiled back as if she were the only person in the world, and in that moment, Dara realized envy could turn to hate if she wasn't careful. Of course, it wasn't Elise and Gwendolyn's fault that they captured male attention. Men were superficial.

It was just that Dara wished she had their power, because she knew about Mr. Brogan. She'd read about him in her collection of newspapers. He was an attorney who had been appointed to Parliament for the Carlow seat upon the untimely death of the previous occupant. He had often been mentioned for his "firebrand" rhetoric and his willingness to take up any cause he found just. He was considered a leader among the liberal faction of the Whigs and was expected to handily win his election to the seat next year. He championed the merchant classes, the weavers, and others who were part of a "middling sort," those who were not landowners but manufactured, traded, and built.

He was the sort of man she could admire.

And he wasn't paying *any* attention to her.

Apparently, Mr. Brogan was a frequent visitor to Lady Whitby's weekly salons. Elise had many questions to ask. He edged closer to her while not actually cutting Dara out of their small circle, and yet she felt excluded all the same.

Dara listened to the conversation with half an ear so she would know when to smile and nod. After all, manners were all she had.

But inside, she felt as if something was breaking. A hope? A fantasy? Her own silliness at being so quickly infatuated? After all, she was a woman of good breeding and taste, even if she did notice that there was blue in the depths of his gray eyes and that the rims were dark, almost black. Eyes like she'd never seen before. Unique, intense . . . with a spark of interest whenever he glanced at Elise.

He was unsuitable, Dara tried to convince herself, even for Elise. Dara was certain he stood politically against anything *a duke* would support. In fact, most dukes would consider him an enemy, which didn't bode well for women who wished to be duchesses.

Besides, he was Irish. She hadn't come to London for an Irishman—

Mr. Brogan laughed at something Lady Whitby had said. Elise and Gwendolyn joined in. Even Molly, standing discreetly off to the side, chuckled.

Dara had been so busy stewing, she hadn't heard it. And she wished she had. She wanted to hang on his every word, to look at him with the devotion Elise was showing.

"Promise you will come to my salon on Thursday," Lady Whitby was saying to Gwendolyn and Elise. She smiled at Dara, including her.

"That would be lovely," Gwendolyn answered for them. "Will you be there, Mr. Brogan?"

"How can I not be?" he said gallantly.

"Then it is settled," Lady Whitby said. "Now, Mr. Brogan, I have some thoughts about that land bill you and your compatriots are championing. You will give me a moment of your time, won't you?" She placed her hand on his arm, commandeering him so he had no choice but to acquiesce. As they walked away, he gave one glance back, looking right at Elise, whose expression took on a dreamy look.

Gwendolyn, too, seemed a bit under his spell. She smiled at Dara. "Well, we have been introduced to someone very important. That is what we've hoped for."

"I suppose," Dara replied, purposefully vague. She began walking, taking the path toward Willow Street and home.

"Wouldn't Mr. Brogan make an excellent husband?" Elise asked.

Gwendolyn opened her mouth as if to agree,

but Dara jumped in quickly. "I suppose, if one wishes to be poor."

"He's poor?" Gwendolyn questioned.

"I'm certain of it," Dara answered.

"But he is an MP," Gwendolyn pointed out.

"An *Irish* one." Dara didn't elaborate. She let the implication hang in the air.

They walked on as if each kept their own thoughts, and then, "He dressed well," Elise said.

"He wears his clothes well," Dara agreed. "However, don't you want more than an Irishman?"

There was a long beat of silence, and then Elise said, "I don't know that there is anything wrong with an Irish husband."

"After all we've done to come to London and then . . . *settle*," Dara answered, ladening that last word with all the dread she could muster.

Elise didn't like her response. Dara held her tongue, giving her younger sister a chance to muddle around in her thoughts.

"I found him very nice," Gwendolyn murmured.

Dara swallowed her frustration. She needed Gwendolyn to support her. "He isn't a duke," Dara reminded them. "What is our purpose? What have we set out to do? What did we promise ourselves?" They had reached their front step. She turned and faced her sisters, challenging them.

"We can't give up. Not yet. There are so many gentlemen we have yet to meet."

"I'm going Thursday," Elise answered.

"You may," Dara responded, sounding more serene than she actually was. "I just ask that you not lose hope yet."

"After what happened with the Byrnes, it isn't easy to be positive," Elise said, but before Dara could argue, the front door behind her opened.

Herald was grinning and Tweedie was almost dancing as she waved a vellum envelope in the air. "Look at what we have," she said. An invitation.

Dara pounced on it. The back was addressed to all three of them and to Dame Eleanor, Tweedie's title. But then, controlling her excitement, Dara handed the invite to Gwendolyn. "You should open it. You are the oldest."

Gwendolyn took the invitation. "Who sent it?" she asked as she led them inside the house and into the front sitting room.

"A very officious footman delivered it two hours ago," Herald reported.

"We know it didn't come from Lady Byrne," Elise said.

"Of course not," Gwendolyn agreed. "However, let us open it and solve the mystery."

There were twin settees in the room. Gwendolyn and Dara sat on one, Elise and Tweedie on the other. Herald stood by the door with Molly lingering in the hall. There wasn't a soul in the house who didn't know how important this correspondence was.

Gwendolyn broke the seal and unfolded the invite. She read it quickly. "It is from Lord and Lady Royston. We don't know them."

"We don't, but I know *of* them," Dara said with rising excitement. "This is the invitation everyone wants. They say it is one of the most important balls of the Season."

"And we are invited? By people we don't know? Without being introduced?" Elise asked. She looked to Tweedie. "Do you know them?"

"I have never heard of Lord Royston."

Elise scrunched her nose in thought. "Then why did he send us an invitation?"

"Does it matter?" Dara said. She took the invite from Gwendolyn, wanting to feel the paper and see the words scratched upon it.

Lord and Lady Royston request your presence . . .

Magic words. And it didn't matter to Dara how it had happened. What was important was that all her planning was finally bearing fruit. "My sisters, we are entering Society. We have arrived."

CHAPTER FIVE

The lines of Society are not imaginary. Do not speak until introduced, do not laugh loudly, do not frown, do not make eye contact until after introductions.

THE RULES (ACCORDING TO DARA)

Perhaps it would be easier if we all wore sacks over our heads?

TWEEDIE'S SUGGESTION

When they left Willow Street for the Royston ball, Dara believed that she and her sisters, and even Tweedie, had never looked finer. The sisters wore their white muslin dresses in the Grecian style. Each had spent the afternoon trimming their gowns with ribbons, which they also used to style their hair. Gwendolyn's ribbons were a soft rose, Elise's a clear sapphire, and Dara's were the green of summer grass.

They chattered with excitement as they set off for the ball in their hired hack. They had accomplished their goal. They were making their way into Society—and who knew what could come after this first endeavor? Dara had promised them they would marry dukes. Perhaps they would.

However, the closer they came to Royston House's grand and well-lit doors, the quieter they grew as a few home truths became evident. "No one is arriving in a hack," Gwendolyn said, something Dara had already fretfully observed.

They had joined a line of stately coaches and dashing carriages waiting their turn to deliver their passengers in front of the magnificent house. "I'm sure someone is," Dara answered, desperately praying that was true.

"It don't appear that way," Tweedie responded, accenting her words with a hiccup—a sign she might have had a nip or two? She clapped a gloved hand over her lips as if she'd been caught. "So sorry." She lowered her hand apologetically. "Shouldn't have spoken. I'm feeling a bit nervous."

Dara wished she'd thought to have a nip herself, especially once they were close enough to inspect the other guests climbing the stairs to the doors. The torchlight reflected off of jewels and highlighted silks, lace, and figured velvets. There were headdresses of bobbing ostrich feathers and headbands of gold and silver—and that is when it struck Dara that instead of being very fine, she and her small family appeared hopelessly provincial and out of fashion.

They were wearing ribbons. How could ribbons compare to sapphires and pearls?

Gwendolyn's hand clasped hers as if asking for courage. Elise had linked an arm in Tweedie's, both of them wearing expressions of doubt.

Well, it was too late to turn back now. Dara knew it was up to her to give them courage. "Heads high. We are the Lanscarrs from Wicklow," she managed.

"I wish I was back there right now," Elise murmured.

"No, *we don't*," Dara answered, meaning those words. Then she added, more for herself than her sisters, "Good things will happen this night. *Good* things."

"I fear we are out of our class," Gwendolyn said.

No one argued. Not even Dara.

A bewigged footman in fancy red-and-black livery trimmed in silver opened the hack door. With a bow, he held out a gloved hand to Dara, who was sitting closest to the door.

She drew a fortifying breath and placed her palm in his, conscious that those in the queue behind their vehicle were now observing her. She let the cool night air wash over her uneasiness before smiling proudly as the footman helped her beautiful sisters out of the vehicle.

Gwendolyn took Tweedie's arm and, while holding the invitation in her free hand, helped their great-aunt up the stairs toward the front door and a waiting receiving line.

There was one horrid moment when Tweedie's flask fell out of her pocket. Dara felt a flash of panic. But then, a quick footman standing along the stairs snatched up the flask and discreetly passed it to Elise before resuming his pose of formality. In an undervoice, he whispered, "Happens all the time."

Tweedie looked back at Dara as if to say, *See, it happens all the time.*

They would discuss this in the morning. However, first they had to live through this evening.

And then they were on the top step and in front of a butler who appeared more officious and grander than an admiral. He lifted a brow before asking quietly, "Your names?"

Gwendolyn offered the invitation. He read the names on the back and then raised his voice to announce, "Dame Eleanor Roberson, Miss Lanscarr, and her sisters, Miss Dara Lanscarr and Miss Elise Lanscarr."

Few in the crowded foyer that appeared to spill into an even more densely packed ballroom looked up in response. They were all more interested in themselves.

The butler motioned them forward, across the threshold, to pay their respects to their host and hostess.

And Dara finally relaxed. No one had told

them to leave. No one had ordered them out. Whether dressed properly or not, they had arrived. They'd done it. *Finally.*

The couple in front of them were babbling to Lady Royston about how wonderful it was to be back in the city. Apparently, the gentleman had been ill with a rash—and he wished to go into details.

"He should have you to tell him the rules of polite conversation," Elise whispered in Dara's ear.

"Lady Royston would probably appreciate it if I did," Dara answered.

At last, it was their turn. Lady Royston was everything Dara had expected a true gentlewoman to be. She was of middling years and possessed extraordinary style. Her dress was a silver sheath over layers of finely patterned material. Pearls the size of Dara's thumb were at her throat, and a band of them formed a coronet in her dark hair.

Next to her was Lord Royston, able diplomat and reputed man of the world. He was a disappointment.

He wore a velvet jacket in midnight blue over too-tight white evening dress, a style that emphasized his bowlegs. His thinning hair was brushed forward as if aping the Brutus style, which was not flattering on him. He had an extraordinary amount of forehead.

Nor was his expression of boredom a ruse. "Aren't we done yet?" he complained to his wife.

"Momentarily," Dara heard his wife say, although her lips did not move and her smile remained intact as she looked to Gwendolyn.

Another footman, standing close to her elbow, whispered what the butler had announced, "Dame Eleanor Roberson and her nieces, Miss Lanscarr, Miss Dara Lanscarr, and Miss Elise Lanscarr."

Lady Royston did not act as if she had never clapped eyes on the Lanscarrs. Instead, she smiled benevolently—a smile Dara couldn't wait to practice in front of her looking glass at home. "Thank you for coming, Dame Eleanor."

Tweedie gave a quick bob. "Very nice, very nice." It was all she could manage. Gwendolyn murmured something gracious about the invitation and glanced at Dara as if needing help over what to do next. So Dara tried to inch her family forward while being a bit intimidated herself.

And all would have been fine if Lord Royston's gaze hadn't settled on Elise. Beautiful, golden Elise. His ennui vanished. He almost elbowed his wife out of the way, a wolfish gleam in his eye. "And who is this?" he asked.

His wife's smile tightened. It was not a pleasant expression, and then she said, "Lanscarr." Suddenly her lips parted as if she'd been struck with a sudden realization. "Ah, yes, I remember."

She remembers what? Dara didn't dare ask.

"I hope you enjoy our company this evening,

ladies." Lady Royston then turned to her husband. "Come, my lord, let us open the dancing." She grabbed his arm, her fingers pinching into the sleeve hard enough for her husband to give a start. He reluctantly tore his attention away from Elise and back toward his responsibilities.

Dara and her sisters discreetly trailed behind the couple, even while there was a host of other guests still waiting to enter the house.

"I would have preferred to not have to go through that," Gwendolyn whispered, her own lips doing a wonderful copy of Lady Royston's cool smile.

"Did I do something wrong?" Elise asked. "He acted quite rude."

"He was. And you were *not* at fault—" Dara began to assure her, until she caught sight of the ballroom in front of her.

This was what they meant by a "crush." The room was teeming with people, colorful fabrics, jewels, and ostrich feathers. Heaven could not be more glorious.

Those who had predicted this would be one of the most important social events of the Season had not been wrong. Dara couldn't believe her good fortune in being here.

Hundreds of candles lit the room. Huge swaths of white silk were draped from floor to ceiling like glorious, moving columns that served as a fitting backdrop to the dazzling company.

There was an air of excitement in the room, as if *anything* could happen this evening.

As if the *ton* had been waiting anxiously for Dara . . .

Lord and Lady Royston moved toward the dance floor. The musicians struck a chord, the guests clapped politely as their hosts took their places, and the dancing began.

"I need a sherry," Tweedie said. "And my flask. I need my flask."

Her nieces ignored her. Gwendolyn and Elise seemed as caught up in the magic of the night as Dara was. They watched the dancing, the servants carrying silver trays of crystal glasses, the fluttering of fans, the happiness of friends greeting each other.

They stood, until Elise asked, "What do we do now?"

That was a good question. They were in a room full of people they did not know. People who were busy talking to each other and not paying any attention to the Lanscarr sisters.

Well, that wasn't completely true. Several gentlemen eyed Elise and Gwendolyn, but Dara knew that unless they were properly introduced, then that was probably all that could happen.

"Tweedie, look around. Do you recognize anyone you know from your days in London?" Dara prodded.

"From close to thirty years ago?" Tweedie shook

her head. "If they are here, they look as old as I do." She glanced around. "No one looks as old as I do."

Dara frowned. She noticed that along the sides of the room were the mothers with daughters to launch in Society. The available young women were cooling their heels, envious of those of their number who had already been asked to dance. Their mothers surveyed the room with the ferociousness of hawks on the lookout for fresh prey. Or rivals. Several gazes narrowed when they saw the Lanscarr sisters.

"Oh, look," Tweedie said. "There is Lady Byrne."

Elise's gaze hardened. "And her daughters are on the dance floor."

Gwendolyn and Dara followed the direction she was looking. Helen and Sophie had partners who were not very attractive. One gentleman did not dance well at all, and the other was as wide as he was tall. However, Lady Byrne stood to the side, watching her daughters as if they were the most beautiful creatures in the room.

And they were dancing while the Lanscarr sisters could only watch.

Elise made a sound of disgust before turning to Dara. "I know what you are thinking, and the answer is no."

"What am I thinking?"

"That we should cozy up to Lady Byrne," Gwendolyn said. "The answer is no."

"I know she is mean-spirited and evil, but we can't just stand here," Dara said in desperation. "If she introduces us to just one person, then we can make our way from there."

"Perhaps a better plan would be to learn who had us included on the guest list," Gwendolyn said. "I doubt if it was Lady Byrne. We also know it wasn't Lord and Lady Royston." All day, as the sisters had been preparing for the evening, they had wondered about who their mysterious benefactor was.

"Actually, I would think our hostess should introduce us to the other guests," Elise said. "Isn't that a rule, Dara?"

"Possibly," Dara hedged, uncertain what the proper etiquette was.

"I will say, Elise made an impression," Tweedie chimed in. "Lord Royston keeps eyeing you." Elise gave a small shudder.

Gwendolyn spoke. "What of Lady Whitby? Perhaps she was the one?"

"I thought she might be as well," Elise answered. "I've been looking for her in this crowd, and I haven't seen her yet. She might not be here."

"Lady Byrne sees us," Gwendolyn warned, and then added with delight, "Look at the scowl on her face. She definitely wasn't the one who invited us."

Elise's response was to wave cheerily. Lady Byrne looked away as if she hadn't seen them.

Instead of being offended, Elise and Gwendolyn almost fell into each other laughing—loudly. Something Dara had warned them *not* to do. Except that it was comical to see Lady Byrne try to ignore them. Her "cut direct" wasn't insulting. She just appeared silly and spiteful.

"I fear we might never know who wished us invited—" Dara started, and then stopped as the strangest sensation swept over her. An awareness. She experienced it from the depth of her being to the tingling of the hairs at the nape of her neck.

She whipped her head around, searching—and saw *him*. Mr. Brogan. *He was here*. Tall, leanly handsome, and obviously popular. Other women eyed him while their husbands or dancing partners did what they must to reclaim their attention.

He must have just arrived. Dara would have known if he had been here before. She was that keenly aware of him. He was speaking to a gentleman who looked like the prime minister.

And then he turned as if he caught sight of Dara. Their gazes held. He smiled.

She could have floated to the ceiling over that smile . . . until she realized he was looking past her—

"There is Mr. Brogan," Elise said happily before adding in a giddy undervoice, "Why, he is looking right at me."

Of course he was.

Every man in the room was eyeing Elise. Most discreetly. A few were like Lord Royston. If they weren't looking at her youngest sister, they were glancing at her oldest. Elise and Gwendolyn were a mighty pair with one so light and the other so dark.

"Perhaps he is the one who had us invited," Elise said, turning to Dara and blocking her view of Mr. Brogan. "We should say hello to him. Come, Tweedie, chaperone us over to Mr. Brogan. I want to make Sophie and Helen and their terrible mother frightfully jealous."

She would have taken off across the ballroom as if it was a Wicklow dance, Tweedie in tow, if Dara hadn't gripped her arm. "The lady does *not* pay the respects first," Dara snapped, her words sharp as the roiling bile of jealousy once again reared its ugly head.

And she was being silly.

Mr. Brogan was too fine a gentleman for her. Of course, he'd be interested in one of her beautiful siblings.

She was the useful one. The planner. After all, if it had been up to Elise, they wouldn't be in London right now but at an Assembly dance in Wicklow—

"He's here," Gwendolyn said, looping her hands around her sisters' arms as if to hide them behind one of the hanging silk draperies.

Elise frowned. "Mr. Brogan? We just said that. And Dara won't let me greet him . . ." Her voice trailed off as both she and Dara realized Gwendolyn wasn't looking at Mr. Brogan.

No, she stared at the ballroom entrance.

It was obvious Someone Important had arrived. People were already moving out of the way to create a path, even as they gathered round.

Dara strained her neck trying to see past those who blocked her view of the door. She even rose on her tiptoes. Elise could see. She had a slight frown on her face.

Tweedie, who was as petite as Dara, whispered, "Who is it? What is happening?"

No one answered, or moved, not even Gwendolyn.

The crowd shifted. Lady Royston became suddenly very visible. She walked toward the entrance, her hands outstretched in warm greeting, and then Gwendolyn, the tallest of them, made a choking sound. "I'm trapped. There is nowhere to go."

Dara was uncertain. "What are you saying?"

Gwendolyn swayed slightly as if needing support and reached for Tweedie. In a low voice that only the sisters could hear, she said, "You don't recognize him?"

Dara frowned at the dashing, broad-shouldered man with crisp dark curls and a hard, square jaw.

Fans fluttered rapidly as the women whispered about him. Men didn't hide their jealousy. Lady Royston looked as if she was practically purring with excitement.

"Should we know him?" Elise asked.

"Most certainly," Gwendolyn said. "Dara gave him quite a blow in Dublin that night."

Dara whirled back to look at the man in disbelief. "He is the man who attacked you? Why is Lady Royston acting as if he is some honored guest? Why is *everyone in the room* behaving in that manner?"

"Well, now we know we didn't kill him," Elise said.

"But what is to stop him from wanting to kill us?" Gwendolyn responded. "Quick, we must leave. Isn't there a garden where we can go to hide?"

"Who is he?" Dara demanded.

Tweedie spoke up. "It is too late to run. He is walking in this direction. I think he is coming right for you, Gwendolyn."

"Oh, good Lord, no," Gwendolyn whispered, her face draining of color.

Dara, Elise, and Tweedie bravely flanked her. "I shall confess I am the one who hit him," Dara promised, even though he seemed to grow bigger and stronger the closer he came. Lady Royston practically danced at his side. She acted proud to have him there.

"Brazen it out," Tweedie warned under her breath, and she stepped her diminutive self in front of her nieces.

"I wish we could hit him on the head again, and this time, do it right," Dara answered, frowning.

Her family gasped their surprise, but Dara was unrepentant. This man was a threat. "Smile," she ordered. "He is almost upon us. Stand tall. We are Lanscarrs."

"The bravest of the brave," Elise echoed. They used a motto their father had taught them.

Except Dara didn't feel brave. This man could denounce them for their attack in front of everyone . . . and the Byrnes . . . and Mr. Brogan.

She reached for Gwendolyn's hand. She had protected her once, and she would do so again.

And then he was right in front of them. "Miss Lanscarr," he said, his greeting easy as he bowed to Gwendolyn. "I am happy to see you here. Lady Royston told me you had arrived."

Gwendolyn stared, unmoving as if she'd been frozen.

Apparently he didn't need her input. "And this is your aunt, Dame Eleanor?" He gave her a bow. "I'm Beckett Steele. It is my pleasure to finally make your acquaintance."

Tweedie stared up at him, apparently as stunned as Dara was by his manner.

"And these are your lovely sisters?" he continued. "Those who lauded their beauty were very much on the mark." But as he spoke, his focus never left Gwendolyn.

She cleared her throat. In a very small voice, she managed, "Hello, Mr. Steele. I'm surprised to see you here."

His smile widened. "Are you now, Miss Lanscarr? You needn't be. After all, I'm the one who had you invited."

Chapter Six

Make amusing conversation while dancing.
THE RULES (ACCORDING TO DARA)

How can one be amusing while hopping up and down?
TWEEDIE'S RESPONSE

Beck was enjoying this meeting with the Lanscarr sisters immensely. Gwendolyn appeared ready to swoon over the news that he had orchestrated their invitation, a sign that the sisters had wondered about it. They were quick ones. Female pirates setting themselves up to plunder the *ton* for husbands.

He found them delightful.

At this point, there was very little he didn't know about the Lanscarr family, even Dame Eleanor. Those who had warned him the sisters were very close had not been wrong. They practically held Gwendolyn up so that she could meet Beck's eye.

Gwendolyn. He liked the sound of her name. The numerous syllables were like music to him, and far superior to *Bunsaway.*

Physically, she was stunning. Once he'd recovered from the blow to the head, he'd wondered if he had remembered her correctly. After all, the only light had been a streetlamp.

He was pleased to realize that his memory had not lied. She was indeed a brunette beauty. Black lashes framed the gold in her concerned brown eyes. Her lips were full and enticing, even as she unconsciously pressed them together as if summoning her courage.

Beck grinned. He'd surprised her. That had been his intent.

In fact, he had caught all of them off guard with his announcement. Elise, the youngest and loveliest, had let her lips form a perfectly round O of surprise. Those who had claimed she was a golden goddess had not been wrong, although Beck's tastes ran more toward her older sister.

Then there was Dara. She regained her composure first. While her sisters struggled with his presence, she announced, "I should have hit you harder."

It was a shocking statement from a very proper young woman. Lady Royston's mouth dropped open in shock, but Beck tilted back his head and laughed.

"They warned me you were forthright," he said.

Miss Dara's brows came together. "Who warned you?"

He didn't answer. Let her wonder.

Fortunately, Lady Royston spoke up with the formalities. Always formalities. "I am so pleased you had me invite the Lanscarr sisters, Mr. Steele. They are charming young women and excellent additions to our company."

"I assured you they would be, my lady," he answered with her same smooth, albeit false, pretense.

But before more banalities could be uttered, a recognizable male voice said from behind him, "Steele, good to see you."

Beck turned, unsurprised to find Michael Brogan—who was at the head of a host of men ready to descend upon Lady Royston for introductions to the most beautiful women in the room.

"Brogan," he said with a nod. He and Brogan did some business together, except Beck did not want the handsome younger man intruding on his plans for Gwendolyn, and he did have plans. Big ones . . . eventually.

"Delightful evening, Lady Royston," the politician said, wise to speak first to his hostess before letting his gaze light on the youngest of the sisters, the golden one. "Hello, Miss Lanscarr. It is a pleasure to see you again. May I ask for this next dance?"

He spoke as if no other woman was standing before him, a clumsy move from the usually adroit Brogan. Of course, Beck was pleased that the man hadn't been focused on Gwendolyn. She was his.

However, everyone, including Miss Elise, was startled when Miss Dara smoothly stepped in front of her younger sister and said, "I would be delighted." She offered her hand.

Brogan hesitated as if he hadn't truly registered that there were several Miss Lanscarrs in front of him. He'd only had eyes for one. However, Miss Dara had neatly trapped him. The Irishman could have corrected the misunderstanding, except he was too much of a gentleman. Meanwhile, Miss Dara wasn't too fine a lady to use the fashionable world's manners to her own advantage.

What had the locals told Beck about her? She was the force in the family. *Fiercely protective of her sisters. Unafraid to do what she must.* He now had no doubt she was the one who had clubbed him in the head. *Though she be but little she is fierce.*

The Lanscarr sisters were one entertaining mystery after another. Beck hadn't felt so intrigued in years.

Brogan offered his arm to Dara and off they went, although he wasn't gentlemanly enough to resist a regretful glance back at the beautiful Elise.

He was right to worry. Lady Royston introduced her to Lord Painswick, a young man from a very wealthy family. Yes, he was boring, but he wasn't a bad sort as far as Beck knew. Then again, everyone had secrets and failings. They kept Beck in business. Painswick's buttons threatened to burst as he led Miss Elise past a group of jealous would-be suitors to join the next set.

That left just Gwendolyn . . . and himself.

She'd been very quiet. He remembered seeing her for the first time in her black garb and being struck by the way she held herself, as if she didn't wish anyone to know she was afraid. He longed to assure her she was certainly safer with him than she'd been with the Weasel and the lads at the Devil's Hand. He didn't expect her to believe him.

"Miss Lanscarr, will you dance?" he asked. He offered his gloved hand. It had been some time since he'd stepped out on a dance floor.

"I believe I should stay with my aunt."

Several young coxcombs moved forward, anxious to offer in his place. Beck blocked them with his body, and shot a frown toward Lady Royston, who, realizing her cue, jumped in to say generously, "I'll stay with your aunt. Go, dance with Mr. Steele. Have fun."

Gwendolyn's brows lifted as if she didn't think

fun and Beck went together. He'd have to prove differently to her.

"They are setting up for the next set," he prompted her.

"Yes, go on, my dear," her aunt said. "I'm fine here with Lady Royston. It will also be a pleasure to see all three of my nieces out on the floor."

Gwendolyn didn't try to hide her distrust, but she was more courteous than Dara. She placed her hand on his arm.

The weight of it felt good there.

Beck led her toward the couples preparing for the next set.

She spoke. "I would appreciate if you would keep my adventure in Dublin to yourself."

"I wouldn't breathe a word," he assured her.

There was a beat of silence and then she said, "Thank you."

"We all have our secrets."

"Does Lady Royston owe you a favor also?"

Several gentlemen, important men, nodded as they passed, acknowledging him with a murmured, "Steele." Did she notice their deference to him? Did she care?

"You shouldn't be so cynical. Lady Royston was happy to invite you."

Her mouth quirked to one side. She knew better. "Has anyone dared to refuse you?"

"Never. And that is because they are happy

with whatever small service I perform for them. It is all about fairness."

She hummed her opinion.

"You are starting to hurt my feelings," Beck mock-complained.

"I've known rock walls who have more tender emotions than you have, sir."

"You are a difficult woman, Miss Lanscarr. I shall work hard to convince you that I do have a better nature." They had reached the dance floor. The set had already started.

"Oh, this is unfortunate," she said, already starting to turn away from him. "We are late for the dancing."

Beck caught her hand. "The next set will start soon. We can watch the dancers."

She hesitated, reminding him of a fawn ready to take flight.

"Please," he pressed.

Uncertain eyes met his, and then her shoulders relaxed. She faced the dancers.

"Thank you," he said.

"I'm being polite."

"I appreciate it."

They fell into silence, supposedly watching the dancing. He found he liked having her stand next to him.

She spoke. "How did you find us?"

He smiled. "I said I was very good at what I did."

"Hunting people?"

"Sometimes other tasks. I earn a living."

She faced him. "Have you noticed how many people are staring at us, and trying not to?"

"You are a newcomer, a lovely one. They stare because they are curious. And interested."

She shook her head with a frown. "It is you. They stare because of you. Who *are* you?"

"Exactly who I said I was. Beckett Steele."

"You must be more than what you say you are. You convinced Lady Royston to treat us as honored guests. How?"

"Are you asking because you admire my way with people?"

"Yes," she agreed. "I wish to understand how to coerce the powerful to do as I wish."

"It is a good talent to have."

She closed her eyes as if annoyed with him and then repeated, "Who are you?"

He could tell her some of the truth. "My father is the Marquis of Middlebury. But I rarely go out into Society. It bores me."

Although he was not bored this evening.

On the dance floor, Miss Elise was smiling and pleasant to young Lord Painswick. She appeared so charming and delightful that Beck knew hearts were being broken. *She* would be the talk of the evening.

In contrast, Miss Dara acted distant. She barely glanced at her partner. Although Brogan was more than a match for her. He smiled smoothly while equally ignoring her. "It is enjoyable to watch your sister and Brogan treat each other with a thick layer of, well, I can't call it politeness. She doesn't appear happy with him. That can't be comfortable for him. Miss Dara is a bit of a spitfire, isn't she?"

Gwendolyn's chin rose. "If you use the word *spitfire* to mean she is passionate about what she wants in life, then, yes, she is. I admire my sister for her tenacity."

"And it is never a trial?"

There was a pause, and then Gwendolyn unbent enough to admit, "It is a bit like holding a comet by the tail. She will have her way."

"And I take it her way is keeping Brogan apart from your youngest sister."

"Dara is very particular about whom we should meet."

"Obviously I'm not on the list."

Gwendolyn tilted her head. "Do you wish to be on the list of possible husbands?"

The idea that Beck was fodder for matrimony made him laugh aloud. "That is one list I avoid at all costs. Besides, I have it on good account that the Lanscarr sisters won't rest until they return to Ireland as duchesses."

Gwendolyn had the good grace to blush. "And where did you hear that?"

"It's not common knowledge yet," he assured

her. "However, it is the goal of every unmarried woman in this room, so it won't be a surprise. Your secret is safe."

"If it wasn't for Dara, we wouldn't be here. She is the dreamer. Does that offend you, Mr. Steele? That we dare to be bold with our plans?"

"Not at all. And the three of you are beautiful enough that you might succeed. However, most dukes I know are deadly dull."

"We haven't met one yet."

He looked down at her, marveling at how the candlelight seemed to make her hair darker, richer. "You will."

Did she hear the admiration in his voice? If she did, she gave no indication, and he was relieved. He didn't like anyone knowing what he was thinking . . . but something about her caused him to let down his guard—

"Did your head hurt very much?"

"In spite of her size, Dara can wield a club, can't she? You needn't worry. I'm not the vindictive sort," he offered.

Her lips twisted as if she suppressed a laugh before saying with a boldness he could only admire, "Vouchers for Almack's would prove you are not vindictive." She referred to the infamous social club that was very difficult to join. The standards for receiving that invitation were very high.

Beck laughed, enjoying her spirit. "You are

learning how to navigate quickly, Miss Lanscarr. However, some things are beyond even my capabilities. In spite of his knighthood, your father, Captain Lanscarr, was a well-known scoundrel."

He regretted his words the moment her manner changed. "Will that harm us?" she asked. "I had assumed few would know who he was."

"Sir John was known in some quarters. However, the hostesses of Almack's are sticklers for many things, including lineage. They would inquire, and I don't know that you wish such inquiries."

Her brows came together as if she saw the good sense of his thinking. "He wasn't a bad man," she corrected him. "He was a gambler, not a scoundrel. There is a difference. And if Almack's shut its doors to gamblers, there would be no one left to attend its socials."

"True," he conceded, and was rewarded with one of her quick, triumphant smiles. "But then you would owe me another favor," he pointed out.

"Always transactional. Careful, Mr. Steele, or I will believe you are not a gentleman."

He laughed. "You know I am not, Gwendolyn."

"You forget yourself, sir. I haven't given you leave to be so familiar."

"I'm not one for rules. And neither are the Lanscarrs." He said it imperially. One equal to another. The music stopped. The previous set had ended. He held out his hand. "Our dance, Miss Lanscarr."

Instead of taking his hand, she backed away. Her manner had changed. The easy playfulness was gone. "I've decided I do not wish to dance after all, Mr. Steele."

He lowered his hand, confused. "Because?"

Had he been too honest? Or was she being coy?

"Perhaps the more distance between us, the better." Before he knew what she was about, she fell into step beside her sister Elise and Painswick as they passed.

Beck let her go. He didn't chase women, and he'd never once wasted energy trying to decipher them.

And yet Gwendolyn tempted him.

He couldn't help watching her move away with admiration. She had bearing, grace. She'd do very nicely for his plans.

As long as he kept a distance.

Lady Royston sidled up to him. "Has my debt been paid?"

"Absolutely." Elise and Gwendolyn had rejoined their aunt, who now appeared busy brokering her nieces with the circle of gentlemen begging for their attention.

He tore his gaze away from Gwendolyn and gave Lady Royston a small bow. "Was the favor I asked a terrible one?"

"Those sisters have created quite a stir this evening, especially with *your* appearance."

He ignored her jab. "I want everyone talking about them on the morrow."

She sniffed her opinion. "They will be. Especially since men think with their little heads and not their big ones."

"Then you wouldn't have owed me a favor," he countered. She had come to him when her husband had declared he was going to leave her for an actress. Royston had planned to elope to Amsterdam and polite society be damned.

Beck had been able to help her husband see sense.

Well, as much as the man was able to be sensible. Royston was the sort who would wander again. Beck knew because his father had been of the same mind. Beck's initial advice to Lady Royston had been to let her husband go. Ignore the gossips, discreetly take on a lover while playing on everyone's sympathy, and spend Royston's money lavishly and generously.

She hadn't appreciated the idea, so Beck had done as she asked.

And now she had done as Beck had asked.

So would Gwendolyn Lanscarr.

And he actually was looking forward to the encounter.

He started for the door. He'd accomplished what he'd set out to do, including passing off the piece of information Brogan had requested from him. In turn, Brogan had done as Beck had asked. He'd singled out the Lanscarr sisters.

The time had come to leave.

Beck prided himself on his ability to slip away unnoticed. *He* decided what people thought. However, before he escaped, he did something out of character—he looked back.

Searching for Gwendolyn, he saw she was being introduced to Viscount Morley, who actually appeared fawningly entranced.

Good. He'd planned their meeting as well, and it seemed to be progressing as he wished.

Beck didn't worry Gwendolyn would be swept off her feet. Yes, the sisters had a chance at becoming duchesses; however, he wouldn't take a wager on the matter. He understood the *ton* far better than they did. The Lanscarrs were aiming beyond their reach, and there would be a fall. The question was, what did he wish to see happen?

He left the ball.

GWENDOLYN SAW MR. Steele slip from the ballroom. He was an enigma. He could either command all the attention in the room, or slip away like a shadow—and yet she'd been aware of his every movement. He'd watched her for a good moment as she'd politely smiled at Viscount Morley and the number of other suitors lining up for introductions.

While the sisters had been occupied, Tweedie had made a friend. Lady Ponsby, a woman of about her same age, stood by Tweedie offering advice. Lady Royston had introduced them, and now Lady Ponsby helped Tweedie navigate the intricacies of chaperoning.

Poor Tweedie. She was more comfortable sitting in the matron's corner with a glass and some gossip instead of playing gatekeeper. Dara was more suitable for that task, but Dara was nowhere to be found.

Gwendolyn wondered where her sister had gone off to—and hoped it wasn't with Mr. Steele—even as she placed her hand on Viscount Morley's arm and let him lead her to the dance floor.

Chapter Seven

Never be indecorous or indiscreet.
THE RULES (ACCORDING TO DARA)

But slap men with fans and bat eyelashes—
that's discreet.
TWEEDIE'S AMAZEMENT

Miss Dara Lanscarr had bowled over her sister to dance with him, only to act disinterested, cold even, through the set. Michael wasn't one to stand on manners, but something was amiss, and he wondered what. Certainly he wasn't at fault. Nor was he accustomed to women taking a dislike to him.

When the dance ended, he gratefully offered his arm to escort her back to her aunt—except when he would have led her to the right, she tugged at him to go left. He frowned, confused.

"Escort me into the Supper Room," she said. It was not a request.

"I don't believe it has been opened yet."

"I'm certain it hasn't." Her blue eyes turned imploring. "I only ask a moment of your time. You will grant me that, will you not?" Her voice had gone low, husky, and for the first time, he noticed her hair carried the scent of clover and wildflowers. The fragrance of Ireland. A siren's call for him if there ever was one.

Steele's letter to him earlier in the day had warned him to be wary of Dara. *Never take your eye off her.* And yet Dara was a debutante, a naïf. Granted, she was a lovely slice of Irish womanhood but nothing Michael couldn't handle. "No, I believe I need to return you to Dame—"

She let go of his arm and took off in the direction of the Supper Room as if she expected him to follow, and God help him, he did. He couldn't stop himself. Curiosity alone propelled him forward.

The door to the Supper Room was closed. That didn't stop Dara from opening it a crack and slipping inside as if on a clandestine mission.

Michael frowned. This was ridiculous. He opened the door outright. He was a man. He didn't skulk around.

A footman setting linens on the buffet table looked up. "I beg your pardon, sir. We are not prepared to serve. We will shortly."

Dara answered before Michael could speak. "That is not a problem. We are not here to eat. I desire a moment alone with this gentleman."

The footman looked taken aback, and then his smile turned knowing. He ducked his head and left through a door on his side of the room. He even stopped a maid who had started to go by him, pulling her back into the passageway with him and giving Michael and Dara privacy.

She marched over to a corner table for two and sat. With the air of a queen, she folded her gloved hands on the table and nodded for him to join her.

Michael took the other chair. "What game are we playing, Miss Lanscarr?"

"You appreciate plain speaking?"

"I don't believe you know any other kind."

"I regret not. However, I had to ask. Men like to believe they are open-minded. They rarely are."

"I am not like most men," he coolly informed her.

"Oh, I know all about you. You are highly respected."

He leaned back. "Are you plying me with compliments?"

"I am saying I know how important you are, especially to Ireland."

"Thank you?"

"You are welcome." She paused as if letting her graciousness sink in before adding, "However, I wish to discourage you from calling on my sister."

He wasn't expecting that. He sat up. "Discourage me?"

"Elise is beautiful in both form and spirit. However, she is not for you."

"And why is that, Miss Lanscarr?"

"Because."

He waited for her to say more. She didn't. He pushed. "Because *you* said so? Because I'm too *respectable* . . . ?"

That drew an indignant sound out of her. "Because I'm asking you to leave Elise alone."

"Still not a reason."

Color rose to her cheeks, and he had to smile, thinking of Steele's warning. If Michael could handle Parliament, he could handle her. "You act as if no one should question you when you give orders, Miss Lanscarr. That was probably true in Wicklow, but we are out in the world. And now, since we are 'speaking plainly,' what is it you have against me?"

Her face grew pinched as if she was offended that he would dare to challenge her—and against all reason, he found himself drawn to her.

He did not like bold women. They got on a man's nerves over time. And Elise was the true beauty, with Gwendolyn not far behind. They had both piqued the male hunting instinct in him.

Except Dara's clear blue eyes could never hide what she was thinking, and he'd wager she was *always* thinking. Hers was a busy mind. An intriguing one.

He also wondered what would happen if he

were to reach across the table and pull on one of the green ribbons tucked in her hair. Would her curls come tumbling down, a cascade the color of good whisky around her?

Michael pushed away from the table, a bit thrown off by the sudden tightness in his breeches.

Dara had no conflicted feelings about him. "We have come to London to seal our family legacy. We are related to the Duke of Marlborough, you know."

"I did not know that."

"Why should you? That is why I am telling you." She didn't wait for a response but said, "I am tired of being poor, but genteel, Irish."

"There are many of them," he noted. "And many are poorer than you." He had been one of them until Lord Holsworthy had come looking for him when he had needed an heir.

"My sisters and I are in London to marry dukes," she announced as if impressing on him how lowly he was.

He didn't blink. "As is every young woman on the Marriage Mart."

"True. But we could. Even better, we want to carve out our *own* directions in life. You may not understand the importance of such an ambition because you are male. No one has ever questioned your authority to govern yourself. However, for a woman of intelligence—and we are intelligent—being able to act on her own mind is the Holy Grail. Elise and Gwendolyn could easily become duchesses just as the Gunning sisters did years ago." She leaned toward him. "I asked you to meet privately with me, Mr. Brogan, to say that I am very sorry, but you are *not* acceptable as a suitor for my sister. You must take your attention elsewhere."

He almost laughed at how serious she was being. However, that would be a bigger insult than arguing with her. So he replied, sounding as friendly as he could, "It is widely acknowledged that I am a good catch." He did not elaborate upon his prospects as Lord Holsworthy's heir. She claimed to know everything about him. He saw no reason to correct her. Let her find out he would someday be an earl.

"But not good enough for Elise."

"I would prefer hearing such a statement from her . . . if it is true."

A spark flashed in her eyes. Before she could lash out, Michael said, "Don't act so offended. *You* wished plain speaking, so here it is. The reason we are hiding in the Supper Room is that your sister would not agree with your warning me off, would she? She might not even share your plans for making her a duchess. These are all your ideas. Your goals, *your* ambitions."

Miss Lanscarr placed her palms flat on the table and stood as if trying to lord her petite frame over him. "*You* don't know what I've done to bring us here. And we are going to make *the most* of the opportunity—which is something, I suggest, any man would do. You can't tell me the men looking for wives aren't vying for the richest and best-connected of the lot. If you all would allow us to inherit what is rightfully ours, we would have our own money, our own homes. Unfortunately, all we have that is ours alone is our looks, and we will proudly use them to our advantage. *Or,*" she said cynically, "are you going to claim that you would pursue Elise if she was plain?"

She had him. Michael liked beautiful women, shallow as it sounded. What man didn't want a lovely wife?

Although, in truth, Holsworthy would be furious if he thought Michael was pursuing Elise Lanscarr. He had his own ideas of whom his heir should marry. Holsworthy brought up names of suitable, well-connected, and very wealthy possibilities for a wife every time Michael called upon him.

But that didn't mean Michael was going to dance to Holsworthy's tune, or Dara's. The decision of whom to marry was one of the most important and personal ones in a man's life—and Michael would make his own choice.

"It is my role, Mr. Brogan," she continued, "to

see us successfully established as rightful members of the *ton*. Leave Elise alone. *I* will not approve a match."

"All the more reason I should pursue her."

Dara sniffed her disdain. "You are teasing me now. Let me assure you, sir, there is nothing to mock about wanting what is best for one's family. Cross me at your peril."

Michael almost laughed. "At my peril? Did you truly just speak such flummery?"

She refused the bait. "And with that, I will say good evening, Mr. Brogan." She made as if to sail from the room, but he couldn't let her have the last word.

"What of love, Miss Lanscarr? What if I've fallen in love with your sister? Are you so far gone from modern sensibilities that you see no value to deep emotion?"

That caught her. An expression crossed her face—one he couldn't quite define. Her gloved hands tightened on the handle of the door, even as she squared her shoulders and said, "You would be lucky to fall in love with my sister. However, what most feel is lust. *That* is what I'm protecting her from. I told you, Elise deserves better." With those words, she threw open the door and slammed it behind her.

Michael stared at that closed door. Even when the footman and maid peeked out to see if it was permissible for them to finish their preparations, he sat. They came out anyway.

He barely paid attention. Deep within him, a resentment was brewing. It wasn't because Dara Lanscarr was an outspoken woman. He valued the female perspective. He didn't consider them inferior beings like so many of his peers. He liked the way their minds worked.

But no one, man or woman, had ever *dismissed* him.

Him, an MP, a highly respected and very proud *Irishman*. And he suspected the latter was her objection—not only was he not a duke, he was Irish. Kind didn't always admire kind.

Whoever came up with the idea that dukes were special? He knew most of them, and the majority were dim-witted. But he would not share as much with Miss Dara Lanscarr. Let her learn for herself.

Resentment turned to rebellion.

If Elise was half as opinionated as her sister, and she must be, she could make her own judgment about him, although he was very aware of how he presented himself. Elise's smiles had always been inviting.

No, the problem was Dara's.

Michael rose from the table. Miss Lanscarr had thrown down a gauntlet. He was going to accept the challenge.

THERE WERE SEVERAL people in the hallway when Dara stormed out of the Supper Room.

She had a moment of alarm when she realized that she was wandering around alone, something only the boldest of young women would do and a violation of her own rules. Two matrons walked by her, moving away from the ballroom, and Dara stepped in behind them as if she was one of their number.

Only then did she draw a breath and reflect on what had just happened. If Elise and Gwendolyn found out that she had warned Mr. Brogan away, they would be furious. She'd crossed a line. It had been high-handed even for her.

The women she trailed behind were going to the Necessary Room that had been set aside for the ladies. Besides wash basins and whatever else, there was a connecting room with a sitting area for women to relax. Fortunately, it was empty. Dara practically fell into a chair, desperately needing this moment of privacy. She leaned forward and buried her face in her hands.

Guilt was as uncomfortable an emotion as jealousy. Dara was not one to fool herself. She'd confronted Mr. Brogan because she knew she could never have him. A man as respected, important, and handsome as he was did not notice dowdy middle sisters like herself.

She had not lied. Elise could do better for a husband than a mere MP—except Dara wouldn't have minded if the man had been anyone else. Mr. Brogan set her pulse racing. Just being as close as she was on the dance floor or across the table in the Supper Room caused unsettling, fluttery feelings inside of her. *Deep* inside of her . . . in places she'd never had such a response before. Being around him was like looking at the sun—she should turn away and yet yearned to bask in his presence.

Dara dropped her hands and sat upright, disgusted with herself. Was that poetry? She hated sentimental, lovesick poems, and here she was practically writing one in her mind.

No wonder she was angry. Anger was better than the way he made her feel vulnerable. During their dance, she'd acted indifferent to him to keep her distance and to help prepare her for what she knew needed to be said to him.

Because she didn't want to spend the rest of her life jealous of Elise.

And then he had asked that question—*What if I've fallen in love with your sister?*

Love. What a wicked little word. It spun her into a tizzy.

Could he have already fallen in love with Elise? She was very loveable. But wouldn't something like "love" take time?

Apparently not . . . because what Dara felt toward him was so intense, it both frightened and annoyed her.

Maybe *she* was the one who was feeling lust? That thought made her feel worse. She was no giddy milkmaid. She was a woman of common sense. And she would not let any man come between her and her sisters.

A crowd of women burst into the Necessary Room, the ostrich feathers in their hair bobbing with their loud gossip. Several of them invaded Dara's sanctuary, and she knew it was time to leave. She was considering the proper way to return to her sisters without appearing as if she was wandering around alone when she heard one of the women say, "Lanscarr."

She eavesdropped as the women discussed how lovely her sisters were. That all the men appeared taken with them. Dara's heart filled with pride. This was what she had wanted. It was what she and her sisters deserved.

A sense of peace settled around her. Her actions toward Mr. Brogan had been justified. She quietly rose and left the Necessary Room. The hallway was more crowded as guests gathered waiting for the Supper Room to open. Dara found a new pair of ladies to follow back to the ballroom.

Tweedie was right where Dara had left her, sipping a cup of punch. She introduced Dara to her new friend, Lady Ponsby. Tweedie wasn't truly a good chaperone. She did not question where Dara had been. Dara would have to support her in her duties. She didn't want her sisters' success to be marred by unintentional mistakes.

While Dara had been gone, liberal libations had done their job on all the guests. The conversation was louder and the dancing more enthusiastic. Dara took it all in with the knowledge that the Lanscarr sisters had arrived. They were now part of Society.

Gwendolyn stood not far from Tweedie and Dara. She and two other young women were being teased by several dashing men who begged for the next dance. Lady Byrne and her daughters stood in a lonely little clump, their sour expressions showing the spitefulness in their hearts as they glared at Gwendolyn.

When they caught Dara watching them, they walked off in a huff.

Good.

And Elise? Dara scanned the room for her youngest sister. She was on the dance floor, stamping and clapping to the lively music of a reel. She appeared breathtakingly happy—

Dara's self-congratulations ended abruptly.

Instead, her blood boiled in her veins.

Elise's dance partner was Michael Brogan.

So this was the way he wished to play. Very well. She was unafraid.

If she told Elise that Mr. Brogan was unacceptable, her sister would listen. After all, Dara had a lifetime of experience guiding her. Elise trusted her.

Of course, Dara needed to be careful with her warning. So she plastered a smile on her face, danced with her own partners, and ignored Mr. Brogan.

Later, as she, Tweedie, and her sisters rode home in the hired hack, all tired after an exciting evening, Dara didn't talk about Mr. Brogan.

No, she focused on the gentlemen she *wanted* her sisters to marry. Viscount Morley, numerous lords, and one duke. The duke had been aged, but by any measure, the Lanscarr sisters had shown to one and all that they could make spectacular matches.

Elise didn't mention Mr. Brogan on the ride home.

And Dara was very happy.

Chapter Eight

A gentlewoman never lifts her skirts above her ankles.

THE RULES (ACCORDING TO DARA)

Unless it is the fashion to flash ankles. We will do anything for fashion.

TWEEDIE'S OBSERVATION

The day after the Royston ball, *The Morning Post* christened the sisters the "Lovely Lanscarrs." The author declared they were exactly what was needed to perk up what had been a rather "humdrum" Season. *Their manners are impeccable, their grace to be envied. Now, the only question is, who will capture the interest of the Divine Miss G Lanscarr? Or claim the hand of Miss E, whose Beauty rivals Venus's?*

Dara wasn't mentioned. It didn't bother her. She was proud of their success. After all, she had orchestrated it . . . well, with a bit of help from Mr. Steele. But Dara had been the bold one.

When she read the article to Gwendolyn and Elise, they laughed at hearing themselves described in such a manner. They also protested Dara not being mentioned. They had always been modest. That was part of their beauty.

Dara lowered the paper. "No door will be closed to us. Watch and see." And she was right.

Over the next few days, invitations poured in. The sisters were invited to every ball, rout, and garden party planned for the next two months. There were even personal invitations to join titled and important people in their boxes at the opera and theater or to dine at their tables—people Dara had read about in the papers. Now she was going to meet them. To move among them.

She wasn't naive. These people wished to use the presence of the Lovely Lanscarrs to draw attention to themselves, to burnish their guest lists, to ensure they were mentioned in the latest *on dits*. This was the way the world worked, she told herself.

And then there were the suitors.

They lined up every day outside Willow Street—gentlemen, officers, and lords—with trinkets, bouquets, and a startling amount of very bad poetry.

They swarmed around the sisters wherever they went. Promenading in the park was no longer a congenial exercise. It was a parade with Gwendolyn surrounded by one group of titled and noble gentlemen and Elise by another.

Dara followed with whoever was left. Surprisingly, she did have her suitors. No one who sparked her interest, but decent men, a few with titles.

She kept it all in perspective. Her sisters always included her, and her goal had never been about herself. No, she was honoring her promise to her Gram, to not let any of them be shuttled off and devalued. They were gentlewomen, and they deserved the favors of their class.

Gwendolyn solved their problem of having too few dresses. In the beginning, the sisters tried to change the look of their muslin gowns with ribbon and lace. However, they soon discovered they couldn't run this way and that for social obligations *and* ply their needles. They also couldn't afford dressmakers or even another maid. Gwendolyn finally pointed out that she saw nothing wrong with a simple white dress, especially for unmarried women. "Furthermore, look at where we live. Willow Street. There is no hiding that we don't have great fortunes. So why are we trying to pretend?"

Her words made sense. Besides, Dara and Elise would rather read than pick out threads and resew frills.

For the next affair, a musicale at Lady Ponsby's, the sisters wore their white dresses without any embellishment. There were some less than kind comments, especially from Lady Byrne about how "frugal" they appeared.

However, the next day, the papers praised the Lanscarr sisters' *graceful and demure silhouettes.* Their gowns became a mark of their style, and were quickly copied by other debutantes, including Helen and Sophie Byrne.

Yes, all was very good and *exactly* as Dara had hoped, except for one thorn in her plans—Michael Brogan.

He took pleasure in annoying Dara every chance he could. Worse, he charmed Elise into being his willing accomplice.

Dara's next confrontation with him happened when she and Gwendolyn had gone on errands only to return and find Elise entertaining Mr. Brogan in the sitting room.

The two sat so close on one of the settees that their knees were touching. He held a hank of wool hooked around his hands that Elise was happily winding into a ball. Tweedie, their chaperone, sat on the other settee, her chin lowered to her chest as if she was dozing in spite of Elise's happy giggles and the couple's whispers.

Only that morning, Dara had made a rule, which her sisters had agreed to honor, that male visitors would only be allowed to call between three and five o'clock. "We must pace ourselves. Be decorous," Dara had said.

It was hours before three. And did "decorous" include giggles and whispers? Especially after Dara had instructed Mr. Brogan to leave Elise alone?

Elise looked more than pleased to entertain him. There was a rosy bloom in her cheeks, a sparkle of pleasure in her eyes. She had rarely appeared more radiant.

And *that* was the crux of the matter—Elise could claim the heart of any man in the world . . . and Dara feared that she had chosen Michael Brogan.

The sight of the couple together on the settee squeezed Dara's heart into a hundred pieces. And she hated herself for it. Elise and she were the closest of the sisters. They shared the same mother. In spite of their being little more than a year apart, Dara had guarded and protected Elise from when they were both toddlers. They slept in the same room.

But the truth was, Michael Brogan could drive a wedge between them. Sisters should not be attracted to the same man. One of them would lose, and it would probably be Dara.

Surprising how much the realization hurt. She was also tired of having to be the bigger person all . . . the . . . time.

The couple was so busy with their wool and

their flirting, they didn't register Dara and Gwendolyn's presence immediately. Mr. Brogan's back was to them, so it was Elise who finally glanced up and then made a small surprised sound. There was no guilt or shame in her face. She was rather pleased with herself.

Mr. Brogan turned in his seat and then rose, the wool still around his hands. He made a gentlemanly bow. "Miss Lanscarr, Miss Dara, I'm pleased I have the chance to see you." He spoke to both of them, but his gaze went directly to Dara—and was it her imagination, or did she see a glint of laughing triumph in the depths of his gray eyes?

Was he mocking her? And using her sister to do it?

The last shreds of infatuation died. In its place was fury and a grim determination to teach him respect.

"Why, it is always a pleasure to see you, Mr. Brogan," Gwendolyn was saying as she removed her bonnet and handed it to Molly to take upstairs with their packages. "Have you been here long?" Dara removed her own bonnet and gloves.

"Not very long," Elise said quickly. "Hardly any time at all." Dara knew Elise made the claim for her benefit. Considering the size of the ball of yarn Elise held, Mr. Brogan had been here for well over fifteen minutes.

At that moment, Tweedie came awake with a snort. Her eyes were wide, and she blinked like an owl until she focused on Gwendolyn and Dara. "Oh, dear, did I nod off? Last night was very late for me."

Gwendolyn offered kind words. Dara gave her a reassuring smile she did not feel. Tweedie must be a better chaperone than this.

And then inspiration hit. She'd show her how a good chaperone should behave.

Dara walked over to the settee where Mr. Brogan still stood. "It was late for all of us, Aunt," she replied as she lifted the wool off his hands, dumped the mess of it into Elise's lap, and then sat down on the settee beside her sister. She even wiggled to take up as much room as possible on the narrow piece of furniture.

"Dara, my yarn," her sister protested.

"Oh, did I tangle it up? I'm sorry. Gwendolyn, please sit so Mr. Brogan will take a chair."

"He had a seat next to me," Elise grumbled.

Dara's answer was a benign smile.

Mr. Brogan caught the hint. His gaze met Dara's as he gave a courtly bow. "Please, be comfortable, Miss Lanscarr. I must take my leave."

Elise started to rise, even with her lap full of wool. "Let me see you to the door—"

"I can see him out," Dara interrupted, already on her feet. She placed a hand on her sister's shoulder to push her back down. "You should see to your yarn." She started for the front hall, expecting him to follow.

He took a few moments, offering his goodbyes to Tweedie and Gwendolyn. He was particularly charming to Elise. "I promise to return, and we will work on your next skein."

Elise simpered her delight, and it took all of Dara's self-control to not roll her eyes in annoyance. She was waiting for him out in the front hall by the door. She offered him his hat, which had been on a side table.

"We appreciated your call, sir," she said loudly enough for her family to hear in the other room, before adding her true feelings in a low undervoice, *"I thought I was very clear with you last night. You are not suitable."*

His gaze narrowed. He took the hat. "Thank you for seeing me out, Miss Dara." And then he added, matching her intense, quiet tone, *"You are not the one who makes all the decisions, especially for matters of the heart."*

Matters of the heart?

Oh, no, that could not be, and then she realized he was toying with her. He was no lovesick suitor. He'd been in control of his emotions every second he had been in the sitting room with Elise.

He'd visited to let Dara know that her wishes held no sway with him. What a scoundrel. What a politician!

She reached for the door handle, smiling with clenched teeth as she said, *"You of all gentlemen know Irish women. We don't like to be crossed."* She raised her voice. "I'm certain we shall see each other at many of the Season's social events." She didn't invite him to return.

He set his hat on his head, tipping it at a rakish angle to give a bit of "devil-may-care" to his look. Was that intentional? Of course.

"I'm certain we shall," he responded genially before adding, *"Ruffling their feathers is the fun of Irish women. You are making this too entertaining, Miss Dara."*

She wished she had stomped on his hat before handing it to him.

Dara opened the door. "Good day to you, sir."

"And to you." He took his leave.

She returned to the sitting room. Elise was fussing with the wool and tangling it up all the more. Gwendolyn was attempting to calm her. "We have rules for a reason—" Dara started.

Elise cut her off. "You chased him away. He hadn't been here that long."

Dara feigned ignorance. "Chased him away? What are you talking about?"

"Mr. Brogan left because you made him feel unwelcome."

Dara shrugged. "You are being fanciful. He is a busy man. So busy I doubt if we shall see him often."

Elise stood, tossing the yarn into a basket. "You don't wish me to see him."

"Now, why would you think that?" Had he said something? That would be quite low of Mr. Brogan.

"Because, Dara," Elise answered, "you all but knocked me out of the way when Mr. Brogan asked me—yes, it was *me* he was asking—to dance at the Royston ball. And then the two of you disappeared after the set."

"We wondered where you were," her older sister confirmed.

Because they hadn't said anything, Dara had not thought they'd noticed. "I had need of the Necessary Room." There was truth in her statement.

A silent communication passed not only between Elise and Gwendolyn, but also Tweedie. They knew her too well.

So she admitted, "He isn't good for you, Elise."

"Why do you say that?"

Because I believe he is trifling with your feelings, that he is playing a game of annoying me . . . and I, too, am attracted to him—

She kept all of those thoughts to herself. Elise wouldn't understand her fears, because Dara was always the watchful one. "I believe you can do better."

Elise pointed a finger at her sister. "I will make my own decisions."

"Of course," Dara agreed serenely, while mentally chalking another black mark against Mr. Brogan's name. "And you have many suitors to choose from." Which was true.

Unfortunately, the next day, in spite of Dara's admonishments, Mr. Brogan joined the line of suitors who cooled their heels outside the Willow Street door. It was almost as if it amused him to do so.

He knew Dara couldn't shut him out, not in such a public forum. He acted as if he enjoyed himself. He chomped on Cook's bread-and-butter sandwiches and listened to the "poets" spout their nonsense. When Lord Painswick wrote a poem comparing Dara's hair to a brown night highlighted by golden stars, Mr. Brogan clapped enthusiastically.

"Damn clever," Mr. Brogan declared. "A brown night." He grinned at Dara while Lord Painswick preened over receiving praise for his work.

And she had to say it. She didn't want to say it, except she couldn't help herself. When she found a passing moment alone with Mr. Brogan, she said, "Nights are not brown."

He grinned with fiendish delight as if he'd been expecting her to criticize his taste. "Only the *un*romantic ones." He considered a second and then added, "The poem seems fitting."

Her response was to bring her heel down hard

on the toe of his boot and smile as he tried to muffle a woof of pain.

In truth, there was very little Dara could do to prevent him from calling on them.

And sometimes, she wondered if she wished to stop him. She felt more alive when she was around him. They all did, even Tweedie.

Mr. Brogan occasionally joined the sisters and their bevy of suitors for walks through the park. Often, he would make a point of falling into step next to Dara. Her sisters believed he was being gallant and trying to win her over for Elise's sake. If they could hear what she and Mr. Brogan hissed at each other under their breaths, they would change their opinion.

"Would you please leave me alone, Mr. Brogan? You do not need to walk with me."

"I'm a gentleman. I should be generous in my attentions. Isn't that what your rules say?"

"My rules?"

"Your youngest sister said you made a list of important rules so that you all could be proper."

Dara made a mental note to tell Elise to never mention her name when speaking to Mr. Brogan.

"My rules say nothing about your need to annoy me."

"Come, Miss Lanscarr, we annoy each other. But then, I annoy you just by being in your presence."

"That is not true. You annoy me because you

are full of your own consequence without regard to others."

"Nonsense, fair lady whose-hair-is-brown-as-the-night"—Yes, he used that phrase with her every chance he could—*"You are annoyed because you can't have your way."*

That last statement was so true it made Dara want to spit with anger. Instead, she whispered sweetly, *"You are an ogre, Mr. Brogan."*

It didn't help that he laughed off her insults. The sound of his very male laughter made her sisters exchange indulgent smiles, as if they were pleased he was winning her over.

The man was a demon—and he stood head and shoulders above all of their suitors.

At night, in their shared room, during those moments when they first climbed into bed, Dara tried to moderate Elise's infatuation with Mr. Brogan by praising her other callers. She pointed out their strengths . . . and tsked over Mr. Brogan's shortcomings, which were, admittedly, hard to find. But she identified some. After all, he was male.

Elise just shook her head and, as time passed, seemed to become even more intent on pursuing Mr. Brogan—which was not the direction Dara wished for her to go. So Dara stopped talking about him. Her little sister was coming into her own, and Dara's suggestions and wishes were no longer carrying much weight.

THEY WERE AT the Earl of Morrow's ball, which was, like so many others, overcrowded with stuffy, perfumed air. Dara had danced quite a bit because, a bit to her horror, Lord Painswick had become marked in his intentions toward her. Apparently his bad poetry had been a form of declaring himself.

Dara had been surprised when he'd shown up by her side this evening. He was from an excellent family, one of the oldest in Britain, but he had an overbearing mother. The Lanscarr sisters had met her the week before, and she definitely let them know she was not impressed. She had looked them up and down with her gold lorgnette and then turned away to address her son about some family appointment.

Now, with Lord Painswick practically trotting at her heels like a puppy, Dara was tempted to ask him about his mother's obvious disapproval—although she thought she understood the source. Unsavory rumors had started circulating about their father. Stories had cropped up about his gambling and his wild ways. Some had heard it suggested that he was not dead, which was cruel, because the sisters missed him very much.

Most of the rumors were traced to the acidic Lady Byrne and were being repeated by other debutantes and their mothers. Dara assured her sisters that the stories made Helen, Sophie, and their mother appear spiteful. But after meeting Lady Painswick, Dara started to have doubts. Could beauty and manners only take a woman so far?

It didn't seem fair.

She was also very relieved that no one had, as of yet, discovered Gwendolyn's adventure at the Devil's Hand. That would ruin them.

It would help if one of the Lanscarrs would make a match. Soon. Except Dara didn't want to marry Lord Painswick, who was being motioned over by his mother.

"Miss Lanscarr, I see my mother has need of me. If you will excuse me?"

"Please, see to your parent and give her my best wishes. My aunt is right here, so I am fine." Dara nodded to Tweedie, who was standing three feet away. She was deep in a cozy chat with Lady Ponsby and Captain Garrett, a retired officer who had known Tweedie's second husband. Dara was well chaperoned.

"By your leave, then." He made a bow and took off in the direction of his mother. He had a hitching walk, an awkward thing to watch. Oh, no, she definitely didn't wish to marry him.

Gwendolyn was on the dance floor with Lord Salcott, a new contender. He was actually a perfect age for a husband. Dara didn't know that much about him, but he was handsome in an open-faced way and of average height. Gwendolyn appeared as if she was enjoying herself.

Dara looked around for Elise. She didn't see her among the dancers. Dara scanned those milling around, thinking Elise could be speaking to some acquaintances. Perhaps Lady Whitby was in attendance.

She was not to be seen.

Turning to Tweedie to say something, Dara had second thoughts. Did she truly trust Lady Ponsby to not gossip about the sisters? She didn't know.

More importantly, Dara didn't know where Elise was . . . and it was best to keep her own counsel until she did.

She searched the room a second time, looking for Mr. Brogan. She didn't see him, although he was supposed to be there. Could Elise have been foolish enough to go looking for him? Could she have found him?

It wasn't that Dara didn't trust her sister. It was more that Elise and Gwendolyn were starting to chafe under the restrictions of having all eyes on them. Elise had been complaining that she tired of not being able to discuss topics of importance. "I hate nattering about the weather. Or other people."

"I do as well," Dara said. "But we must be careful. We don't wish to be labeled bluestockings."

"Dara," Gwendolyn said, "we *are* bluestockings. Especially you, with your collection of newspapers."

Elise had laughed at the description and agreed. However, Dara wasn't worried about herself. She'd promised to take care of her sisters—and right now, she was concerned about Elise. Dara prayed she wasn't doing something foolish, and the only way to protect her was to find her.

Tweedie was still engrossed in her conversation, and so Dara did what she needed to do. She slipped away, moving behind a group of women and acting as if she was part of their party.

No one paid attention to her. The fashionable world focused on Gwendolyn and Elise.

So Dara worked her way to the Necessary Room. No Elise.

She wound her way toward the cardroom. She was not surprised that Elise wasn't inside. Nor did another search of the ballroom reveal her. She had not returned to Tweedie's care.

That left the garden.

The Earl of Morrow had a well-planned and extensive garden right in the center of the city. The Lanscarrs had been invited to Lady Morrow's garden party several weeks ago, so Dara had a sense of all the hidden places one could be. Guests had been taking a turn in the garden all evening. Paper lanterns had been hung in the trees, and everyone had been commenting on how lovely it all was.

And then Dara saw Mr. Brogan. He went out the garden doors. Alone.

His expression was . . . intense. Almost as if he had a purpose in leaving. A furtive one.

Dara couldn't help herself. She followed him . . . afraid that he had a tryst with Elise.

And not knowing what she would do if he did.

Chapter Nine

A gentlewoman should never indulge in imprudent freedom with a gentleman.
THE RULES (ACCORDING TO DARA)

Some rules should be broken.
TWEEDIE'S THOUGHTS ON THE MATTER

Michael had spent weeks making the rounds of ballrooms and routs, his least favorite activities. However, it might finally have paid off this evening.

Sir Duncan Carnuck, a Scottish MP who had been in Parliament for close to two decades, had left his seat in the cardroom and gone outside as if to take a turn around Morrow's garden. Michael had been surreptitiously watching the man for a good month now, and Sir Duncan had *never* left his cards before.

Could this be the change of behavior Steele had urged him to notice?

There was only one way to find out, and that

was to follow Sir Duncan. Michael trailed the Scot out into the garden. The path for guests was well lit with paper lanterns, except Sir Duncan went in the opposite direction. Into the garden's dark corners.

Michael had been drawn into this subterfuge because someone, certainly a person in power and with authority, had been embezzling from the War Office's coffers. The theft had been going on for years and had only recently been noticed by a clerk relatively new to his position in the Treasury accounting office, Thomas Ferrell.

Ferrell was shrewd enough to catch the discrepancies. "Over time," he'd told Michael, "I realized there was a pattern to it all."

His curiosity sparked, Ferrell had taken the initiative to investigate the name of a firm on one of the accounting vouchers. The address had led to a small, abandoned building down by London's wharves and was owned by one Ralston Granville, the name of a sailing captain who had been dead for decades. It didn't make sense.

The clerk had come to Michael because he'd believed the Irish MP could be trusted. "My supervisor, Mr. Plummer, doesn't want to hear any of this . . . and then I realized, he would have to be in on it too. So I shut my mouth. Told him it was my mistake."

"Why don't you go to the authorities with this information?" Michael had asked.

"I have a wife. We are recently married. I can't have this coming down on me. I need this job, and who will listen to me? I read what you say in the papers. The public likes you. And I expect you to be as incensed as I am about this," Ferrell had said.

To be honest, Michael hadn't believed the clerk immediately. Ferrell estimated that close to fifty thousand pounds might have been embezzled. That was an outrageous amount of money to just disappear, even over what could possibly be close to two decades. Furthermore, with each new cabinet, there were new ministers. How could such a theft go on this long?

Puzzled, Michael had enlisted the help of Beck Steele, a man he'd known since their school days together. Steele was an interesting person. The bastard son of a marquis, he moved between society's classes, including rubbing shoulders with its darkest elements. He trafficked in information. Michael also knew Steele was a loyal Englishman.

When Steele heard Ferrell's story, he was immediately intrigued. He advised the clerk to pretend as if he knew nothing. "Brogan will handle this."

And so, Michael did.

Steele's investigation had turned up that Andrew Plummer was Sir Duncan's cousin. Sir Duncan was on the Commons Treasury Committee. He'd been the chairman for over a decade. "I'll wager he's our man," Steele had said. "We just have to prove it."

The only tactic Michael could think to try was to watch Sir Duncan and track his movements. Frankly, he didn't think the Scot was canny enough to put together such a scheme. The organization of the requisitions and vouchers called for someone who understood the intricacies of government funding.

Steele had discovered that Sir Duncan was not particularly wealthy. He gambled too much—but not enough to lose such a vast amount. And while Andrew Plummer lived well for someone in government service, he wasn't hiding the amounts Ferrell suspected had been stolen.

No, Michael was convinced that others were involved, and he wanted to know who.

He had his man Teddy and his secretary, Elliot, take turns watching Sir Duncan during the day. However, the evenings, the balls, and the social affairs were on Michael's shoulders.

Fortunately for him, the Lanscarr sisters had made the dreariness of Society entertaining. Surprisingly so. Especially Dara. He'd never met a woman with so much determination. She was like a petite general instructing her sisters on how to conquer the *ton*.

She was doing it, too. After his initial shock over her directness wore off, he rather liked it.

Yes, the Lanscarr sisters were beautiful, but Dara was also intriguing.

She might wish to be a member of English Society, but she reminded him of every Celtic woman he had ever admired. She was fiercely loyal to her sisters and protective, even against him. Of course, sometimes, her temper could use a bit more common sense—

Ahead of him in the garden, Sir Duncan suddenly stopped. Moonlight through the trees lit his figure. This part of the garden was not carefully manicured, as if Lord Morrow planned to keep it natural. It was easy for Michael to hide by stepping back into the haven of a weeping willow whose long thin branches brushed the ground. He held his breath, hoping Sir Duncan hadn't noticed him, and cursing that his hiding might let his quarry escape—

A ball of energy slammed into him.

It was so unexpected, he lost his balance and crashed to the ground, even as he turned to fight back.

That is when he realized this was no ordinary attacker. Dara Lanscarr had tackled him and now lay on top of him. She rose up and said furiously in the darkness, "*Where is she?* Where is my sister?"

"Would you be quiet?" he whispered.

"I will not." She raised her voice. "Elise, come out. I know you are here."

Damn it all. Sir Duncan would now know someone was after him.

Michael sat up, the movement unceremoniously dumping Dara onto the ground covered by piles of dried leaves around them. He rolled to his feet, and went to peer out the willow screen.

Sir Duncan was nowhere to be seen. Michael's only hope was that the man hadn't known he was being followed. He turned to Dara, who had come to her feet and was brushing off her skirts. "Did you say my name?" He couldn't remember if she had given him away in her attack.

She looked around and, instead of answering, said, "You can come out, Elise. I'm not angry. I just want to save you from scandal."

Michael frowned. "You know she isn't here."

"Then where is she?" Dara was not keeping her voice down, so he hushed her.

"If you wish to save her reputation, perhaps you shouldn't be shouting her name out in the garden."

"She's not here?"

"Are we having two different conversations?" Michael kept his voice low so she might pick up the hint.

Instead of apologizing, Dara moved to the trunk of the tree and looked around it as if her sister was hiding on the other side.

"Miss Lanscarr, I am unaccustomed to having

anyone *doubt* my word." This time he didn't keep his voice low.

Whirling around to face him, she answered as an explanation, "I thought she was here, with you. If she is not here, where is she?" At last, she whispered—when it didn't matter any longer. This woman was infuriating.

"How would I know where she is? You are the one trying to run the world." He didn't bother to hide his disappointment over losing sight of Sir Duncan. If she had been quiet, if she had stayed by her aunt's side, then he might have discovered who was involved with the Scotsman.

"I didn't mean to barrel into you. I feared you were with Elise and I was trying to protect her. You were just physically closer than I thought. You should have moved."

"If I'd known you were going to attack me, I would have," he answered tersely.

She pointed a finger. "I did not attack. Now, where is my sister?"

"I haven't seen her all evening. However, having some understanding of your sister's personality, I doubt she is in the garden with any man. She'd be too afraid you would do exactly what you did."

At last, Dara had the good sense to look somewhat embarrassed . . . and he was surprised he felt a bit sorry for her. Sorry enough to offer a bit of advice. "Miss Lanscarr, there is no need for you to be anxious over your sisters."

"Family protects family," she retorted.

"Yes, yes, of course—except they are well-mannered and intelligent. Your worry is misplaced. A person, no, *you* can overdo it. You should see to yourself. For example, right now, you are standing under a tree in the deserted area of the garden alone with me. What of *your* reputation?"

Her brows came adorably together as if she hadn't considered the matter in that light. Michael didn't know whether to be insulted *or to kiss away her confusion—*

His thoughts broke. He was startled by how quickly the idea of kissing her had materialized. Or that she had adorable eyebrows.

He took a step back.

Michael was not in the market for a wife. Yes, he had called upon Elise but some of that was to provide a reason for him suddenly going out into Society. And, perhaps he did have a bit of interest because few men could look at the youngest Miss Lanscarr and not be attracted to her. *However,* his true purpose for being at this or any ball was to catch a traitor.

"My reputation?" she repeated. She lifted her pert nose. "My reputation is fine. No one saw me leave the ballroom."

"Said many a young woman who found herself ruined."

Dara did not like being contradicted, especially with common sense. She made a dismissive sound. "Am I in danger from you, sir? Are you going to kiss me?"

There was that word *kiss* again.

And suddenly, it seemed like something he might wish to do. Just for curiosity's sake, he told himself—except, that wasn't true. Dara fascinated him. She had from the moment she'd confronted him in the Supper Room. She was bold, unabashedly loyal, and vibrantly engaged in life with her schemes and her dreams. She was the Lanscarr he looked forward to seeing when he called.

The one he'd enjoy in his bed.

Dara's lips parted as if she could read his thoughts. Her tongue wet her lower lip. A softness came to her features, and what had been a flippant comment now took on real meaning. And he knew what she was thinking because here in the shadows and moonlight under the willow, he was thinking the same thing. She would let him kiss her.

He wanted that kiss, and it would ruin everything between them. The bickering masking attraction; the way he lured her into crossing her imaginary boundaries; their contests to outwit each other. All of those actions made it easy for Dara and Michael to pretend they weren't drawn to each other. He saw that now.

He also believed that infatuation was not enough to toss aside dreams. She deserved her duke. Besides, she wasn't the sort of woman a man toyed with. She was Quality.

He turned away. "We should go inside." He moved toward the curtain of willow branches. Dara didn't follow.

He glanced back. She appeared rooted to the ground, her gloved hands by her sides. "She likes you," she repeated softly.

At first, he thought she referred to herself. Then, he understood—she meant Elise.

Michael released his breath slowly. Dara was so completely loyal. Could it be that he'd read her wrong? She might not have considered kissing him at all and he'd imagined his own desire into her slightest gesture, conjuring feelings that weren't there. The idea rattled him. He was the adroit politician. She was a green lass from Wicklow, of all places.

So perhaps he sounded harsher than he should when he answered, "You would be wiser to think of your own self. Of what you want."

She stiffened as if offended by his tone, and then she said, "I am." She moved forward, head high, her customary swagger back. Miss Dara, general of the Lanscarrs. "Shall we return?"

"Of course," he answered, irrationally annoyed. But then, she could do that to him. One moment he could find her charming, and in the next, her pride and sharp tongue made him want to—kiss her.

God, he was a damn fool.

He reached to pull back the willows when he heard the sound of women's voices, their accent the music of Ireland.

"Are you certain she came down this way?"

"That is what the gentleman on the portico told me. He saw Miss Dara go down the darkened path."

Dara grabbed his arm. "It is the Byrne sisters." She motioned for him to lower the willow branches. They both strained to listen.

"Who do you think she was going to meet?"

Beside him, Dara said, "That is Helen Byrne speaking."

"Girls, if we are going to catch those sneaky Lanscarrs being who they are, we must keep our voices down."

"That is Lady Byrne." She pulled him back into the tree's sheltering shadows. His arm went around her waist. It was a natural movement as they huddled together and listened to the Byrnes perform their little reconnaissance.

"Are you sure she came out here?" one of the daughters complained.

"Sophie, of course I am. I saw Mr. Brogan leave. He was acting very clandestine—"

Michael made a mental note to march outdoors in the future.

"—and then Dara followed him."

"Well, they don't look as if they are here now," Sophie said.

"No, I think not," Lady Byrne agreed. "Let us return to the house before someone wonders what *we* are doing out here."

There was agreement, and Michael started to relax until Dara whispered, "Don't move. I don't trust them. They are canny wenches."

He obeyed, and realized it was not a problem to stay here this close to her. Not a problem at all.

She was tense in his arms. He edged closer, telling himself he wanted to reassure her.

And then she looked up at him.

He couldn't tell what she was thinking, and yet her hip rested alongside his. Her shoulder was tucked under his arm. Her breast pressed against his chest. Her nipples had hardened. He could feel them—

"If they were out here, they would have responded to our leaving," Lady Byrne said, her voice like a shot in the quiet.

Both Michael and Dara gave a start, but instead of moving away from each other, they drew closer. "I told you," Dara mouthed.

"Let's go in," Lady Byrne ordered crisply. This time, the words were followed by the sound of footsteps moving away.

Dara released the breath she had been holding.

She leaned against him as if she valued his presence. "I warned you. Canny."

He nodded—but he wasn't thinking of the Byrnes or even Sir Duncan or anything other than that, right now, she was in his arms, and she felt good.

She turned, looked up at him. She did not move away, and before he could reason himself out of the action, Michael lowered his lips to hers, uncertain, and yet wanting this very much. A kiss. That was all he told himself he wanted, except a humming of desire was building deep inside.

No, that wasn't true. The very fiber of his being had been responding to her from the moment she'd charged into him.

Dara didn't stop him. Her lips parted, and it was almost like here in the moonlit shade of the willow, they were away from the world.

Away from "rules."

Her mouth melded against his, fitting exactly right. She leaned forward, her sigh soft—and was this not a sign she had yearned for this as much as he had? That he had not misread her cues?

No, he had not. For once, Miss Dara Lanscarr was not arguing with him.

Michael lifted her up on her toes, the better to taste her. She reached to wrap her arms around his neck, and the kiss deepened.

She surprised him with her passion. With the

way she responded to his kiss. When his tongue touched hers, she didn't draw back but met him, innocently, seductively copying his motions.

The world faded. In this moment, there was only the moonlight, the June breeze through the willow, and the weight of this woman in his arms.

Like Dara, Michael prided himself on his control. He was an ambitious man, which was the reason he could admire Dara's determination.

However, right now, Hussars could have charged through the night-darkened garden and Michael would not have let her go. She felt too good.

And then he felt the heel of her hand against his shoulder. She pushed, and he released her.

Dara turned away, almost stumbling. Michael offered his hand to steady her, but she warned him back, her palm up.

His heart beat in his ears. Every inch of his body where she had touched him seemed needy, hot, and restless. The kiss wasn't finished. Not yet.

She spoke, and the spell broke. "Elise."

"Miss Lanscarr, I—"

"I don't wish to see you again, Mr. Brogan," she said, a tremble in her voice. "Don't call. Don't speak to any of us." In a blink, she was through the willows, and gone.

Caught off guard, Michael felt as if he had been turned to stone.

She had rejected him.

Even after that kiss.

For the first time, he realized how a woman could play a man for a fool. A simple kiss had upended everything he'd believed about himself. It had sparked something intense inside of him that he'd never experienced before—and she had walked away.

Anger replaced confusion. Dara Lanscarr thought herself too good for him? Well, he was too good for her. Besides, an attachment was not what he wanted. He had an embezzler to catch. A career to manage.

And yet the silliest little word went through his mind—*love*—coupled with the unbidden thought that he could love a woman like Dara Lanscarr. And he didn't understand why. There were other women more suitable for him. Women who didn't issue ultimatums. Women who were *biddable*.

Still, that kiss . . .

Shaken, Michael left the willow haven. He did not go toward the house. Instead, he found the garden gate and let himself out.

DARA FELL INTO step with a group of matrons who had gone out for a turn in the paper lantern side of the garden. She was very quiet, unassuming, and no one commented on her presence. Or questioned where she'd been.

However, inside, she was a tumbled mess.

She'd been kissed before. Pecks on the cheek, and once, Tiernan Enthistle, her second cousin, had kissed her on the lips. But his kiss was nothing like Michael Brogan's. Neither was her reaction. She'd been disgusted by Tiernan's lips. That was not how she felt about Mr. Brogan's.

Even now, as she was regaining some common sense, she had the desire to turn back, to find him, and beg him to kiss her again and again.

And Elise would hate her for it.

The lit path was quite busy. There was a good deal of flirting going on among couples. Dara remembered her original mission to find Elise. She did not see her here.

She did discover a side door that allowed her to enter the house in case Lady Byrne and her daughters were watching the garden doors. She moved swiftly into the ballroom. Tweedie, Gwendolyn, and Elise were huddled together.

Gwendolyn looked up and spied Dara first. The others turned, Tweedie with relief.

Once Dara had joined them, Elise asked, "Where have you been? We looked everywhere for you."

A bit of justified anger felt good. "I was looking for you," Dara answered. "I couldn't find you."

"I've been here the whole time," Elise said.

"I don't think so," Dara responded. "You weren't

here when Gwendolyn was dancing with Lord Salcott."

Elise scrunched her nose. "I went with Lady Abigail and her mother to see the earl's library. Lady Morrow gave us a small tour."

Gwendolyn made a sound. "I'm jealous. Is it as fine as we heard?"

"It puts our lending library to shame," Elise said. "Although Lady Morrow says her husband is not a reader. He just like owning books."

Tweedie shook her head. "How sad."

At that moment, Lord Painswick joined them to ask Elise to dance, and off they went. He shot Dara a look over his shoulder as if silently asking if she was jealous. She wasn't.

Tweedie went to tap a servant on the shoulder for more punch. Gwendolyn took that moment to confide in Dara.

"I believe Elise was actually hoping to run into Mr. Brogan. That is why she left without telling anyone where she was."

Dara hummed her thoughts. Mr. Brogan was a dangerous topic for her right now.

"She is so focused on him," Gwendolyn said. "I don't know if he is good for her, Dara—"

"He's not," Dara cut in. She definitely had an opinion on this topic . . . because she realized that after what had transpired in the garden, she didn't know if she could see Mr. Brogan with Elise. Or how Elise might react if she knew Dara had kissed him. This was not a good scenario. "We must deter her from encouraging him."

Gwendolyn leaned closer. "I don't think he is pursuing her. If anything, *she* is pursuing *him*. Talk to her. I've said something."

"And?"

"She informed me she would make her own decisions. I'm certain she is disappointed he isn't here tonight."

Dara was not going to correct Gwendolyn's assumption. "I will discuss her behavior with her." She would not let Mr. Brogan divide her family.

Of course, how to approach Elise? All of them were headstrong. However, the attention Elise had been receiving had caused her to start taking on airs. She was becoming quite full of herself.

Gwendolyn found it annoying. Tweedie had even corrected Elise a time or two. However, Dara had remained quiet. Elise was young and, right now, the beauty of the Season. What was wrong with a woman feeling a bit of her own power?

Except, as exciting as the London Social Season had sounded back in Wicklow, to actually participate in it was tiring. They saw the same people repeatedly. No wonder the *ton* seemed to live for gossip. It broke the monotony. Several said this Season had not yet had a good scandal . . . and it was Dara's intent that she and her sisters not create one.

CHAPTER TEN

Ladies do not pursue gentlemen.
THE RULES (ACCORDING TO DARA)

Oh, please, we all chase each other.
TWEEDIE'S ASIDE

Mr. Brogan had obeyed Dara's command to not call on the house on Willow Street. He might have been glimpsed at one of the parties, but he did not approach them, to Elise's disappointment.

Whenever Elise expressed concern over Mr. Brogan's sudden aloofness, Dara changed the subject. She would not even mention his name. She also didn't confess about the kiss, even to Gwendolyn or Tweedie. It was her secret, and it was one that wouldn't let her go.

She lay in bed in the room she shared with Elise, listening to her sister's untroubled slumbers, while she tried to remember the minutest details about that kiss.

Mr. Brogan had smelled of the night air, the earthiness of the willow wood, and ginger. Hugging her pillow, she smiled at the thought. She'd long noticed his shaving soap had a manly spiciness that celebrated cloves and ginger. Or was that scent just unique to him?

His arms had been strong. There was no padding beneath his jacket. And even though he was almost a head taller than her, they had fit together nicely.

And thinking this way was not sane. Because, every day, Elise hoped for him to call.

Dara believed that, in time, Elise would eventually stop looking for him. Someone else would capture her heart. That was Dara's hope.

As for herself? Dara tried not to think on her future. She would marry. Eventually. It might not be a duke. A Season in London meeting real dukes had destroyed her illusions of them. They were men, like all the others. Although, they were, perhaps, a tad more disappointing since they were indulged by one and all.

Meanwhile, life went on with social engagements, gentleman callers at three o'clock every afternoon, services on Sunday, and trips to the lending library.

All seemed as if it would be fine, until Elise came down the stairs on Monday afternoon, dressed for going out.

Dara was annoyed. "Elise, it is a quarter past

two. Our doors will open to callers shortly. Are you intending to return in time? You are also taking Tweedie or Molly with you?" Dara didn't see anyone following Elise.

Elise put on her gloves before confronting Dara's questions as if it took great courage. "I'm not going to be here for callers. Lady Whitby will be by shortly to pick me up."

"For what? And for how long?" Lady Whitby's salons were rumored to take hours. "We are due at Lord Freeman's musicale this evening. He has an Italian singer in."

Elise answered as if she could no longer contain herself. "I *don't* know if I will be available to attend. Lady Whitby is hosting the Reverend Roland Hastings, who will discuss his views on education for the poor in this country and I wish to hear him. Dara, *I* need to speak to people about *issues* that matter. I'm exhausted talking about dress patterns and asking puffed-up men about the weather."

Gwendolyn had started down the stairs, a book in her hand. She stopped halfway to listen.

Dara made a commiserating noise. "I grow tired of mindless chatter myself. However, we have replied to Lord Freeman's invitation. He is expecting us." He had told Dara he was most anxious Gwendolyn and Elise attend because he wanted them to meet his nephew from the country. The extremely wealthy nephew was rumored to have a most unfortunate lisp and an overbearing sense of self-importance. Dara had kept that information to herself or else her sisters would never have agreed to attend. She seemed to be collecting secrets.

"Then you will have to make my regrets," Elise answered as if it was a simple matter.

"You should have told me sooner. Or at least warned me of what you were thinking."

"I didn't because I feared you would carry on this way. I can't sit on the settee for another afternoon and listen to gentlemen drone on about themselves. I need to *think*."

Or was she going to chase after Michael Brogan? That was Dara's first suspicion.

After all, it was well-known he attended Lady Whitby's salons. The Reverend Hastings's topic would appeal to him. It would appeal to Dara, but she had made a commitment—one Elise had made as well.

"You can't just leave Gwendolyn and me to entertain the gentleman callers," Dara argued.

"I can. We've been entertaining them for weeks. And do you know what I've observed? Most of them aren't that serious about us. They are either old, have unfortunate habits, or, like Lord Painswick, have relatives who would move the heavens to prevent a match between us. Besides, Gwendolyn and I are not interested in any of them. I prefer cerebral men. Men who serve their government."

"Like Mr. Brogan?" Dara's voice sounded more brittle than she had intended.

Elise didn't blink. "Absolutely like Mr. Brogan. And I believe our sister is interested in mysterious men."

"What does that mean?" Dara asked and looked up at Gwendolyn, who started down the stairs.

"She is jesting," Gwendolyn said. "She is talking about Mr. Steele, whom we have not seen since the Royston ball."

"Lord Salcott may call." Dara was hopeful. "We know little about him. That makes him mysterious. The two of you are a dashing couple on the dance floor."

"His stays creak," Gwendolyn said.

Dara felt her face fall. "He is trying to look his best."

"They are noisy."

"I'd hate to see him without them if they are that loud," Elise murmured, and earned a furious frown from Dara.

"That comment is not helpful."

Gwendolyn ignored their little battle. "In truth, Dara, I wouldn't mind not receiving callers today either. May we just tell them that we are not at home?"

"But they expect us."

"And you are saying they can't do without us for one day?" Gwendolyn acted somewhat regretful. "I will go with you and Tweedie to the musicale, but I would appreciate a few hours to read. Perhaps I am like Elise. I tire of listening to poetry about my 'elegant neck' and to men anxious that I think the best of them."

"This is a mutiny," Dara declared. She took a few frustrated steps away from her sisters. "We came to London to meet exactly these men."

"That was before we realized how boring they were," Elise said.

"They are ten times better than Squire Davies," Dara shot back.

Elise shook her head. "I'm not certain about that."

"You would change your tune if you found yourself watching his brood of children," Dara predicted.

Gwendolyn spoke up. "You are so angry, Dara. What is wrong with not accepting callers for one afternoon? Elise has a good reason to attend Lady Whitby's."

Yes, Michael Brogan.

Dara whirled toward Gwendolyn. She lowered her voice. "The Reverend Hastings is not why she wishes to go to Lady Whitby's."

"I understand," Gwendolyn said. "However, you must stop trying to control our every action. Or what we think or what we say."

Dara rocked back. Gwendolyn had always supported her. Elise might grouse, but Gwennie backed her up—until now.

"We all need room to breathe, Dara," Gwendolyn offered as an explanation.

Elise came up beside her and touched Dara's arm. "Please, one afternoon. That is all I ask. I need to speak to him. To discover why he has not called."

She hadn't even bothered to say who "he" was. Or to pretend he was the Reverend Hastings.

"A lady doesn't chase a man," Dara murmured.

"I'll be circumspect," Elise promised. "Besides, you have all these rules, and you are always the first to break them."

Dara was shocked by the charge, even though there was a good deal of truth in it. And Gwendolyn and Elise didn't know *all* the rules she had broken, usually in trying to protect them. Such as the night of the kiss.

A knock sounded at the door. "Lady Whitby is here," Elise said.

Herald started coming from the rear of the house and whatever task he was doing, but Elise waved him back. She opened the door herself. One of Lady Whitby's coachmen stood there.

The liveried servant said with a bow, "Her ladyship is waiting for you, Miss Lanscarr."

"Thank you." Elise looked back at her sisters. "Don't worry. Lady Whitby shall be my chaperone." And then she was out the door, closing it behind her, before Dara could issue a protest.

Dara stood very still. Elise would find Mr.

Brogan—and then what? Would Mr. Brogan say anything to Elise? She crossed her arms, concerns over what might happen threatening to overwhelm her with apprehension.

With great gentleness as if sensitive to Dara's feelings, Gwendolyn said, "Tweedie is snoring in her nap. Do you wish me to wake her? It is half past the hour."

Dara frowned. What was it Gwendolyn had said? She needed room to breathe? Dara hadn't experienced an easy breath since their father had disappeared and Gram had died. Life had been a scramble. Worse, she seemed to be the only one to see the pitfalls that lay ahead.

She looked to Gwendolyn. "It was unfair of you to let her accuse me of not following the rules. I always try."

"I know you do. But we all do. They are just so stifling."

"Stifling?" Dara felt her temper rise. "Gentlewomen all over this city obey those rules."

"And many of them are deadly dull for it."

Dara almost choked on her sister's directness. Seeing Dara's reaction, Gwendolyn held up a hand. "Please, let us not argue. We've all been trying very hard, especially on a constrained budget. However, let us not accept callers this afternoon. Elise and I just need a small break."

"And what will you do instead?"

Gwendolyn held up her book.

What could Dara say? She nodded and, with a happy sigh of relief, Gwendolyn went back upstairs.

Herald had not truly returned to his task. He was wise in the way of the Lanscarrs. He stepped from where he'd been discreetly listening. "What would you like me to do, Miss Dara?"

It went against everything she had strived for to say, "Please tell any callers we are, unfortunately, not at home today."

She also knew she could not stay here and listen to the knocks on the door. She was too inwardly furious. Things were growing out of hand.

"I need to walk," she said abruptly. She needed action. She needed to move. She ran up the stairs to fetch her bonnet and gloves and to round up Molly.

Fifteen minutes later, Dara wore her green cotton pelisse over her second-best white muslin gown and her straw bonnet. The soles of her walking shoes felt thin and worn as she briskly headed through the park's entrance. *What I would give for a new pair of shoes.*

Molly had to skip a step or two to keep up.

The walking did help clear Dara's head.

She *should* concentrate upon herself. Isn't that what Mr. Brogan had suggested before the kiss she was trying *not* to think about?

Her sisters had doubts. *Fine. Dara* would be the one to marry well. She would be the duchess, and then she would be generous and see to their well-being. Of course, she was not going to support Elise over anything as nonsensical as living independently and hosting salons. She knew her sister. Under Lady Whitby's tutelage, Elise would foolishly start blathering on about free love and women having the right to vote.

No, Dara as a duchess—or even a countess—would not support anything immoral. If Elise complained, Dara would tell her she should have married her own duke.

Dara wished their father was alive. Elise listened to him. So did Gwendolyn. Dara was certain that Captain Sir John would have approved of what she had been doing. Gram would have, even though her sisters acted as if she badgered them—

"Excuse me, Miss Dara," Molly said. "Could you please slow down? I have a stone in my shoe."

The maid's request snapped Dara into the present moment. She had been so worked up, she hadn't really been paying attention to their surroundings. They had already reached the bridge over the Serpentine. "Yes, of course. Do you need to sit?"

"I can lean against the railing," Molly answered.

While waiting for the maid to remove her shoe, Dara took stock of her surroundings. Even though it was a bit early for the fashionable world to promenade around, there were a good number of people out and about. A group of dandies who always overdressed for a mere walk in the park were huddled together while one shared some story. There was a shout of male laughter, and they all moved closer to the speaker as if not wanting to miss a word.

Other women walked with servants, and there were families out with the nurses for a stroll. The children ran ahead or in circles, enjoying being outside.

On the other side of the bridge, on a nice patch of grass, two men were apparently discussing a horse. The animal was a handsome bay. There were also a number of carriages with their tops down.

And Dara realized that she should have been paying attention to the world around her instead of stewing in her own thoughts. It was one of those summer days that made one happy to be alive—

The thought froze in Dara's mind as she realized the rider on the horse was Mr. Brogan.

Of course. Here she was, finally feeling as if all was not lost, and he appears. The man was an annoying pest.

She frowned. The path would take her right by him. She wasn't ready to face him yet. She needed to be composed, sophisticated . . . *distant*.

At least she now knew he wasn't at Lady Whitby's . . . although he could be there later. She refused to let herself think about it. Or him.

Or that Elise was probably anxiously waiting for him to arrive—

"I'm ready to walk, Miss," Molly said.

"I've changed my mind. I wish to return to the house." Dara pivoted and started back the way they came. She ran the chance that a caller might see her. Well, so be it—

A woman screamed and began shouting, *"My baby! Help!"* She stood on the very edge of the Serpentine's bank, her arms reaching out.

Dara's heart caught in her throat when she saw why the woman was in a panic. About ten feet from the shore, a child of no more than three or four was flailing in the water. Little hands reached up as if to grasp hold of air even as its head sunk below the surface, and then nothing. The water closed over the child.

Turning to the dandies who had wandered over to see what was happening, Dara begged, "One of you go after the child."

They looked at her in horror. The tallest mumbled he couldn't swim and, "Who knows how deep it is?"

Another just shuddered his response and advised her to send for the Humane Society. It was a good suggestion. The Royal Humane Society kept boats at hand for just such rescues—but how long would it take to summon them?

How long did the child have now that it was underwater?

The sobs of the mother had set off an alarm to everyone within hearing distance, and yet Dara realized no one was coming to help, at least not in time. They craned their necks, and some ran over, but there was no action.

She glanced at where the child had gone under and knew she could not stand on this grassy section of bank and wait. She knew too well the danger.

Dara could also swim. Her father had taught her. He'd insisted. Swimming wasn't her favorite thing to do, but she was too aware of what would happen if no one did anything.

She tore off her bonnet, heedless of pins. She dropped it and her reticule on the ground, shouting at Molly to watch her things, and leaped into the water.

Chapter Eleven

A lady should always speak, sit, and move with elegance and propriety.
THE RULES (ACCORDING TO DARA)

A lady should be more than a mere chair cushion.
TWEEDIE'S RESPONSE FOR BREAKING SUCH A RULE

The water was deeper and colder than Dara had anticipated. Her heart seemed to stop as she tried to adjust to the temperature. No wonder the child had run into trouble.

Water filled her shoes, weighing her down. What was she doing? This was madness.

And then a calm voice inside her said, *Save the child.*

Doubt was replaced with a fierce determination.

Her skirts swirling and floating around her, Dara kicked hard, moving toward where she'd last seen the toddler. Waterweeds brushed her legs. She hated the feeling of them.

When she thought she was close to the child,

she drew a deep breath and went under, keeping her eyes open in the murky water. Her fingers brushed material before she saw the body. She grabbed hold, raised the tot up, and began the task of moving the short distance toward shore.

It was not easy. Dara's wet clothes and the child's heaviness kept pulling her underwater, and yet the shore was right there. Close enough to throw a stone.

Above her, a male voice ordered, "Take my hand."

She reached for it, thankful for the help. She was practically lifted out of the water, one arm protectively around the child, only to find herself looking into Mr. Brogan's face. He'd even waded into the Serpentine to help.

She frowned, water running in rivulets down her face. This wasn't how she'd anticipated their next meeting. Someone took the toddler from her arms, and then the mother started screaming again.

Dara forgot her annoyance over seeing her nemesis. Her attention went to the small body laid on the ground. The boy's face was blue. He wasn't breathing. And everyone else stood around not doing anything.

Wasn't this the theme of Dara's life? No one did anything so she must do it?

She pushed away from Mr. Brogan, splashed the two steps to shore, and dropped to her knees by the boy. What had she read about how the Royal Humane Society revived drowning people? There had been an article in one of her precious papers. What had it said? Rescuers pushed on the chest?

It would be a sin for this little life to end before it started. Trying to remember the article's details, Dara placed her hands on the chest. The body felt tight, as if full of water. She shut out all the voices around her, even the mother's cries, and told herself to think. To reason this out. She pressed. The length of her hand spread across the whole chest, and she started trying to pump life into the boy. Of course, the child was male. A girl would have had the sense to stay on land—

"Here, Miss, I'm here now," a male voice said. "You are doing great, but we have this." Dara ignored him. She was too busy praying for her charge to breathe. *Room to breathe.* Apparently that was the motto of the day.

"Miss Lanscarr." She was surprised that Mr. Brogan had knelt on the muddy bank beside her. His face was inches from hers. He appeared so crisp. He was even wearing his hat while she felt soggy and smelled of the lake. "This man will take over. He knows what to do—"

A choking sound grabbed everyone's attention. The gentleman from the Humane Society quickly turned the child to his side. Foul water, mixed with whatever had been in his stomach, rushed out of his mouth, and then he began crying between horrible coughs.

A cheer went up, and it was only then that a dazed Dara realized exactly how many people were gathered around her. There were the dandies—those useless sots—who had refused to act, and Molly, but also so many others. All pushing and shoving as if wishing for a closer look to see what was happening.

She needn't worry about the boy. The color had returned to his face, and he was now in danger of being smothered to death against his mother's breasts.

The man from the Humane Society said, "That was well done. Had you read one of our pamphlets?"

Dara shook her head. "There was an article in one of the papers." A shiver went through her.

"Ah, good. We are trying to share our message everywhere. You saved his life, Miss. There is a good chance I wouldn't have been able to revive him without your help."

Dara nodded. She was tired. So tired.

And all eyes seemed to be on her. They all jostled for position to stare—

A coat was put over her shoulders. She huddled into it, thankful for the warmth without knowing she needed it.

"Let me see you home, Miss Lanscarr," Mr. Brogan said. His voice was close to her ear.

She nodded. She wanted to go home.

His strong hand under her arm helped her up. Her shoes were soaked through to the point the leather could not be repaired. Gwendolyn would grumble about the expense. Dara couldn't blame her.

She straightened and then realized that Mr. Brogan had given her his own coat. "Thank you," she murmured. She had to appear a mess. Her hair hung down to her shoulders in a tangle of loose and still pinned curls. Her dress was probably ruined as well. She looked down, and then caught her breath in shock.

Wet material clung to her figure in an indecent fashion. Half her skirts were hitched up on one side so that the stocking of her left leg was revealed for all to see. She reached down to shake them out and then realized that the white muslin made her gown practically transparent. She was wearing a petticoat, but it seemed small protection, especially against the smirking dandies. What disgusting creatures they were.

Mr. Brogan put his arm around her to guide her away, but before they could take a step, the child's mother grabbed Dara's hand. She began kissing it and saying, "Thank you so much, my lady. Thank you."

"Yes, yes," Dara murmured, wanting her hand back. She was suddenly ready to be done with this whole matter. Overwhelmed by it, actually.

Mr. Brogan stepped in, gently freeing Dara's hand. "Here, see to your son while I help my friend." With that, he shouldered his way through the crowd.

"Miss Dara?" At the sound of Molly's voice, Dara stopped. "What shall I do?" Molly asked. She was holding Dara's bonnet and reticule.

And Dara would have answered, except she couldn't. She had started to shiver.

Mr. Brogan's hold around her shoulders tightened. "Walk back to Willow Street," he instructed. "You may carry those with you." He directed Dara toward his horse, held by the man who had been with him earlier. "Do you believe you can ride?"

She shook her head. She didn't think she could do anything.

Before she knew what he was about, he lifted her in the air and sat her in the saddle. A beat later, he climbed up behind her. His hands took up the reins, his arms and chest sheltering her, and off they went at a brisk trot.

It felt good to be away from everyone. The staring of so many eyes was unsettling, and now Dara was starting to have a bad premonition about all of this.

Dear God, what had she done? She was glad she'd saved the child . . . but is that what gentlewomen did? Save a life and have men leer at her?

"I didn't like those men." She didn't even

realize she'd spoken aloud until Mr. Brogan answered her.

"Franklin and his acquaintances? I will have a word with him. You needn't worry."

Dara hadn't said she was worried, except Mr. Brogan had known exactly what she'd meant. And therefore, she had reason to worry.

She hunkered down in his coat. Now, besides the incessant shivering, she had a strong desire to cry. Unfortunately, Lanscarrs didn't cry. Gram had taught her that. No crying allowed. It was far better to be resourceful.

Except Dara didn't know if that was true after a person had made a public spectacle of herself.

"The man with the Humane Society was right," Mr. Brogan said quietly. "If you hadn't acted quickly, that child would have died. You were heroic, Miss Lanscarr."

Was that admiration in his voice?

Honesty made her admit, "I wish I'd taken a different route when I entered the park."

"Nonsense. You were right where you were supposed to be."

Encouraging words . . . except, why did she have this strong sense of dread?

Once through the gates—after all, one did not gallop through Hyde Park—he put heels to horse and they set off at a good clip, neatly working their way through the traffic. The fine merino wool of his jacket formed a barrier between herself and whatever mysterious fear had gripped her. The material held the scent of warm spice and masculinity. *His* scent. Her shivering eased.

He reined his horse in. A boy from the street shouted, offering to walk his animal.

Mr. Brogan tossed the lad a coin. He lowered his voice for her ears alone. "We are at your door. I'm going to dismount."

She sat up, surprised at how heavily she'd been leaning against him.

Mr. Brogan lifted her from the saddle and carried her to the door. She should protest that she could walk. She didn't.

With one arm, he used the knocker. The door opened, and Herald made a surprised sound. Cradled in the jacket, Dara listened to the voices over her, to Gwendolyn's cry of alarm, to Mr. Brogan's quick explanation of what had happened at the lake, to her family's sounds of concern. She closed her eyes, letting their words wash over her.

"I recommend you take all measures possible to see she doesn't come down with an ague," Mr. Brogan said. "A brandy would be wise as well."

"I have sherry right here," Tweedie volunteered. "Where is Molly?"

"The maid? She's walking home with Miss Lanscarr's bonnet," Mr. Brogan said.

Gwendolyn took command of the situation. "Will you be so kind as to carry Dara up to her room, Mr. Brogan? I don't believe Herald is up to the task."

And that is when Dara roused herself to speak. "I can walk." She hoped that was true. Really, all this fuss was silly.

To her relief, Mr. Brogan set her on her feet. She wobbled a moment. Nothing seemed solid, especially herself. His arms hovered in case she needed help. His coat hung heavy on her shoulders. She was relieved to see Herald's lanky frame coming down the stairs with a shawl. It was just the thing.

She relinquished Mr. Brogan's coat and slipped the shawl around her, overly conscious that she looked a fright. She could see the concern on Gwendolyn's face. "I'm fine," she murmured.

"You will be fine when you drink this," Tweedie said, pressing an overfull glass of sherry into Dara's hands. There was a noise behind them. "Ah, here is Molly. Girl, run and tell Cook to start boiling water for a bath." Tweedie had never sounded so in command. Especially when she returned her attention to Dara and saw she was still just holding the glass. *"Drink."*

Dara took a sip of the sherry. She wasn't fond of it, or any spirits for that matter. She never overindulged because she disliked not feeling as if she was in control of herself. Unfortunately, she hated the hazy way she felt right now.

But the sherry did help. She took another sip. Her sense of detachment started to ebb.

She dearly wished to lie down. She gave the half-empty glass to Gwendolyn and started for the steps before remembering herself. She turned back to Mr. Brogan, whose expression of what could only be genuine concern was disconcerting. "Thank you for your help." She didn't wish to be beholden to anyone, but she especially didn't trust being beholden to him. Dara prided herself on being strong and brave . . . but the face of that poor child. The blue, blue lips—

Don't think about it, she warned herself.

Mr. Brogan answered her with the right things. That it was his honor to be of service and so on and so forth, but Dara didn't linger. A roaring had started in her ears. She couldn't faint. Her pride wouldn't let her. She managed to make it up the steps. She turned the corner, out of sight of those in the foyer, and there, she leaned against the wall. She had only a few more steps to take to reach her bedroom. She'd make them, but she needed to rest and to think of something else besides how close the boy had come to death.

Downstairs, she heard Gwendolyn thanking Mr. Brogan for his timely help. Sound carried very well up the wood staircase.

"I'm very concerned for her," he said. "She was brilliant. I heard the mother's screams, and then

Miss Dara jumped in the lake to save that child herself. The boatmen would not have arrived in time. Even though I was on horseback, I might not have arrived in time."

"Dara is very brave," Gwendolyn agreed. There was pride in her voice. "But this is hard on her. She likes being in the background."

"If she had stayed in the background, that boy wouldn't have survived. She has *nothing* to be ashamed of."

And then Dara listened as Gwendolyn said, "It is more than that. This isn't Dara's first drowning. There was another when she was younger, say twelve. A village girl whom we all knew well drowned in the local pond. She and Dara had been playing when the girl went after a ball that had gone into the water. Dara ran for help, but of course it was too late. She was—" Gwendolyn paused as if caught in emotion, then continued, "Inconsolable." There was a sigh as if Gwendolyn felt Dara's shame over letting her friend die.

Dara leaned her head against the wall. Tears welled in her eyes, then ran down her cheeks. She never thought of Moira anymore. Life had gone on, as it did. Gone on without Gram. Gone on without their father.

But overhearing Gwendolyn, she understood why she had been so desperate to help. Even why, when she had seen the article about the Humane Society, she had realized its significance.

"Father came home shortly after the incident," Gwendolyn said briskly, "and decided the best way to cure Dara of her grief was to teach all of us to swim. He'd spent a number of the years in the Indies. He'd met my mother there. It took some time to coax Dara into the water. She is still not fond of it, not like Elise or me."

"Then what she did today was an uncommon act of courage," Mr. Brogan said. "Please give her my regards and let her know I am honored to have been of some small service."

"Thank you, Mr. Brogan. We appreciate you seeing her home," Gwendolyn said. There followed the sound of the door opening and closing. He was gone.

Dara heard Gwendolyn start up the stairs. She pushed away from the wall and stumbled to her room. She had just managed to cross the threshold of the bedroom she shared with Elise when she stopped, exhausted. Gwendolyn gently guided her forward and helped her to undress.

"This dress is ruined," Dara said.

"Not necessarily," her sister answered. "We shall see what we can do."

"I wish you hadn't told him about Moira."

Gwendolyn didn't respond. Instead, she reached down to undo Dara's wet shoelaces. Dara waved her away. "I can take off my own shoes."

Her sister sat back. "I told him what I thought he needed to know. He was very concerned for you. We all are. And everyone is in awe of what you did, Dara." There was a beat of silence. Then she said, "You don't have to be strong all the time."

"I'm not trying to be." Dara didn't meet her eyes. She tugged hard on the knot, making the wet lace all the more difficult to undo, and then threw her hands in the air in exasperation.

Gwendolyn swiftly untied the knot before reaching for the next one.

It was on the tip of Dara's tongue to confess about the kiss. She didn't know why. Guilt, probably. Or perhaps something else, something she didn't wish to consider. Instead, she murmured, "I've been rude to him."

"You have been protective of Elise—who is admittedly headstrong and needs some watching. She likes him very much."

"She can do better. She can have the best England has to offer."

"Perhaps that is not what she wants. I like him."

Would Gwendolyn like him if she knew about the kiss? Dara combed her fingers through her wet hair and then started to remove what pins were left. "A crowd gathered. They all stared at me as if I was an offering at an emporium."

Gwendolyn stood and fetched Dara's dressing robe. "Come downstairs and bathe. You will feel better."

"We must attend Lord Freeman's this evening."

"Dara—"

"We *must*. I will be ready, and I'll smell better. Lake water is not a perfume I wish to continue to wear."

"You don't believe it would be wiser to send our regrets?"

"We can't miss an opportunity, Gwendolyn. We only have this *one* Season to succeed—"

"You are too single-minded. Please, Dara, think of what is good for you."

"I do." Wearing the dressing gown, her feet bare, she started for the door and stopped. "Someday, I won't ever have to bathe in the kitchen again. I'll have servants to carry my bath up to me."

"Yes, and they will be carrying buckets of warm milk."

Dara smiled. "That would be nice." And then she had to ask, "Do you regret leaving Wicklow?"

"No," Gwendolyn answered. "Not for a moment."

At least Dara hadn't gotten that wrong. She went down to the kitchen, where Molly had set up a privacy screen for her bath.

Dara made quick work of her bath. She wrapped her wet hair in a linen towel, returned to her bedroom, and then lay down. She didn't sleep easy. Her thoughts drifted to Moira, and she mourned that she had forgotten those memories.

She had finally started to drift into a deep sleep

when the door to the bedroom was thrown open with such fury, it crashed into the wall. Elise was there, the very picture of rage.

"How could you?"

Dara sat upright groggily. "Could I what?"

"I'm so ashamed. Everyone is talking about you and Mr. Brogan. It's humiliating."

Giving a small shake of her head, Dara tried to make sense of Elise's anger. "Humiliating? What?"

"You knew I admired him. *You knew.* You have done everything you could to discourage me. Now I know the truth. You wanted him for *yourself.*"

Her words sent Dara's mind scrambling—Elise must have learned of the kiss.

Dara started to climb out of the bed, but her younger sister gave her a shove that sent her back to the mattress. "Rules you created out of your imagination, I've come to learn."

Gwendolyn came running to the door. "What is going on? Why is there all this shouting? And when did you return home, Elise?"

"Dara has betrayed me." Elise spit the words out. "Everyone is talking about seeing her in Mr. Brogan's arms—"

She knew. God help Dara, she knew.

"—riding on his horse, no less. How long has this gone on, Dara? How long have you been behaving this way?"

"What? *No*," Gwendolyn said stoutly. "Dara has done nothing wrong."

But she had. She'd kissed Mr. Brogan . . . and now, Elise knew. Dara dropped her head in her hands. Elise would never forgive her.

"Then why are they saying it?" Elise demanded. "Three people came to Lady Whitby's salon and said they saw them with their own eyes. Mr. Brogan was riding down Willow Street."

"Because he was bringing her home," Gwendolyn said. "And also, because those three people have small minds and nothing else to do with them but think of nonsense." Gwendolyn then shared with Elise what had transpired that day.

Elise acted stunned. She sat on the bed as if mortified by her own behavior. "This is outrageous. How could people make something so wicked out of Dara saving a child?"

Gwendolyn shook her head in exasperation. "To stir up trouble. Isn't that why any rumors about us have been going around?"

Turning to Dara, Elise said, "I'm sorry I pushed you. I was just so—" She paused as if searching for the right words. "I mean, when they said you were with Mr. Brogan after he'd been expected at Lady Whitby's . . . I may have jumped to a conclusion?"

Dara raised her head, and realized Elise didn't know about the kiss. It was still a secret. "As Gwendolyn said, they wished for a reaction from you."

"I fear they received one." Elise shook her head. "I'm sorry, Dara. I was so angry, I attacked you. I shouldn't have. That isn't like me, except, he means so much to me. And he has stopped calling on me."

Gwendolyn moved into the room. "Elise, you can't be so serious about him. Not until he declares himself first. You should withhold some of your affection. Protect your heart."

"Did you, perhaps, say something you shouldn't have at Lady Whitby's?" Dara dared to ask.

"I was embarrassed. They made it sound as if the two of you were chasing each other around the park."

"Dara?" Gwendolyn burst into laughter.

Elise groaned. "I know. My reaction was ridiculous. I shouldn't have been so unguarded. Dara, please, I am sorry."

She was right; she shouldn't have said anything. Elise rarely lost her temper, but when she did, she was not reasonable.

But she did not know of the kiss. Dara could laugh, she was so relieved.

She gave Elise a hug. "When we show up at Lord Freeman's musicale and act as if everything is exactly as it should be, then the gossips will have nothing left to say."

"They said you were practically naked," Elise confessed sheepishly. "I didn't believe that."

"Her dress was wet," Gwendolyn answered

crossly. "She had many layers of clothes on. I know because I helped to peel them off of her."

Elise took Dara's hand. "You are actually a heroine, then. And as much as I don't want to listen to singing in Italian tonight, I will be beside you. We shall let everyone know the Lanscarr sisters ignore ridiculous rumors."

"And that we think you are wonderful, Dara," Gwendolyn said.

"Yes," Elise echoed enthusiastically.

"Then we'd best start dressing for this evening." Dara stood. Fatigue weighed her down, but she would manage. She always managed. "It shall take me some time to style my hair. It is still damp."

"I shall help," Elise volunteered. She rarely offered, and she was the one with the most talent.

With harmony restored, the sisters began preparing for the evening. However, right as they and Tweedie were ready to go out the door to the waiting hack, a messenger arrived with a letter addressed to them.

Gwendolyn broke the seal. She read it and then looked up in shock. "It is from Lord Freeman. He has disinvited us for the evening."

Dara took the letter from her and quickly read herself.

"What does he say?" Elise asked.

Stunned by what had been written, Dara handed it to her.

Elise frowned as she read and then said, "He is disinviting us for unbecoming behavior? His wife insists?"

"Isn't his wife the one with the two lovers?" Tweedie wrinkled her nose in disgust. "Now isn't that a false appearance of virtue."

"I find it startling he writes to tell us that if we attempt to attend, he will have us refused at the door," Gwendolyn said.

Dara sat on the steps right where she stood. A thousand thoughts bombarded her, none of them good.

"What does this mean?" Elise wondered.

"That we are ruined," Dara answered. *"Ruined."*

"Because Lord Freeman's wife decided to be a stickler?" Elise huffed her opinion. "We have numerous other invitations. We are the 'Lovely Lanscarrs.'"

Dara prayed she was right.

Chapter Twelve

A gentlewoman should never call
attention to herself.
THE RULES (ACCORDING TO DARA)

If she doesn't, how will she be noticed?
TWEEDIE'S BELIEF

Elise was not right. Lord Freeman's was the first of many disinvitations.

Herald was kept busy the following morning with a number of privately delivered letters letting the Lanscarr sisters know their presence was not welcome.

Some of the writers were apologetic. Most were imperial, dismissing the sisters, as one writer put it, as "you unfortunate upstarts who have been found out—at last!"

Gwendolyn tore up that letter, adding the bits to a growing pile.

"At least we know who our friends are not," Elise said.

"Exactly," Tweedie agreed.

"Perhaps if I wrote each of them and explained the circumstances," Dara suggested helplessly. She was horrified. She'd done this. Not her sisters. They were all being branded because of her one impetuous act.

Gwendolyn came over to sit next to her on the settee. She turned Dara to meet her eyes. "You did nothing wrong. *Nothing.*"

"Exactly," Elise agreed. "You saved a child." She motioned to the stack of torn letters. "Once everyone hears the full story, you will be vindicated. Until then, Tweedie, Gwendolyn, and I are at your side."

"I'm there as well," Herald said from the doorway with a bow.

Dara wanted to cry. She was touched by their love, but also, they didn't understand. They believed this could be fixed, but she had heard stories. She'd studied Society. She knew that many people involved in incidents were never forgiven whether they were in the right or not. Especially debutantes. No matter what corrections could be made, the rumors of this would follow her and her sisters *forever.*

Another knock sounded on the door. Herald went to answer it. Elise said, "There can't be many more rejections to receive. This should all stop before noon—oh, *Lady Byrne*?" Elise's voice went up to a high note when her ladyship appeared standing next to Herald in the doorway. Without waiting to be invited, she'd just followed him in.

Looking uncomfortable, Herald bowed and announced, "Lady Byrne is here."

"It's fine," Gwendolyn said to the servant. He nodded his gratitude for her understanding and withdrew.

Meanwhile, the sisters all respectfully stood. Tweedie sat, curling her lip as if she smelled something foul.

Lady Byrne entered the room with the manner of someone offering condolences over a death. "I know it is early, but considering the gossip, I felt it my duty to your dear grandmother to come running over here."

Gram had detested the Byrnes. Elise and Gwendolyn stepped to Dara's side, protectively flanking her.

Tweedie spoke up. "I didn't know you listened to gossip, my lady."

"Oh, I don't. However, this is quite salacious. Almost unbelievable. Of all the members of your family Miss Dara is the most well considered. I cannot imagine you doing anything as coarse as what they whisper. Especially with a man who was showing such marked attention to your younger sister."

For a moment, Dara's world seemed to spin.

This was how she was being discussed at breakfast tables and afternoon calls. *This* was what she had wished to avoid.

Elise hooked her arm around Dara's. "Do you truly believe my sister would behave in such a manner?"

"Where a man is involved, several would." Without invitation, Lady Byrne took a seat on the opposite settee beside Tweedie. She moved with the contrived grace of an actress playing a part in a tragedy. "After all, in spite of your pitiful background, you girls came in search of titled husbands—"

"As did your daughters," Gwendolyn answered.

"Oh, quite true. But my daughters are not fortune hunters, as you are. I mean, what Dara did to lure Mr. Brogan is quite disturbing."

"She did not *lure* Mr. Brogan toward anything," Elise said. "She saved the life of a child."

"And Mr. Brogan was kind enough to see her home," Gwendolyn added.

Lady Byrne's eyebrows raised in patent disbelief even though she smiled and murmured, "Lovely to have that resolved." She sat up as if remembering something. "I should share that I've heard from your cousin Richard. He was shocked to hear you had taken up residence in London."

"Who told him?" Elise asked, matching Lady Byrne's air of feigned dismay.

Her ladyship ignored the mimicry. "He wrote that he has been very worried since the three of you and your aunt disappeared. Can that be true? Would you leave your guardian without a word?"

No one answered. Not even Tweedie.

Lady Byrne shook her head. "You can expect him to arrive in London shortly. He promised that he would come to take the three of you in hand, hopefully before you can further shame your family. This whole incident of walking around in damp skirts in public will certainly cause him further distress." She stood, her shoulders back, her smile vicious. "That is all I had to share."

"Then you won't mind that we don't walk you to the door," Gwendolyn said coolly.

Her ladyship laughed. She started out and then paused in the doorway, looking directly at Dara. "Seems some believe Miss Dara was scampering after Mr. Brogan in Lord Morrow's garden the other night?"

It took all of Dara's self-possession not to move a face muscle. Lady Byrne couldn't know. She was guessing.

Tweedie rose and stepped in front of her charges. "I chaperone my nieces properly. I shall not have the likes of you insult them."

Lady Byrne gave a mocking little shudder as if demonstrating she was not afraid of Tweedie's threats, and then left. Out in the hall, Herald already held the door open for her.

The moment the door closed, Elise said, "I hope she chokes on her spitefulness."

"I will tell Richard this was all my idea," Dara said.

"I do not believe she said anything to Richard at all," Tweedie replied.

Gwendolyn looked to their aunt. "What do you mean?"

"Your cousin is the laziest man in Ireland. Do you really think he would spend the money to come fetch you?" Tweedie slowly turned to sit down, her movements stiff. She claimed she was slowing down because of all the late hours. Dara desperately hoped that was true. She couldn't stand the thought of causing Tweedie pain on top of everything else. Her aunt said, "No, what we should do is hope for the best. It is the only thing we can do."

"Well," Gwendolyn said with a shrug, "at least today we don't need to be worried about gentleman callers."

She was right. There was no line of callers at three o'clock. There were no knocks on the door. No deliveries of flowers.

Even the letters rejecting them had stopped coming.

At three o'clock, Tweedie suggested a trip to the lending library. "Take Molly with you."

"I have no desire to go out," Dara said.

"But you should come with us," Gwendolyn said. "Tweedie is right. A walk will be good for us."

"I'm not ready to be seen by anyone," Dara said. "I'm too uncomfortable."

"Dara—" Elise started.

"I agree with her," Tweedie said. "You both go on. Let Dara have a chance to lick her wounds. The world will be waiting for her on the morrow."

Her sisters put their arms around her. "You didn't make a mistake," Gwendolyn said fiercely. "They are the ones who are wrong."

"Yes," Elise echoed. "Hold your head high."

Dara smiled as best she could. She valued their support. She was also keenly aware that she would be highly annoyed if one of them had caused her to be banished from Society. The realization was humbling.

Her sisters left with Molly to walk to the library. Dara had a stocking to darn, but she had trouble focusing on the task.

She'd done nothing wrong. She would jump into the Serpentine to save the child a second time if need be. Still, that the fashionable of London wished to believe she, of all people, would dance around in public half-naked was annoying. She felt herself start to move from grief to frustration. The gossip was unfair, and cruel.

Then again, hadn't she occasionally believed gossip that was so ridiculous it couldn't be true?

Never again, she promised, stabbing her needle into the stocking. Forevermore, she would give lascivious stories the benefit of the doubt—

A knock sounded on the door.

Tweedie had been reading a paper. She removed her spectacles from the end of her nose and looked to the hallway expectantly. Dara placed her darning in the small basket next to where she was sitting.

Herald appeared in the doorway. "Mr. Brogan is here."

"Ah, good, I have been expecting him. You may send him in." Tweedie folded her paper and set it aside. She then stood, Dara joining her. "Pinch some color in your cheeks," she ordered Dara. "You don't want to be looking so sad."

Before Dara could obey, Mr. Brogan was in the doorway.

He held his hat in his hand. His immaculately cut bottle-green jacket fit his shoulders to perfection and highlighted the deep auburn of his hair. His boots were highly polished, as if he had not traveled far. She realized with a start that other than in the ballroom, she had never seen him so carefully turned out. He wasn't one to fuss about his clothing.

Serious gray eyes went straight to meet hers. In that moment, she knew he'd heard the rumors. Her humiliation was complete. Heat rushed to her cheeks.

And then Tweedie spoke. "I'm going to let the two of you have a moment of privacy." Mr. Brogan reached to help her great-aunt. Tweedie began walking toward the door.

"Privacy? Why?" Dara was confused. Her aunt shouldn't leave them alone—and then she understood. He had come to offer marriage. That was the reason he was impeccably dressed.

"Oh, no. *No.*" Dara moved to the other side of the room, holding one finger in the air like a governess as if to dissuade him from doing something regrettable. "This is not necessary."

Tweedie paused by the door. "It is," she insisted gently. "But don't worry. All will be well. You can make a decision after you listen to what he has to say." With that, she went out the door. Herald followed her down the hall, and Dara was alone with Mr. Brogan.

Who didn't act like himself. He was too grim.

"Miss Lanscarr, thank you for seeing me."

"You sound *ridiculously* formal." She paced a few steps, wishing there was a doorway on this side of the room. "And, no, you don't have to do this. I said that a moment ago, didn't I? No, no, no."

Mr. Brogan countered, "Actually, I do. I'm also not going to let you refuse my offer."

Dara stopped pacing. "You won't let me reject you? Are you daring me?"

"Not hardly. I know better." He tossed his hat on the settee as if he needed both gloved hands to gesture. "Miss Lanscarr, I agree we have found ourselves in a ridiculous situation. The gossip has made me angry."

"Not any more angry than it has made me. But you have power. Speak up," Dara said. "Tell people that it isn't what they think."

"I have tried. However, I've discovered that stopping a juicy bone of a story like this, no matter how fantastical and unbelievable, is beyond even my powers. Nor do I believe those spreading the rumors—and they are being spread, *diligently*—will have a change of heart and admit they were wrong. I'm discovering how vicious the mothers of debutantes can be. We are caught in a wicket that is not of our making." He took a step toward her. "You and your sisters are being ostracized."

She flinched on his last word. It was so ugly. "This will go away," she insisted faintly. "It *will*. Some other scandal will come along and move the attention from us."

"Can you wait that long?"

There was the crux of the matter. They couldn't. They had resources for one Season, one opportunity to create new lives for themselves—unfortunately, both time and money were rapidly running out.

"I cannot stop the rumors," he said. "I was involved in them. The only solution is to change the substance of them. *Marriage,* Miss Lanscarr. We marry and you regain your respectability. In turn, so will your sisters."

"That doesn't even make sense."

"I know, and yet among our class, marriage is the antidote to scandal. So, that being said—Miss Lanscarr, would you do me the honor of being my wife?"

For one long second, Dara felt her heart open. *He was asking her to marry him*—Michael Brogan, the shining star of Parliament, the most handsome, and challenging, man of her acquaintance. The one she longed for all the way to her soul. *He* was willing to let her be his wife.

Dara yearned to walk into his arms, whose strength she knew from yesterday when he'd gallantly taken her home. She even wanted to bury her face in his chest and burst out in tears.

But she couldn't.

She would not.

Her pride wouldn't let her . . . and also her loyalty to Elise, who all but worshipped him. Elise had been furious when she'd first heard the rumor linking his name with Dara's. A marriage would send her spinning.

However, the most important reason for refusing him was that his proposal had been uninspired. True, she'd told him she did not wish to marry him, but if he *had* to ask, he could have put some emotion into it. A bit of warmth.

"No, Mr. Brogan, I can't marry you."

His formal facade dropped. He made an annoyed sound. "Do you remember when I first arrived? Just now? I said I would not let you refuse my offer. That was only a few moments ago, you know."

Now he was showing emotion. Aggravation. She'd known she could bring it out in him. She crossed her arms, aware that she was rejecting the only way out of the mess she was in. Then she thought of Elise. It gave her the courage to say, "You behave as if I don't have a choice."

"You do not."

"Hmm . . . that is funny. I *have* made a choice, so I think I do."

He took a step toward her. *"Dara."* He did not say her name as if they were lovers, or ever could be.

"Michael," she responded in kind.

He shook his head. "You are the most *exasperating* woman in London."

"Obviously not wife material," she countered coolly. And then, because she was who she was, she told him the truth. "Elise admires you. I won't hurt her."

"Dara, I have made no promises to your sister."

"You don't have to. We women imagine what we will. Elise sees herself with you."

"You speak of choices, and yet I am denied mine? What if I don't see myself with Elise?"

This was dangerous ground. "You are asking me to be your wife out of obligation—"

"What if I wasn't?"

For the first time in her life, Dara was robbed of speech.

Was he saying what she believed he meant? She feared examining his words or giving them too much credence. Every man wanted Elise.

And yet his face had an expression she couldn't define. Oh, his frustration with her was there, but also something else. His gaze dropped to her lips. Deep inside her, muscles tightened in response.

He spoke, his voice low and tight, almost as if he struggled within himself as well. "If you don't marry me, you will be ruined. I can't let you be destroyed after you so heroically saved a child's life."

Bitter disappointment struck her with what seemed to be a hundred little darts. She'd misread his intention—again.

She took a step back. "You are like David, ready to take on the Goliath of Society, to stand for what is right—"

"To stand for you."

He wasn't going to make this easy. She felt the

sting of tears. She blinked them back to continue doggedly, "Except, unfortunately, there is too much at stake for me." *Such as her heart*. "Society's disapproval means nothing compared to betraying a sister who trusts me." Elise had become a good excuse. A true one, and much safer than Dara honestly confessing her feelings for him.

"She will understand, Dara."

"I think I know her better. She won't. You are quite a prize, Michael Brogan. On top of being important and impossibly handsome, you aren't afraid to let a woman speak her mind. Who among us can resist that? Especially once she learns how well you kiss?" Her throat was tight. She was just barely holding herself together. She looked away from him. "Marriage is a drastic measure for a few rumors. It also makes a mockery of the sacrament."

"Dara." He said her name as if it was caress. He moved closer to her. She watched him approach, almost afraid to breathe.

He stopped. They were practically toe-to-toe. "I will not let you drown in the gossips' meanness any more than you would have let that child drown."

"And so you are trying to rescue me?"

"No." His arm came to her waist. "I am actually trying to rescue myself. Dara, I *want* to marry you."

Her first thought was that she wasn't hearing him correctly, that she had imagined his confession. And then he did the one thing she had wished him to do from the moment he'd arrived—he kissed her, and all her protests over why he shouldn't evaporated into the pleasure of having him hold her close.

It was as good as the night under the willow. Maybe better. She pressed her body against his. Her breasts felt full and tight. She reached her arms around him even as he bent to gather her closer—

The front door opened. Voices. She didn't care. She never wanted this kiss to end. She could stay in his arms forever—

"Mr. Brogan?" Elise's voice said happily. "Is that your horse outside?" The sound cut through the beating passion in Dara's blood.

He had to have heard as well, and yet seemed as lost as Dara in their kiss.

Consequently, they didn't break apart as quickly as they should have, even as Elise almost danced into the room with pleasure to see him and caught Dara in his arms.

Chapter Thirteen

Always be chaperoned when a gentleman comes to call.

The Rules (according to Dara)

And try not to be caught by one's sister in the arms of the man she had hoped to marry.

Tweedie's suggestion

Michael released Dara. He turned, shielding her with his body.

Dara would have happily hidden, except she wasn't a coward. She came out to stand by him. Both her sisters stood in the doorway. Elise's expression was almost comical for its shock. Gwendolyn stayed close to Elise as if ready to grab her if she charged forward or catch her if she collapsed.

Tweedie and Herald came hurrying as fast as they could to the sitting room and then stopped in the doorway.

Everyone seemed posed as if in some horrible

dramatic tableau until Tweedie brought them back to life with a soft "Oh, dear."

The shock left Elise's face, replaced by fury. *"What is going on?"*

Mr. Brogan's gloved hand reached for Dara's hand. "Please wish us happy. Dara is to be my wife."

Elise doubled over as if in pain. Dara started to go to her, but Mr. Brogan held her back, warning her to stay beside him.

So it was Gwendolyn and Tweedie who attempted to calm Elise. Gwendolyn who whispered, "It will be all right."

"How could she?" Elise demanded.

"There was no other choice," Tweedie answered. "You must be practical."

Gwendolyn faced Michael and Dara, her smile forced. "This is wonderful news—"

"No, it isn't," Elise announced, righting herself.

"My dear—" Tweedie started soothingly, only to have Elise shake her off and step away.

Every muscle in Elise appeared knotted tight. There was hurt in her expression, the pain of betrayal.

Mr. Brogan spoke, his tone carrying the weight of authority. "I ask you to be happy for us. We are going to marry within the week."

Within the week? Startled, Dara looked up at him. "So soon?"

"It would be best," he answered, half apologetically. "I'll arrange a special license."

She nodded. He was thinking of quelling rumors, rumors that were, surprisingly, already widespread. Rumors that had no justification.

When she had Elise alone, she would explain that this was not her idea. She was actually agreeing to this marriage *for* her sisters. Dara didn't wish them to be destroyed with her.

"If you have any anger," Mr. Brogan said, speaking to Elise, "direct it at me. Dara is an innocent in all of this."

"Do you truly believe that?" Elise asked, her tone scornful. "Because I don't." She looked to Dara. "Gwendolyn and I were prepared to stand beside you. I value you more than what those toadying gossips say about us. And then you steal him from me? This is beneath you, Dara."

Each word was a barb because, to Dara, it was true. Every charge she made.

Gwendolyn attempted to explain. "Elise, this has been difficult for Dara."

"Difficult?" Elise shook her head. "I was fine with my life back in Wicklow. Dara was the one who wanted us here. The one who pushed it." She pointed a finger at Dara. "I now realize you also did *everything* in your power to keep me from the one man in London I've found interesting. I admire him, Dara. I—"

"Elise, let's go upstairs," Gwendolyn said, her hands clamping down on her sister's shoulders.

Elise shook her off. "I listened to you, Dara, because I *trusted* you. I believed that having a suitor who was not approved by my sisters, my *beloved* sisters, was not right, even though he was perfect for me. Just perfect. Now I learn what you really wanted was him for yourself. And he isn't a duke, Dara. Isn't that what you insisted you wanted? You lied about that, too."

Dara rocked back on her heels. "I—I didn't want him. I was going to marry a duke—" She closed her mouth. It all sounded silly right now. The truth was, she'd hurt her sister. That was what was important. "I am only trying to do what is best for you."

"Then why did you accept his offer?"

"Because circumstances gave me no other choice."

"Oh, please. Circumstances, Dara?" Elise shook her head. "I know you. There is more to this and you are lying to me. You are a *coward,* and a terrible sister." On those words, Elise stormed up the stairs.

Dara felt as if her breath was caught in her chest. Gwendolyn stood in indecision. She looked at Mr. Brogan. "I'm sorry you were a witness to that. Please, excuse me." She went hurrying up the stairs after Elise.

Tweedie sighed. "Mr. Brogan, perhaps if you would give us some privacy?"

He looked down at Dara, concern in his eyes. "I didn't mean for this to happen so brutally . . . However, now it is done."

She held up a hand. "May we talk later?"

"Yes, of course." He did not appreciate her response. He stood as if there was something more he should say.

Tweedie came up to him. "All will be well, Mr. Brogan. We just need time for some things to settle. I'm certain you understand."

He appeared reluctant to leave, but then seemed to realize that was what he was being asked to do, and he should honor Tweedie's request. He bowed and walked over to the settee for his hat. He left the room, pausing to glance back at Dara before he went. Herald followed him out.

Once they were alone, Tweedie said, "Elise doesn't mean what she said."

"She does." Dara shook her head, blaming only herself. "She is right. I did discourage her from Mr. Brogan, but not for the reason she believes—"

Except, that wasn't true. "Or perhaps exactly for the reason she suspects." She looked to Tweedie. "He is a remarkable man."

"I grant you that," her great-aunt said.

"But is he worth a rift with my sister?"

"What would you do if you were in her place?"

"I *was* in her place, Tweedie. I believed he was

calling on her. I've liked him from the beginning and so it has been hard to watch."

"Ah, now I understand why you were so surprised by his visit today. You thought he'd been calling on Elise all those afternoons."

Dara frowned. "He wasn't?"

"Child, don't be foolish. The two of you have been flirting with furious whispers you thought no one could hear."

"That wasn't flirting. We were arguing. Genuinely arguing."

Tweedie shrugged. "You were paying attention to each other. I believe the man is more than willing to marry you. Granted, there is this scandal, but he doesn't appear as if he has been coerced. In fact, to be candid, Dara, marrying you is something of a commitment. You are a headstrong woman. I'm impressed with him. He didn't show one sign of fear when he presented himself today."

"But what am I without my family?" The question haunted Dara. "Elise's accusations are right." She had wanted everything about this Season to go well. Instead, she had ruined it.

At that moment, Gwendolyn came down the stairs. She gave Dara a wan smile. "Everything will be all right," she promised. "Elise had her mind made up about him—unbeknownst to us. I mean, we knew she had a tendre for him. Even I hadn't realized how strong a one."

Dara had known. She understood Elise better than anyone else in this family.

"This has been a shock," Gwendolyn continued, "but she will work it out." She removed several pieces of paper from the secretary and picked up pen and ink. "She wants to write. I think it wise." Gwendolyn went upstairs.

MICHAEL WASN'T ONE for introspection. He considered the facts of a situation, made up his mind, and then acted.

That was what he'd done over Dara Lanscarr.

He'd been stunned when he'd first heard the outlandish rumors. When he'd gone to his club and men he'd always considered reasonable and somewhat staid snickered and elbowed him like overgrown schoolboys, he knew Dara had a problem. Their behavior angered him, especially since she had been heroic. She should be lauded, not ridiculed.

The loudest voices were those of fathers who had daughters in this Season's Marriage Mart, daughters who perhaps felt they weren't receiving their due because of the attention the Lanscarrs generated. The bitter among the *ton* were very happy to mock three genteel Irish women audacious enough to test their fortunes in London. The innuendoes were not going to die down quickly. Not without action.

So he'd made his decision, and had been bemused to realize it had been an easy one to make. It was as if something inside him was glad to take Dara to wife. One moment he'd thought of himself as alone and happy; in the next, he discovered she was perfectly right for him.

The kiss had something to do with that. The second kiss convinced him they were a very good match. He wondered what a third kiss would prove, and he was anxious to find out.

Of course, that was before Elise had thrown her tantrum.

His conscience was clear on the subject of the younger sister. Yes, he'd initially been attracted to her, but as time had passed Dara had proved the more interesting Lanscarr. Other than a mild flirtation at the beginning of their acquaintance, one started under his guise of taking a more active role in Society, he'd made no promises to Elise.

In fact, as time passed, he'd started calling on the Lanscarrs with the purpose of annoying Dara, and he'd been very good at it. Good enough to even fall in *love*—

Michael shook his head, feeling a bit embarrassed at the direction of his thoughts. He wasn't given to flowery words. Or strong emotions.

And yet he had very clear feelings about Dara.

Feelings of attraction, interest, lust . . . and, since that word kept cropping up in his mind, possibly love? Actually, he wasn't certain what love was. The word was used often by Society until it had little meaning. Except *he* didn't use it. It was not part of *his* vocabulary, and that he would think of it in relation to Dara, whom he was anxious to see again, was telling . . . because she *had* to marry him. She must. Without an honorable marriage, this story would follow her, even home to Ireland. He also didn't wish to be refused.

Michael had been so caught up chewing over his feelings for Dara, he didn't realize he had arrived at his destination until he almost passed it by. Brooks's was his great-uncle Lord Holsworthy's club. Before Michael put an announcement in the papers—and he couldn't wait to announce his betrothal to Dara—he should break the news to his benefactor. Holsworthy was a stickler for being respected.

He found his lordship in one of Brooks's side rooms. His great-uncle had tufts of white hair poking out from under an old-fashioned bagwig. He was closing in on seventy-five and not aging well, possibly because he kept a bottle of port beside him at all times. He was a tall, narrow man with a pronounced belly. Like his wig, his clothing was definitely out of fashion.

By all accounts, Holsworthy might be the wealthiest man in Britain. Michael didn't know if that was true. Holsworthy was very close-lipped about his affairs. Michael had experienced his great-uncle's largesse over the years, even though, as an MP, he no longer needed an allowance. Still, it had been nice to have the help for his schooling. Holsworthy also paid a living for his mother and for his half brother, Ian, who was fifteen years younger than Michael's thirty.

Almost two decades ago, the earl had sent a representative to Ireland for him. Holsworthy's son had died, and he had come looking for the next male in line, his great-nephew, Michael. Holsworthy had plucked Michael out of Ireland and set him up in school in England. Education had been a true gift, and Michael was always respectful of his uncle.

But he'd never forgotten his mother's warning that Holsworthy always extracted a price. "Neither your grandfather nor your father, bless their souls, trusted him. They said he only looked out for himself. Be certain *you* look out for yourself." Wise words that Michael heeded, even though he and his great-uncle rubbed along well.

Today might test the relationship.

The earl sat in his usual spot, a well-worn upholstered chair next to a wall of books. Michael had no doubt that his uncle had read most of them. He had a book in his hand even now.

Holsworthy sensed Michael's presence and looked up from his reading, his spectacles on the end of his nose. He had his shoe off and one stockinged foot propped on a footstool.

"I was just thinking of you," Holsworthy said in greeting. He turned down a corner of the page to mark his spot. The book belonged to the club; however, Holsworthy treated Brooks's as if it was his personal domain. "Come, sit. Rogers," he called to a waiting porter, "bring young Brogan here whatever he wishes. No, bring him a brandy. Another for me as well."

"Should you?" Michael asked, taking the indicated chair.

"I'm already in pain. Damn gout. Brandy may help it." Holsworthy set his book on a side table. "I was almost ready to send for you. Any more on your suspicions that there is a thief in the government?"

Michael shifted in his chair before answering. Last week, frustrated by his lack of progress over the embezzlement, he had discussed it with his lordship. The earl had held some of the highest positions in government. Michael had hoped his experience might have given him some insight that could help.

Holsworthy did have some thoughts, but ultimately had suggested Michael leave it alone. "You don't know this Ferrell."

"I believe what he is telling me," Michael had said.

"That is your mistake."

Except weeks ago, Steele, whom Michael explicitly trusted, had assured him the funds were indeed missing, giving credence to Ferrell's suspicions. How Steele knew was a mystery, just like everything surrounding the man. He'd sent that information at the same time he'd suggested Michael keep his eye open for three Irish lasses ready to make their mark on Society. It had not been a hard favor to perform . . . and one that had led to Michael's current circumstances.

He looked at his great-uncle. He trusted Holsworthy. The man had always kept his confidences. Then again, Michael hadn't offered many. He was also beginning to wish he hadn't brought up the embezzlement with the earl. The fewer who knew, the better.

"There hasn't been more information." Michael shrugged. "Perhaps Ferrell was just being overzealous."

"Such is the life of a government clerk," his lordship quipped.

Rogers arrived with overfull glasses. Michael accepted his and set it on the table beside his chair. "So, I have news—" he started, but Holsworthy overrode him, as he often did.

"The time has come for you to marry."

This extraordinary statement gave Michael pause. Could sharing the news of his impending marriage with his great-uncle be this simple?

"I agree," Michael said.

"The question is, to whom?" Before Michael could open his mouth, Holsworthy continued, "I have decided that Lady Henrietta Georgeham would be best. Georgeham is a powerful voice in the Lords and, of course, has the correct political persuasion. Very important, you know. When I suggested something, he informed me that he is not fond of lawyers. Your time before the bar is a liability. He's that stubborn on the matter. However, I knew his father when we were—"

He would have gone on and on. Holsworthy had a full glass of brandy and an audience. Many a time, Michael had had to use all of his political prowess to extricate himself from his mentor's soliloquies.

"Marriage is *exactly* the subject I came to share with you," Michael injected neatly into the conversation before the earl could go on too much longer.

His great-uncle frowned. "Subject?" Holsworthy had already forgotten the topic, something he was doing more and more lately. He took a huge gulp of his brandy.

"Marriage," Michael dutifully reminded him.

"Ah, yes," Holsworthy said and launched into it as if they hadn't been discussing the topic. "I believe you should offer for Lady Henrietta Georgeham. A dark-haired chit. I like dark hair. They say she is fairly good-looking. I haven't seen her, of course—"

"Lady Henrietta has pleasant looks," Michael confirmed dutifully—however, she was not as attractive as Dara Lanscarr.

In fact, to his mind, few were as lovely as Dara. Elise and Gwendolyn had stunning looks, but there was something about Dara's character that set her apart. And her opinionated ways. He could picture her meeting his great-uncle. He chuckled just thinking about it—

"What is so humorous?" Holsworthy demanded.

"Humorous?" And then Michael laughed when he realized he was the one who had lost a bit of the thread of the conversation. He leaned forward eagerly. "My lord, I hope you will wish me happy. I have asked Miss Dara Lanscarr to be my wife. We shall be married posthaste."

The earl pulled back his head, giving himself several chins, and then uttered one word. "*No.*"

Michael frowned and then said quietly, "I have asked her. We are marrying."

"You will not," Holsworthy said. "I don't know her."

"The Lanscarrs are from County Wicklow—" Michael started. In truth, he didn't know every detail about his bride-to-be. Furthermore, if Holsworthy had heard of Captain Sir John Lanscarr, then he might truly balk. All sources claimed he was a rogue. A fun one, they would add, as long as you watched your pockets.

But his great-uncle took the conversation away

from him. "Nothing good comes out of Wicklow." Holsworthy sat up, his gout forgotten. "Furthermore, you will not have an Irish wife. Especially this one. I know everyone of importance in Ireland, and I have never heard of the Lanscarrs. What we *do* need is for you to marry a young woman with dark hair, a fortune, and connections. An *English* fortune and connections," he amended as if there was any doubt. "This is about the future of my title. I want alliances. We almost lost the game until I tracked you down. I do not want my title reverting to the Crown. Damn monarchy."

"You needn't worry," Michael said.

The earl ignored him. "Holsworthy is an old, old title. I wouldn't let just anyone wear it, and that goes for your children as well." He sat back, and with a dismissive wave of his hand, he picked up his brandy and said, "You will not marry this Lanscarr person. You will talk to Lady Henrietta. I've already discussed it with her father, and he is pleased with the match." He drained his glass.

Michael was usually good at holding his temper. Holsworthy was of that generation who were often arrogant and domineering. He'd been extremely stern when Michael had been a boy, but those days were long past. And while Michael, out of respect, always took his benefactor's opinion into consideration, the decision of whom a man should marry was a personal one. Michael reserved it for himself. After all, he would be sleeping with the woman.

He did not wish to sleep with Lady Henrietta.

In fact, he was looking forward to having Dara in his bed. Feisty Dara. She would not be a passive partner. It was not in her nature. The image of her in his bed took hold of his imagination.

"I'm sorry, my lord. The decision is mine to make. I have already asked Miss Lanscarr to be my wife."

"Un-ask her."

"You know I cannot. That would be a callow thing to do."

"Then *I* will un-ask her."

"You will not."

Holsworthy jerked as if he hadn't heard Michael clearly. Deep lines furrowed his brow. "You disobey me?"

Ah, yes, here was the man his father's side of the family had chosen to be estranged from. His mother had made certain Michael knew all the stories.

"It is not disobedience to honor my word," Michael replied.

"On that matter you are wrong. You are my heir. You will do as I say."

"On many matters, but not on this one." In fact, Holsworthy might not be aware of it, but Michael had been doing exactly as he wished for quite some time. It had been serendipity that their politics dovetailed . . . a bit. The earl pontificated and Michael acted as he thought best, often keeping his own counsel.

Holsworthy gripped the arms of his chair. "Does this have anything to do with the rumor I heard that you were cavorting with a wet and naked woman in the park? Was she this Lanscarr woman?"

"Miss Lanscarr was wet because she'd rescued a child." *What is the matter with everyone?* Michael was on the verge of exploding. "If I had jumped into the Serpentine to do the same thing, the polite world would be applauding my bravery. She even resuscitated the boy. The boatman claimed that if it hadn't been for Miss Lanscarr's quick action, the lad would not have survived. There was not a moment to waste."

"I hear the child was of no consequence. Just a shopkeeper's get."

"Would you wish any child to be dead?"

"I don't want a dead child." Holsworthy poured some port into his empty brandy glass. "However, there are things a gentlewoman, a *true* lady, should not do. Rescuing other people's spawn is one of them."

They were moving into a dangerous discussion. Holsworthy's attitude toward the fairer sex was archaic. He saw wives for breeding and little else. His own wife had not had a long life, and

Michael had never heard him speak of her, let alone mourn her.

Of course, here was the gist of the problem between them—Michael liked women. He appreciated their perspective. His mother had held opinions of her own. He enjoyed her frequent letters giving him not only insight into the workings of Carlow, where he'd been raised, but also her thoughts on issues in front of Parliament. She could not withhold her opinion, even if she tried, and she never tried.

Dear God, he missed her. No wonder he enjoyed Dara.

He also believed she would like Dara very much. The thought of the two of them together gave him great pleasure—

His uncle spoke. "Do you believe I have no recourse?" He held his glass of port in front of him, his expression malevolent. "I created you. I can take it all away."

"Created me? That was the act of my mother and father."

"I'm the one who educated you. Who gave you opportunities."

"You have, and I appreciate them. However, I'm a duly elected Member of Parliament. I earned my position."

"At my instigation."

That wasn't true. Michael had made his own choice. His uncle had just approved of that choice.

Still, his purpose was not to alienate the earl. "You have been a remarkable influence, and for that I am deeply grateful. However, I will choose whom I marry."

There was a long, laden silence. Beyond the room, Michael could hear voices of men greeting each other, heavy footsteps on wood floors, and the rattling of trays and glasses. He did not turn away from his uncle's stare.

Then Holsworthy said in a quiet, disappointed voice, "I thought you were worthy. You are not. I disown you." He downed his port.

Michael frowned. *Disown him?* "You can't turn me away. I am your rightful heir in the eyes of God and the Kingdom. Even if you hadn't come into my life years ago, Parliament would still have given me your title upon your death."

His uncle grumbled something about "damn fools and upstarts" before saying, "I can cut you off from my money. I will remove my support of your mother. I'll have your half brother tossed out of school. Then I will take anything of mine that isn't entailed and, upon my death, have it doled out to orphans. Of course, that would please you, wouldn't it? Then again, you would be eating *nothing* but bread crusts."

He eyed Michael as if expecting him to be trembling in his boots over the loss of an allowance, however generous. "You can still earn your way back into my good graces by marrying Lady

Henrietta. Otherwise—" The earl snapped his fingers for emphasis.

Just like that.

For this man, Michael had left his home, his country, his mother, his brother. He had done all Holsworthy had asked of him and performed admirably.

But in that moment, he couldn't imagine marrying anyone other than Dara Lanscarr. Was it stubbornness? Most certainly . . . However, he wanted to marry her. His every instinct said she was "the one."

The one. He'd always wondered about marriage. His parents had enjoyed a short but happy one. After his father's death, his mother had remarried to another good man. Once, when Michael was thirteen and heartbroken over a village girl, he'd written home. His mother's letter had consoled him with the information that someone who could be so callous with his heart could not be "the one." She'd gone on to write that "the one" would make him happy but also feel grounded and whole. "The one" would return his affections. She'd speak to something deep within him. "It won't be all feverish passion," his mother had written. "Even your soul will want her."

There was very little Michael didn't like about Dara. His attraction for her had grown over the weeks.

She fit him—physically and intellectually.

Unfortunately, marriage was a gamble. He had friends who were unhappy in their marriages and had expected the opposite. He didn't want to be like them. Yet her kisses had set his imagination afire, and other parts of him as well. She was worth any risk.

And that brought him to the matter of the moment.

He faced his great-uncle. "I am marrying Dara Lanscarr."

Holsworthy's grip on his glass tightened. His face took on a dull red flush. "You will vacate your apartments." The earl spoke as if he was the voice of Doom. "Do not expect your allowance from me. Or the allowance I give your mother. I will not pay your half brother's tuition for the next year."

Michael pretended to consider the matter. The truth was, his uncle didn't pay for the rooms he rented. He'd never drawn on the money Holsworthy had insisted he take since he hadn't needed it. His uncle did provide support to Michael's family, but Michael had the resources to support them.

He stood. "You may cut me off," he said to the earl. "My life is not for you to order."

"If you leave without agreeing to do as I say, I will not allow you back here. I will have you ejected if you attempt to come through Brooks's door."

"You may do as you wish," Michael said, his easy manner masking a growing anger. He bowed. "Thank you, my lord, for all the support you have given me over the years." With that, Michael turned on his heel and started for the door.

"This isn't over," Holsworthy said, his voice rising and bouncing off Brooks's wood floors and paneled walls. "You will not marry Miss Lanscarr. Do you hear me? *You will not.*"

Michael headed for the stairs, conscious of the curious looks of the gentlemen in the main room and lingering in the hall. Several nodded greetings to him, even as Holsworthy's threats echoed around them.

He hated dragging Dara's name into such a public forum. However, once she was his wife, he'd challenge anyone who dared to defame her.

Chapter Fourteen

A lady may cry off. A gentleman cannot.
The Rules (according to Dara)

If people would think before *they marry, the world would be a more pleasant place.*
Tweedie's theory

Elise moved out of the tidy house on Willow Street for Lady Whitby's that night.

Dara and Tweedie were in the sitting room when she came down the stairs with her portmanteau. They had both pretended to be reading. Perhaps Tweedie was. She was wearing her spectacles.

However, Dara was hiding. She felt both mystified and stunned by the turn of the day's events. She was marrying, but she hadn't agreed to marry, not actually. She'd never given her assent. Not verbally. And she didn't feel good about any of it, especially since Elise was so distraught over the matter.

Dara had attempted to talk to her, to explain—but Elise had shut herself in their room and had refused all entreaties to come out.

Finally, Gwendolyn had suggested Dara should wait downstairs. She would talk to Elise. That had been two hours ago.

Since then, Gwendolyn had descended with a letter from Elise to Lady Whitby. Elise had insisted Herald personally deliver it. Dara was sure it was full of bitter renunciations of herself as a sister. Although if it helped Elise to work through this anger, then Dara would bravely shoulder whatever burden was heaped upon her.

Lady Whitby had sent a reply, which Gwendolyn had dutifully carried up to Elise. She had been instructed to shove the letter under the bedroom door. For a while, Dara had lingered on the stairs, listening to Gwendolyn attempt to talk sense into Elise. Gwendolyn was the peacemaker in the family. As a half sister, she'd earned the trust of Dara and Elise when they had their occasional quarrels.

Although this was something different from a disagreement over petty issues. This was about who the sisters were, their roles, and expectations, the loyalties they owed each other.

Then, Elise came down the stairs holding her bag. A distraught Gwendolyn followed right on their sister's heels. "Where are you going?"

"That is no longer your concern," Elise informed her haughtily. She dropped her bag in the hall, right where everyone in the sitting room could see her, to pull on her gloves. She already wore her bonnet and pelisse.

"Of course it is my concern. I'm your sister. You live here," Gwendolyn answered.

"Then I absolve you of all responsibility for me," Elise declared. So dramatic, so ridiculous.

Dara closed her book and came to her feet. The open doorway gave her the impression she was watching some sort of terrible play. Elise didn't even look in her direction, and Gwendolyn was completely focused on their youngest sister. Dara started to move forward. Gwendolyn shouldn't have to bear the brunt of Elise's temper alone.

At her movement, Elise confronted her. *"Don't come close. Don't speak, not even one word."*

Dara stopped, taken aback by the revulsion in her sister's voice.

Elise threw back her shoulders. "You didn't even *like* him."

"He wants to protect *us* from—" Dara started to say in her defense.

"And you think that makes it better? How selfish are you?"

The accusation crippled Dara. She'd been raised to think of her sisters first. On her deathbed, Gram had charged her to take care of them. And she'd promised . . .

Gwendolyn eyes were alight with fury as she said, "Elise, you go too far—"

"He was mine, Dara," Elise said as if Gwendolyn hadn't spoken. "The one, *only one*, I wanted. And *you* get him? You, who know very little of his politics or what stances he has taken? Or what an admirable, noble man he is? Why, he doesn't even *look* at you the way he looks at me—"

"Elise," Gwendolyn snapped.

Dara held up a hand, conscious that Tweedie now also stood, her expression one of grief. "It's all right, Gwendolyn. What Elise says is true. Mr. Brogan has been quite taken with Elise, as most men are. She is far more attractive than I am. You both are."

"That is not true," Gwendolyn replied. "And beauty is as beauty does."

She shot that last at their youngest sister, who ignored it . . . because Elise was caught up in self-righteous anger. It was a dangerous place. Dara knew; she'd spent time there more than once.

Elise made an impatient sound. "Stop criticizing yourself, Dara, or holding yourself up to us in comparison. You are as lovely as Gwendolyn and me. This has nothing to do with looks. I'm angry because you don't know what a good man he is—"

"You are wrong—"

"—He never fit your ideal. You are clueless about anything beyond your senseless rules—"

"That is not true—"

"—Then again," Elise spoke over her, "you are obviously willing to break every one of them when it saves *you* from disgrace. After all, what rule is there that says you steal the man your sister loves?"

"You *can't* love him," Dara countered, stung again by Elise's claims. "You barely know him—"

"And you know him better . . . ?"

She did. She had kissed him. But before Dara could lash back and say something that would truly be unwise, Tweedie interrupted them.

"Stop this." She pounded her frail hand on the side table, demanding they pay attention to her. "Scratching each other's eyes out won't make this better. Elise, she didn't plan on Mr. Brogan making an offer."

"What choice did he have?" Elise countered. "Once his name was linked to her disgrace, he had to do what is honorable. He is trying to save *her* reputation even though it is *her* fault all the rumors are going around."

Gwendolyn choked on her exasperation. "Her fault? That she rescued a child and small minds are ripping her to shreds? What would you have her do? Let the child drown? She couldn't do that. None of us could do that. Not after—" She paused, glanced at Dara, and then said, "Not after what happened that day in Wicklow."

Elise's face was a mask of hard lines, and not a particularly beautiful one. "I wouldn't want to see a child drowned, but Dara didn't have to accept his proposal. Not if she loved *me*."

She sounded pouty, because she was so hurt. Dara understood. "I do love you, Elise. You are my sister. I also *haven't* accepted his offer—"

"It appeared to me you had accepted it," Elise lashed back. "He even announced it to us."

Dara ignored her anger to finish her thought. "Tomorrow I will speak with him. I will say that I'm sorry, but I can't marry him."

"Then he'll run from all of us," Elise said sadly. "Do you not see the situation he is in? He believes he is saving you. And even if you refuse him, you have ruined it for me. He'll not have me now."

"Elise, I love you," Dara pleaded. "You are more important to me than any man."

"Oh, no, Dara, the only thing important to you is your precious scheme. That we *all* marry."

Dara's temper reignited. Her nerves were stretched thin, and she was willing to do what she could to please her sister, except have Elise continue to attack her. "That charge is *not* true. We all agreed—"

Tweedie threw her book on the floor with enough force it sounded like a door slamming. *"Stop this bickering. It is beneath all of you."*

The three sisters turned to stare at their little aunt, who was practically shaking with anger. "Elise, I was here when Mr. Brogan brought Dara back to us after the drowning incident. He had nothing but admiration for Dara. And even though you three tease me about my frequent bouts of closing my eyes, I do watch what is going on in this house. Yes, Mr. Brogan has looked at you with what I will call 'hot' eyes—"

"Hot eyes?" Elise repeated as if offended.

"He had that heated look men, or stallions, take on when they see an attractive filly. Where they snort and paw the ground."

"Gentlemen don't do that," Elise said.

"They do, my dear, they do," Tweedie assured her. "However, it takes more than hot eyes and longing looks to convince a man to take a wife. I'm surprised you haven't learned that by now."

"But he hasn't ever paid any attention to Dara before."

"Do you realize how spoiled you sound? Mind your manners, girl." Tweedie didn't wait for a response but continued, "And he has paid plenty of attention to your sister."

"Only because she bickers with him."

"Sometimes bickering isn't what it seems on the surface. There is more than looks to attraction. I should know. I've had three husbands, and that is three more than any of you have had, even all together. Mr. Brogan knew what he was doing this afternoon. He *wanted* to ask for Dara's hand."

Elise's lower lip started to tremble, and Dara yearned to put her arms around her. Gwendolyn wasn't so moved. She shot Dara a look warning her to stay right where she was.

"I've never met a man I've admired as much and I *never* will," Elise said.

"Pshaw," Tweedie declared. "One day you will meet someone who cares more about your character than your looks, and that man will be *worthy* of you. And who knows? He might be a duke. Or a prince. Or a king. Or a *ditchdigger.* That is the fun of life. We never know what is coming."

"I thought I *had* found the man worthy of me," Elise confessed in a small voice before being interrupted by a knock at the door. She released her breath with a heavy sigh. "Finally."

"Finally what?" Gwendolyn asked.

Herald appeared from wherever he had been discreetly hiding. He moved around the sisters to open the door. Instead of a servant, Lady Whitby was there. She stepped inside, took a pitying look at the sisters, and then murmured, "I will wait on the step."

"You don't have to wait. I'm coming," Elise answered. Waving Herald away, she picked up her valise, moved to the door, and then paused, addressing her sisters. "Lady Whitby has kindly offered to let me stay with her. I need a bit of distance from all of this. I'm certain you understand." She looked directly at Dara and whispered, "I can't share the same house with you, let alone the same room. It hurts." On those words, she was out the door.

"Elise," Dara started, wanting to call her back, to have her see reason, but her sister was down the step and following Lady Whitby into her coach.

Gwendolyn came to Dara's side and put her arm around her. They watched the coach drive away. Elise didn't even glance out the window at them.

"This isn't your fault," Gwendolyn said.

"No, it isn't," Tweedie agreed heartily. She had joined them in the doorway.

"I must make it right." Dara looked at her loved ones. "I never said yes. I never accepted his proposal."

Tweedie made an impatient sound. "Don't be foolish. And now I really do need to lie down. Gwendolyn, don't let her, you know, be silly." With that, she started for the stairs. "I will be down for dinner."

"She's right," Gwendolyn said. "No one forced Mr. Brogan to make an offer."

"Elise is so hurt." Her sisters had been the one constant in her life. And having Elise leave? Dara felt as if a part of her had gone out the door.

"She will work her way out of this."

Dara didn't see how, not unless she took action.

That night, Dara had trouble falling asleep. She was too aware of the empty side of the bed. She understood why Elise was so angry. Her hopes had been dashed, and Dara knew that disappointment.

Nor was Dara at peace with the solution that would make Elise happy, because her sister was right—there would be no winner.

The problem kept Dara awake most of the night.

Consequently, she came down the stairs almost an hour and a half later than her usual time for her breakfast, feeling heavy-lidded and without any enthusiasm. She had reached a decision. She had one purpose for this day. She needed to inform Mr. Brogan that she could not accept his marriage offer. Salvaging her relationship with her sister was more important than her reputation.

She was halfway down the stairs when Gwendolyn, her eyes bright and her smile wide, popped out from the sitting room. She held several envelopes, which she spread out in her hands like a fan.

"Can you believe this?" she said.

"What is it?" Dara asked, too sleep-befuddled to be quick.

"Invitations. We are being re-invited. There are also congratulations on your match with Mr. Brogan."

Dara stopped on the step. "Has the announcement been published?"

"I don't believe so," Gwendolyn answered. "There hasn't been time."

"And yet people know?"

"Good gossip spreads fast," Gwendolyn said.

Dara wanted to wail her frustration . . . because her decision to refuse Mr. Brogan would probably anger Society. Everyone adored him.

At that moment, there was a knock at the door. Herald opened it and received another letter, which he handed to Gwendolyn. She closed her invitation "fan" to accept it, setting them on the hall table.

She paused to look at the seal and then cracked it open. Her brows lifted. "It is from the Duchess of Marlborough."

Dara practically flew down the last steps. She was wide awake now. The duchess, their mother's second cousin, had not ignored their letter. "What does she say?" she demanded as she trailed after Gwendolyn into the sitting room.

Scanning the letter, Gwendolyn said, "The duchess writes that she is still in the country, and she appreciated our letters of condolence—"

Another knock on the door interrupted her. Dara ignored it. "What *else* does she say?"

"That is about all." Gwendolyn looked up, confused, and then shrugged. "It is as if our letter just reached her and she wished to acknowledge us?"

"At least she knows where we live," Dara answered, taking the missive from her. She wanted to see the words, to know how a duchess made the loops on an *h* or an *l*, and the sort of ink she used. It must be very special ink. Something fitting her station in life.

The door knocker was lifted again. While Herald hurried to answer it, Gwendolyn was going through the other mail. "These invitations, I've never seen the like. This one is for the Countess Fitzgibbon's ball Friday night."

"The Countess Fitzgibbon? She invited us? Why, she has barely given us a passing glance, and only the cream of the *ton* have been invited. Oh, and look here." Dara held up a heavy, embossed card. "This is for Lord and Lady Reeve's rout this evening. Didn't they disinvite us?"

"They have changed their minds," Gwendolyn said with great satisfaction. Apparently she hadn't lost sleep over Elise. "Lady Reeve included a note saying she regrets any ill feelings and prays we will attend."

At that moment, Herald appeared in the doorway to announce, "Lady Byrne is here to see you." Of course, her ladyship was practically at his elbow. She wore a gown and pelisse of Pomona green that did nothing for her complexion, especially topped off with a yellow chapeau.

"Why don't we have a door on this room for privacy?" Gwendolyn muttered under her breath, because they could not claim to be away from home when they were sitting right there for any guest to see. She rose, plastering a smile on her face. "Hello, Lady Byrne. My, you are a lark today, are you not?"

Her ladyship gave a trill of laughter as she walked into the room. She took a seat without invitation. "One must be early when they realize their dear friends have news to share."

Dear friends? Knowing how spiteful Lady Byrne was, Dara's first thought was the fear her ladyship had heard about Elise leaving. Dara and Gwendolyn sat on the settee across from her.

Then, to Dara's relief, Lady Byrne clarified her meaning. "I hear we should wish you happy? Your betrothal to MP Brogan? It is all anyone could talk about last night. Such a juicy bit of gossip, especially since I left here yesterday believing all was lost." She paused, and then she asked slyly, "Is it true he and Lord Holsworthy had a terrible row over you?"

Dara frowned. She had no idea what Lady Byrne was talking about. Neither did Gwendolyn, who had the good sense to say, "I fear we have not made Lord Holsworthy's acquaintance."

Lady Byrne's eyes brightened. "You do not know Lord Holsworthy? Why, Mr. Brogan is his heir. The earl of Holsworthy is one of the wealthiest men in England. Certainly you knew about Mr. Brogan's expectations." She leaned forward as if she had the power to ferret out the truth from them.

She didn't.

"One should not brag about expectations," Dara responded sweetly, relying on one of her "rules."

Lady Byrne's smile widened to show her full set of teeth. "Apparently they made a spectacle of themselves in Brooks with Lord Holsworthy shouting that he would not support a match. In fact, the betting book in that establishment and others are rumored to predict that you will not marry." She made a sound as if dismissing those rumors. "Men and their wagers. So ridiculous. Ah, but then, you understand. You are a gambler's daughters. I wonder what your father would have wagered."

Dara was speechless and a touch horrified by all the gossip surrounding her. Gwendolyn was not. She gave Lady Byrne her own serene smile and said, "That is a mystery since he is not here to share his opinion. As for us, we can let you know the chances of success after considering both sides of the issue. That's what gamblers do."

"And?" Lady Byrne prodded.

"I would never wager against my sister Dara."

Dara wanted to cheer.

Lady Byrne was undeterred. "Lord Holsworthy threatened to disown Mr. Brogan if he married Miss Dara. It would be a pity to give up an earldom."

There wasn't much Dara didn't know about

Society. Studying it had become her life's work for the last year. "A man can't disinherit a legitimate heir. The Crown makes those decisions."

"The Crown does not control the money or any land that isn't entailed," Lady Byrne replied. "It would be a pity if you claimed such a catch only to find yourself poor."

Gwendolyn spoke up. "Dara and Mr. Brogan are a love match. Money is of no importance to you, is it, Dara?"

"Oh, no," Dara agreed, wide-eyed. "I admire Mr. Brogan for his personality. We'd be happy in a cottage in Wicklow, all tucked in around a peat fire." Let her spread rumors about that statement.

Lady Byrne stared at her as if that was the most outrageous thing she'd ever heard any woman say. However, she'd accomplished what she'd set out to do—delivering insults while prying for information. "Well, then, you will have a fine future after Mr. Brogan gives up a fortune for you." She rose. "I rushed over here because I believed you should be warned about what is being said. As a mother, it has been difficult to watch you girls struggle. Thank you for accepting my call, even so early."

Dara and Gwendolyn had stood with her. Gwendolyn matched her false tone with one of her own. "We always enjoy a visit with you, my lady. Please, give our best to Helen and Sophie."

"Oh, I will."

As soon as Herald closed the door behind their guest, Gwendolyn mimicked Lady Byrne as if the lady were among her friends. "Can you believe she did not know he would become an earl?"

Dara clutched her chest theatrically and responded, "Those Lanscarr sisters are *so* naive. Such a *pity* they don't understand Society."

And then the two of them collapsed into laughter, and it felt good. After all the stress of the past day, Dara needed the release. They were loud enough that Tweedie came downstairs to see what was so humorous. Soon she was laughing with them.

Dara was the first to sober. She glanced around at the group of them, and keenly felt Elise's loss.

They noticed her expression. Gwendolyn said, "It isn't your fault. Elise has always been headstrong, just like we are."

Dara paused a moment and then confessed, "I'm beginning to wish we never came to London."

"You?" Tweedie said.

Dara nodded. "I didn't anticipate that this venture would divide us." She drew a deep breath and then made her decision. "I am going to refuse the offer. I can cry off, and it will not reflect poorly on Mr. Brogan."

Her announcement was met with silence.

Gwendolyn exchanged unspoken thoughts with Tweedie and then said, "Is that what you truly wish to do? Or are you just so desperate for peace with Elise?"

Memories of matching wits with Mr. Brogan, of his smiling when she scored a point against him . . . and of being in his arms, feeling safe and protected, flashed through Dara.

Then she thought of her sister, of her hurt.

Instead of answering, she went to the secretary by the window and pulled out a sheet of paper. She wrote to Mr. Brogan requesting he call upon her as soon as he was able. She sanded it, blew on it, and sealed it—and only then did she realize she had no idea of his address, just as she hadn't known he would be an earl or that he would inherit a fortune.

Elise was right. Beyond feelings, Dara knew very little about him and, therefore, she *was* making the right decision. She wrote his name on the letter.

Standing, she said, "I'm past ready for my breakfast." She handed the letter to Herald for delivery, trusting he would see it safely to Mr. Brogan.

IT WAS LATE in the day when Dara heard a reply from Mr. Brogan.

His first comment was a request that she refer to him as "Michael," his given name. He'd addressed her as Dara.

She stared at the two words scribbled in his bold hand on the page. *Michael. Dara.*

He then went on that he was unavoidably detained with committee work. Could they meet at the Reeve ball that evening? He and the Reeves were great friends. They could find someplace private there.

It wasn't the answer Dara had anticipated. A ballroom was not the place to have the discussion she wished to deliver. There would be too many people watching. And according to Lady Byrne, the betting books alone would ensure they would be the center of attention. Their conversation could become very awkward if not handled right. Still, she couldn't march to the Commons to track him down. She would have to wait.

Therefore, because the evening might prove fraught with emotion, Dara took extra care preparing herself for the ball. She asked Molly, who was usually tasked to fuss over Elise, to help with her hair.

They decided to style Dara's thick tresses loosely with yellow ribbon rosettes pinned in the curls. Dara chose to wear the simple white dress the Lanscarrs were now noted for, and once Molly had finished, she felt she looked her best.

She wondered if Elise would be in attendance. Possibly.

Several times over the course of the day, both Tweedie and Gwendolyn had muttered their disappointment in Elise. They didn't understand her Medea-like anger, but Dara did . . . because prior to yesterday, she had been bracing herself for Michael choosing her sister and having to live the rest of her life with that choice.

Now he would be lost to both of them. There weren't that many men like Michael—yes, she could think of him by his first name. She liked the sound of it. *Michael* was a strong name without being hard, and it fit him. He'd never talked down to her. He took his responsibilities seriously. He had come to her aid when she'd needed him. He had done what was necessary to protect her.

Carrying out her decision would be very difficult, but so would spending her life estranged from her sister.

Dara picked up her shawl and went downstairs.

THE REEVES' BALL was another ridiculous crush. Apparently, this Wednesday evening, no one had anything to do but sip their hosts' punch, dance, gossip, and unknowingly wait for Dara to reject Michael's offer.

Only a few weeks ago, this sort of entertainment had seemed exciting. Now Dara found herself rather jaded about the experience. She was uncomfortably aware that her presence was eliciting a good deal of attention. Whispers seemed to flow around her. Lady Reeve fawned over her, letting her know that "our dear Mr. Brogan has not arrived yet."

Gwendolyn was quickly claimed for dancing. Several hinted to Dara that best wishes were in order. No one asked her to dance. Apparently, she had been branded "claimed."

It also puzzled her that no one inquired after Elise. Her sister had been popular. Now, either everyone knew about the rift and they were staying mum, or—and this was the more likely scenario—no one even noticed her absence because they were more interested in themselves.

Dara wondered why she had ever thought London Society was better than Wicklow.

At that moment, she caught sight of Michael. He had apparently just arrived, but he wasn't looking for her. Instead, he walked through the room, keeping to the far back wall as if trying to escape notice. There was a door that led out into the garden. He left through it.

What was he doing? He seemed furtive. Exactly the way he'd acted the night under the willow tree when she'd suspected he'd been slipping out to meet Elise.

Dara had never been known for her patience, especially once her curiosity had been engaged. She had also grown past her rule that ladies needed to be chaperoned everywhere in a ballroom. Besides, being "claimed" should give her a touch of freedom.

"Excuse me," Dara said to Tweedie. "I must step away a moment." That was their polite code that one needed to seek the Necessary Room. "You don't need to come."

Tweedie nodded, distracted by the sight of Lady Ponsby winding her way toward them. She always looked forward to seeing her friend at these gatherings.

Dara pretended to move away sedately only to hurry to the door leading out into the garden once she felt she wouldn't be noticed. The cool evening air was a blessing after the stuffiness of perfumes, colognes, and bodies beneath so many candles. She appreciated the escape.

Michael wasn't on the portico. She skirted the couples and a group of gentlemen enjoying the night there. At the foot of some steps, a stone path disappeared into the shadows of trees. She remembered that Lord Reeve fancied himself a great arborist and delighted in his collection. His garden was famous for exotic trees of all shapes and sizes.

And somewhere among them must be Michael.

She set out looking for him. She'd actually prefer their discussion away from the house.

The trees bordering the walk were overgrown and dense. At many of the soirees she had attended paper lanterns were usually strewn through the gardens. Not so here. All was dark and quiet. She couldn't even hear the musicians clearly. If ever there was a garden designed for midnight trysts, this was it. Conscious that her white muslin would stand out in the night, she tried to stay to the shadows.

And then suddenly, Michael was in front of her.

Before she could speak, he placed a hand over her mouth. His other arm encircled her, pinning her close to him. "Quiet, you must be quiet," he desperately whispered in her ear.

A beat later, she realized they were not alone. He had been spying on someone.

CHAPTER FIFTEEN

Pay heed to the rules of engagement.
THE RULES (ACCORDING TO DARA)

Young people will do what they will.
TWEEDIE'S BELIEF

Michael could hear Dara's heartbeat. It sounded overloud when he needed them to be noiseless.

Or was it the sound of his own pounding heart?

It had been luck when he'd first arrived that he'd caught a glimpse of Sir Duncan Carnuck by the ballroom door leading into the garden. He had not known the gentleman would be in attendance this evening. In fact, Michael's first intention upon arrival had been to seek out Dara.

However, when he saw Carnuck slip out as if not wishing to be noticed, Michael realized that he might have regained the chance he'd lost the week before. There must be another meeting. He'd disrupted the other one.

He thought it clever that Sir Duncan and his accomplices met at social gatherings. They hid in plain sight.

And Reeve's garden was perfect for skulking around, what with all his beloved trees. Michael had easily trailed behind his quarry this time, ducking under branches and winding around trunks.

Fortunately, Michael was far enough behind so that when Sir Duncan greeted another man, he didn't walk up on them. He'd ducked into the shadows before they could sense his presence. There he'd strained to hear any conversation, and realized they were close to a back garden where a gate led to a passageway.

The man Sir Duncan had come out to meet held a lantern. He kept the light far enough away so that Michael wasn't able to see his features. His clothes were those more befitting an ostler than a gentleman.

"He sent a lackey?" Sir Duncan was saying, his displeasure clear. He had always had an air of superiority. Michael did not like him. He admired his politics even less. Sir Duncan and he had verbally tussled more than a time or two.

However, the word *lackey* had made Michael want to look closer. He had a sense there was something familiar about the stranger. It was in the way the man held himself. Could they have met before?

He'd thought to edge toward them when he'd heard soft steps approaching. He moved back and caught a glimpse of white muslin. Dara. Of course.

Fortunately he'd caught her before she had stumbled into the meeting. He held her close. The two men had gone quiet. Michael didn't dare breathe. Dara leaned against him as if she, too, sensed danger. He adored her for trusting him.

After a moment of stillness, the lackey said, "I thought I heard something." He didn't speak like an ostler. His speech was deliberate, concise.

"Probably lovers," Sir Duncan responded. "The gardens are full of them at these events."

"We should meet some place quieter."

"I prefer a bit of company," was Sir Duncan's reply. "Especially for this sort of business."

Michael moved deeper into the shadows, his arm guiding Dara to move with him.

"So, tell me, why did he demand a meeting?" Sir Duncan said. "And make it quick. I don't have time to cool my heels. My wife will notice my absence."

"Everything needs to be shut down," the lackey answered quietly.

"Shut down? Has it come to this?"

"No, my lord. It has come to *this*."

Michael didn't understand why the lackey

had placed the emphasis on *this*. He wanted to move forward, to see if anything like money was changing hands—

Sir Duncan cried out, *"What . . . ? Why . . . ?"* And then quiet.

Michael frowned. He wished he could see.

Another hushed male voice spoke. "Yer done?"

"Pack him up," the lackey ordered. "We can't leave him here. Get rid of the body. Toss it wherever you see fit."

Only then did Michael realize what had happened to Sir Duncan. "Stay here," he ordered Dara before charging forward.

The men were through the gate, one holding the lantern and one dragging Sir Duncan's body by the shoulders. A hackney coach waited in the passageway for them.

"Stop!" Michael shouted. "Stay where you are."

They immediately dropped the body and started for the vehicle.

Michael ran to the gate. He leaped over Sir Duncan to grab at the lackey.

It was a mistake. The man dropped the lantern and whirled on Michael. The lantern light flashed on the blade of a knife. He brought it down and might have delivered a fatal blow except for Dara's warning. *"Michael."*

Her presence distracted the attacker enough that the blade sliced through Michael's coat sleeve, just barely grazing the skin.

The lackey looked at her. Her white muslin was like a beacon in the night. He scooped up the lantern and threw it at her. It hit the ground, exploding. Michael whirled around, worried for Dara, giving the lackey the opportunity to jump into the vehicle. With a snap of the reins, the two men were galloping down the passageway.

Michael ran to Dara, who was busy stomping on broken glass and flames. "Are you hurt?"

"No, I'm just trying to save the garden from catching fire."

At that moment, Sir Duncan groaned. Shocked that he was still alive, Michael swung back to him, dropping by his side. The lackey had slit his throat. "Can you speak?" Michael asked desperately. "Who did this to you?"

Footsteps came running through the garden. "What happened?" a man asked.

"Someone attacked MP Carnuck," Michael answered. The less that was known, the better.

"I saw two fellows trying to drag a body out," a man from the passageway said. He pointed to Michael. "This one tried to stop them."

Where once the garden had seemed empty, it was now filled with people.

Michael turned his attention back to Sir Duncan. His lordship's eyes were wide as if he had something he wished to say, but couldn't—and then, the tension left his body. The light died in his eyes, and Michael knew he was gone.

He also realized he needed to reach Thomas Ferrell, the government clerk who had alerted him to the embezzlement. What was it that the lackey had said? *It has come to this?*

The swiftness of the attack, that Sir Duncan, an MP, had been murdered, left Michael shaken. Anything could happen.

Dara had come over to stand by him. "Michael, are you all right?"

Was he? No. Suddenly the night was filled with danger. If the lackey had caught sight of Dara, he might go for her, too.

Michael looked to the gentleman closest to him, Lord Painswick. "Please see to Sir Duncan. Someone will need to inform his wife that she is a widow."

His lordship nodded, his expression both concerned and confused.

Michael took Dara's hand. "Come." He started to lead her through the gate.

Of course, she balked. "We are leaving? We can't leave. Not unless I tell Tweedie and Gwendolyn. When they hear about this, they will be worried."

Michael looked to Painswick again. "Please tell Miss Lanscarr I have her sister with me. Now come, Dara. We don't have time to lose." He needed to check on Thomas Ferrell.

He also needed to watch his own back. And Dara's.

Nor was he going to wade through a ballroom of people asking questions. Not when time might be of the essence.

"Are we in danger?" she wondered.

He didn't answer, but as he went through the gate, she followed, and he was damned grateful she did.

Michael led her to the end of the passageway. On the street, they found a hack for hire and off they went. Dara settled on the seat across from him. "What is happening? And don't tell me I don't need to know."

He was irritated to have the dark direction of his thoughts interrupted. However, she was right. This night was going to change both of their lives. "Mr. Ferrell and I had business that could have seen Sir Duncan charged with treason."

She didn't bother to hide her surprise. "What did he do?"

"Requisitions were written for military funds that didn't go for that purpose. Instead, they were misdirected by the clerk who preceded Ferrell and, quite possibly, by his immediate superior to others. Ferrell, a true sleuth if ever there was one, discovered a reference to Sir Duncan. One reference. His name in paperwork."

"Why was he murdered if he was part of the plan?"

Michael shook his head. "Considering the

amounts stolen over the years, Sir Duncan should have been the wealthiest man in England. He wasn't. There had to be others, and they don't want the trail to lead to them. They know I'm on to them."

And then he was struck by a connection. Unbidden, and unwelcome.

He frowned.

"What is it?" she asked.

"Just a thought," he murmured, not ready to look too closely at it. Or to involve her. "What is important is that we warn an honest and good man that he could be in danger. Without Ferrell, Sir Duncan and his friends could have continued to rob our country. He is the only one who pieced together all the links, and he did it at risk to himself. If he'd been found out, he would have been fired."

"But you believe someone knows his identity?"

He looked to her. She wasn't flustered by any of this. Instead, she sat coolly poised, asking questions that made him think.

What he wouldn't tell her, what he hadn't told *anyone*, was that tomorrow, he and Ferrell were scheduled to present what they knew to one of Michael's contacts in the War Office. Gammon and Michael had known each other for years. Michael trusted him.

No one should have known about the meeting, and yet the timing of Sir Duncan's attack was suspicious.

Could this all be much deeper than he had feared? What if Gammon couldn't be trusted?

"What are you thinking?" she asked.

He wasn't going to share. There was no sense in alarming her more than the events of the night already had. But his response surprised him. "I'm glad you are with me." And he was. Her calmness steadied him.

Not only that, but once again, in a garden, he'd held all of her. She had been soft curves, moonlight, greenery—and quiet trust.

He had an urge to hold her again.

She shifted, folding her gloved hands in her lap as if uncomfortable, and he realized he stared. He'd been drinking her in, thinking of how he valued her in this moment. "I need to discuss an important matter," she said. "It is why I followed you into the garden. I was hoping for a moment of privacy."

"What is it?" he asked, thankful of something else to consider than the fate of his investigation.

She raised her chin a notch as if bracing herself. "I'm sorry. I won't be able to accept your offer of marriage—and before you think I have accepted it, let me remind you, I didn't. I didn't say anything. *You* did all the talking. So I'm not really crying off. I mean, I never said yes—and don't I *have* to say yes to agree to anything?"

He watched with amusement. "You are wrapping yourself into a knot over this."

"I think I am being very forthright."

"You are. Unfortunately, you must marry me."

"Unfortunately, I can't. Please, understand, Mr. Brogan—"

"Michael."

"What?"

"You have been calling me Michael. I like it. Don't change."

"I feel I must. I've officially refused your offer."

"Officially?" He lifted a brow, both charmed by her seriousness and a bit annoyed. This was a settled matter. She would marry him. He'd grown accustomed to the idea. He had complete faith she would as well.

"Well, I never agreed to marry you. Therefore, we should not be so familiar with each other."

"Like running off alone together in a carriage?" he suggested.

She scrunched her pert nose at him. "You are trying my patience. I'm not responsible for this." She waved a finger to indicate the interior of the hack.

His response was to settle into the corner and let his long legs take up the space between them. He wasn't going to give her what she wanted. He liked her. Exceedingly. Perhaps might even—

He paused, a bit unnerved by his thoughts, at the truth of them. A look at her vexed expression made him smile . . . and then it wasn't so difficult to admit he was falling in love with her.

He thought her beautiful. He enjoyed watching the way her thoughts played across her face. Dara lived life fully.

She also had all the other important requisites of an attractive woman. Her skin was creamy, her teeth straight, her hair thick. However, she hadn't shied away from anything this evening. Not even murder. There had been no hysterics and no ridiculous swooning.

What man couldn't love such a woman? It would defy logic.

However, she did deserve to have her concerns treated with respect. "Why do you wish to call off our betrothal?"

"I didn't agree—" she started and then made a face as if she found arguing about the matter frustrating. She tried a different tack. "It's not that I'm not honored."

"Understood."

"It is just that I fear we would—"

"Stop right there. If you are going to say you fear we wouldn't suit, you will disappoint me."

"Why?"

"Because you would be lying, and I detest liars."

"*All* liars?"

"Every one of them," he assured her.

A wicked gleam came to her eyes. "But you are a politician."

"I find them the worst." And that was very true. Someone stealing from the government? From the military, even while they had been battling Napoleon? "So, do you not like me?"

She hesitated, and then said, "I do like you."

That pleased him. "Why do you believe you must reject me?"

Her features saddened. "My sister Elise is in love with you."

"She is infatuated with me. There is a difference."

"Agreed. Except, Elise doesn't know that. What she feels is truly real to her. She refuses to stay in the same house with me. She believes I stole you from her."

Michael sat up. Now might not be the right time for this conversation, but they were having it. "I don't love her," he answered.

Her eyes met his. "You don't love me either."

The words *Actually, I do* came to the tip of his tongue. Was she ready to hear them? Her feelings were very raw, and her responsibilities to her sisters were paramount. Best he waited. Instead he said, "You would truly sacrifice your reputation for your sister? She would want that from you?"

"I love my sister. All that I've done, or as my sisters would say, everything I've prodded them to do, has been for my family. Which leads me to something I learned today about you that I find disturbing."

"About me?" What had someone told her?

"I have no wish to be the reason *your* family suffers." Before he could ask a question, she plowed ahead. "I have been informed your benefactor has threatened to cut you off because of me. Sir, I have no desire to be the cause of such an action. Especially since there are a dozen other women more suitable than me for you—such as Elise. You should marry Elise."

Michael fell back on the seat with disgust. Of course word of Holsworthy's tantrum was being bandied around. The man had an obsession with keeping his business quiet, so a scene like that in his club would send tongues wagging.

However, Holsworthy did not dictate his life. Neither did Dara, and he was a bit annoyed at her attitude. It was one thing to organize her sisters' lives, another to organize his. "Just like that"—he snapped his fingers—"I should go off and marry whomever you say I should?"

"I'm not trying to tell you what—"

"Or whom my uncle has picked for my wife? His choice is Lady Henrietta. I would be bored before we repeated our vows."

"Georgeham? Why, Lady Henrietta is nothing like Elise. My sister is special in person and spirit. If you don't wish to marry her, you'll find someone you like, but I would avoid Lady Henrietta. She is a bit dull."

Dara was probably right; however, her opinion

didn't matter because he knew whom he liked—*her.* And so far, she hadn't said anything to convince him otherwise. In fact, her devotion to her sister made him care for her all the more. Someone needed to teach Dara how special she was.

He leaned forward, tempted to confess his thoughts, to let her know that he was far from averse to this match—except, before he could speak, the vehicle rolled to a stop. "We shall return to this conversation," he promised. "But don't worry about my being cut off by my uncle. I will provide for us." He opened the door and was returned to reality.

Ferrell was not going to be pleased with Michael's information. He hoped it wouldn't frighten the clerk. He needed him for the meeting tomorrow. Ferrell was the one who understood the intricacies of Treasury accounting and could explain what had taken place.

"Stay here," Michael ordered Dara and climbed out. He started to reach for his hat when he realized he had left it back at the ballroom.

He raked his hand through his hair and walked to Ferrell's door. He knocked. They'd held one of their meetings together here.

Mrs. Ferrell answered the door. She recognized him, even though they had not been introduced during his visit. Ferrell had sent her upstairs.

"Mrs. Ferrell? Michael Brogan. May I speak to your husband?"

"You could if he had come home. He's late. Very late."

"Perhaps he had some appointment for this evening?"

She looked at Michael as if he had grown three heads. "I wouldn't be worried if that was true, sir."

"I see—" Michael started, not wishing to alarm the woman, when Dara's voice interrupted.

"When did you expect him home?" Of course she hadn't stayed in the hackney.

With a sound that let Dara know he didn't like his orders being ignored, he took a side step to allow her into the conversation—since she was going to put herself there anyway.

Dara gave him a small smile as if to say, *Sorry, I don't listen to anyone,* and repeated her question.

But Michael had a few tricks of his own. To Mrs. Ferrell he explained, "This is my betrothed, Miss Lanscarr."

Dara tensed, but she didn't contradict him, especially since Mrs. Ferrell perked up a bit at the information. Her manner relaxed. She stepped from the door. "I'm sorry I haven't invited you in. Please, enter."

"Another time," Michael answered, catching Dara's elbow before she accepted the invitation. "In fact, I'm certain your husband is working late."

She smiled as if she appreciated Michael's reassurance. "He often does. The man is serious about his position. He dreams about numbers. However, he usually warns me when he won't be home at his normal hour."

"Please tell him I called," Michael said.

"Is there a message I may give him?"

Ferrell would not appreciate Michael sharing his warning with the wife. Nor did he trust that if he wrote it, she would not read it. Dara was a constant reminder to never underestimate a woman.

No, it would be best to see if Ferrell was at his desk at Whitehall. It would be a short trip down the road.

"I shall call upon him tomorrow," Michael said to her. "Good evening to you, Mrs. Ferrell."

"Good evening, sir."

Michael turned away, drawing Dara with him. Mrs. Ferrell closed the door.

He walked Dara to the vehicle. "We are going to find Mr. Ferrell, correct?" she said. She didn't wait for his answer. "His wife was lovely, and very worried. We need to help her."

"*I* need to help her," he replied pointedly.

She gave him a look as if he was delusional, then said, "It is too late for anyone to be working. I'm worried."

"Agreed." Michael put her in the hack. "Whitehall," he told the driver, and instructed him to follow the route one might walk between Ferrell's residence and his office. "Go slowly," he ordered. Perhaps they would see Ferrell on his way home.

However, that was not to be. Their way took them by a group of people gathered at the entrance to an alleyway. One of them was the watch, and Michael had a bad premonition.

He leaned out to shout to the driver. "Stop!" He looked to Dara. "*Definitely* stay here." He ignored the face she pulled and hopped out.

Walking up to the watchman, Michael asked, "What has happened?"

"This gentleman found a body in the alley," he answered. He nodded to another gent who was standing off to the side, his expression grim as if he had found himself involved in something he wished not to be.

"A man's body?"

"Aye," the watch said.

"Have you identified him?"

"We have not, sir."

"May I see? Michael Brogan, MP."

The introduction helped. The watchman nodded respectfully and led him a few paces into the narrow opening between the buildings. There was Ferrell, sitting against the wall, his legs at an awkward angle. His clothing was dripping with blood from knife wounds all over his chest.

"I know him," Michael answered. "His name is Thomas Ferrell. I will have someone come for him."

"Thank you, sir. It is a shame to see this. We usually don't have murder down here."

"You will wait until my people can fetch him?"

The watch nodded. "I've sent for the Runners. They should be here shortly." That was good. Michael had connections with Bow Street. He gave the watch a few coins for his trouble and returned to the hack.

"It was him, wasn't it?" Dara asked.

"Yes."

Tears welled up in her eyes. "Two men in one night. What is happening?"

Michael didn't answer. He had the same question himself. "We need to tell his wife."

She nodded. "The poor woman. Did they have children?"

"I don't know." The thought of how little he knew about the brave Ferrell made him sad. He should have done more. Been more wary.

Not only that, but the last thing Michael wanted to do was break the news of her husband's death to Mrs. Ferrell. He felt awkward.

He needn't have worried. Dara handled the matter.

In the gentlest, kindest way, she told Mrs. Ferrell the news. There was a moment of shocked silence, and then Mrs. Ferrell broke down into tears.

Dara held her until she could cry no more. "Do you have friends?" Dara asked gently. "Someone who can gather your husband's body?"

"His brother lives next door. The red door."

"Michael, will you fetch him?" She turned back to Mrs. Ferrell. "Does he have a wife? Or do you have good friends?"

Mrs. Ferrell nodded, not specifying which before giving in to fresh tears.

It didn't matter. Michael was happy to escape, although telling the man that his brother had been murdered wasn't easy either. The wife came over to be with Mrs. Ferrell. The brother went off to knock on friends' doors to help him carry the body home.

Within the hour, the Ferrell house was filled with women ready to support his wife during this hard time. Dara was in the center of it all. She was introduced to them and included in their concern for Mrs. Ferrell. She and Michael were there when the body, wrapped in canvas, was brought through the door. Dara even organized laying him out on a table in the sitting room.

Michael was in awe of her. She was strong, competent, and beautiful.

The hour was well past midnight when they left.

"The hack is still here?" Dara asked in surprise.

"I paid him to be here," Michael answered.

"That is expensive. Another reason why you do not wish to be disinherited."

Michael smiled, impressed. "Do you gnaw on every bone?"

"Apparently so," she answered as he helped her into the vehicle.

After the door shut and the vehicle began moving, she said, "I hate whoever killed Mr. Ferrell. They have destroyed that woman's life."

"Yes."

"What are we going to do for her?"

"Catch them. Make whoever is behind this answer in a court of law."

She leaned back against the seat. "It doesn't seem enough."

He understood. He also knew that he would have to cancel his meeting with Gammon. Without Ferrell, he didn't have proof. Ferrell had known the details. He'd had the facts to answer any questions that might be asked.

Dara stared out the window a moment and then said, "Where are we going? This isn't the way to the Reeves' rout. We need to fetch our hats, and I know my sister and aunt are worried."

"After Sir Duncan's death, the Reeves' dance probably came to an abrupt end."

"You may be right." A somber silence settled over her. She looked tired, as if matters weighed on her. She closed her eyes.

Michael hated that he was going to add to her worries. Dara was not going to be happy with his decision once she realized what he had in mind. If she thought she was right about a matter, she didn't give up.

Neither did he.

They were quiet the rest of the way. The movement of the carriage seemed to lull her to sleep. Michael yearned to pull her over to his lap to keep her comfortable.

Just as he was working up his courage to tempt her wrath and hold her, the hack came to a halt. He jumped out and paid the driver, who was very appreciative. Michael reached into the cab and tapped Dara's shoulder lightly. She gave a start, then stifled a yawn and said apologetically, "I'm sorry, I must have had a bit of a doze." She took his hand and let him help her from the vehicle.

She even took a step before she stopped, puzzled. She looked around the street. "Where are we?"

Michael laced his fingers with hers so that she couldn't run off. He waited until the hack drove away before answering. "I have rooms here. You will stay with me. I need to keep you safe."

Chapter Sixteen

A lady should never call alone upon any gentleman, for any reason, especially at his residence.

The Rules (According to Dara)

Unless she wishes to find herself in the most delicious trouble.

Tweedie's thoughts

Dara stared at him, uncertain if she'd heard him correctly. Michael's hold on her fingers tightened, and that is when she knew he *had* said what she'd believed she'd heard.

Her response was succinct. "Are you mad?"

Michael considered the question. "I don't believe so."

"Return me to Willow Street *immediately*. I will make some sort of *suitable* excuse to my aunt and sister, and we'll just pretend this night never happened." Yes, that was the answer. Dara would pretend nothing happened, including Mrs. Ferrell's terrible grief.

Except it *had* happened. Dara was *worn thin* by all that had happened. It resonated through her.

Although hiding beneath the bedcovers in her *own* bed seemed far more preferable than heaping another controversy upon herself. If anyone saw her walking into his quarters—

"I need to ensure your protection—" he started.

"I do not wish or desire your protection, Mr. Brogan—"

"*Michael.* My name is Michael. You can't go backward now. You have started using it. You must continue on."

Dara gave him the "eye," the look she saved for her sisters when they annoyed her. "And who says I must?"

"It is a rule," he replied with a shrug as if he was merely the messenger.

"I have never heard of that rule." She tried to pull her fingers free, turning from him. He wouldn't let her go. Instead, he swung her around to face him.

"Then I am happy to help in your education."

Education? That is when she knew. "You made that rule up."

He turned her again, moving as if they were on the dance floor. "You made that rule up—*Michael,*" he said, tutoring her.

She tried to pull away. "Michael is a name for the miller's son," she announced witheringly.

"That is not true. I am an MP, my father was an

MP, and we are both named Michael." Again, he swung her around as if they were in a reel.

"Your mother should have stopped him."

"My mother's name is Siobhan. Now, that is a good Irish name." He brought her to a halt in front of him. He looked down at her, his expression serious. "Yes, I made the rule up . . . because I don't want you to push me away, Dara. I ask you to think about yourself. What do you want?"

The moon was full and cast a silvery light on the two of them standing on the midnight street. And she wanted to whisper, *I want you*. Such a dangerous thought, one that would create a chasm between herself and people she loved.

But was it wrong to think of herself?

She closed her eyes and bowed her head. He pulled her toward him so her forehead rested on his chest, and they stood together like that. It was good. Loving, actually.

For a moment, she let herself pretend she didn't have a heartbroken sister or any responsibilities. What if all she had to do was think of him?

"I don't wish to hurt anyone," she whispered.

"That isn't the way life is, Dara. Each of us risks being hurt. That is how we learn grace and the ability to go on. You can't protect Elise by denying yourself. It won't work. Your constant sacrifice isn't what she needs."

Dara looked up at him. He was a handsome man, yes, but there was something deeper about him that made him remarkable and special to her. A strength that she could respect.

She also hadn't realized she was crying, until he gently brushed a tear on her cheek with the pad of his gloved thumb. "Trust me," he whispered, and, for once, Dara didn't argue. When she was this close to him, she was powerless to do anything else. She was tired of fighting, especially with herself.

"Come, let us go inside," he said. "It has been a long night."

She allowed him to lead her into the neat brick house with its stone columns. It was pitch black. He took her hand. "My rooms are upstairs. The landlord and his wife have the ground floor. Watch your step," he warned before guiding her up the stairs.

He turned a handle and opened the door into spacious, well-appointed rooms. The window draperies were a green-and-gold stripe, a fire was in the hearth as if someone had been waiting up for him, and there was a plate of cheese and bread along with a decanter on a side table. The settee was overlarge and upholstered in leather. A masculine piece, for a very masculine man.

A trim servant with a bald pate surrounded by a halo of dark hair entered the room. "Ah, sir, you have arrived." His step slowed as he saw Dara. He, too, had the lilt of Ireland in his voice.

"Dara, this is my valet, Teddy. He sees to everything in my life. Teddy, this is Miss Dara Lanscarr. She has agreed to be my wife. Can you believe it?"

"I had feared you were unmarriageable, sir," Teddy answered without a blink. "However, Elliot asked me to inform you that he has secured the special license."

Michael smiled at Dara. "See? Not such a surprise."

She nodded, feeling a bit overwhelmed and very tired.

"Teddy, first thing in the morning, you must see the Reverend Lucas and request he marry us. It must be done on the morrow."

"Yes, sir," Teddy said. "That should not be a problem. Is there anything else I may do for you?"

"Yes, tell Elliot to cancel the meeting with Gammon." He explained a bit of what had happened this night.

Teddy looked concerned. "Without Ferrell, the trail is cold, sir?"

The lines of Michael's mouth flattened. "Possibly."

That was all he said, and yet Dara sensed that he wasn't convinced it was over.

Michael continued, "Dara wishes to write a letter to her sister and aunt to let them know she is safe. I will ask you to deliver it this night."

"Yes, sir."

Michael crossed to the hearth, took a candle off the mantel, and lit it off the fire. "Here, Dara. You can write to your family in my office." He led her into a connecting room with a huge, very messy desk.

Teddy followed. "He won't let me tidy it, ma'am," he said in explanation.

"That is because I know where everything is," Michael answered. He moved a stack of papers to a table in the corner of the room and then blew on the blotter before presenting the chair. "Here you are. Everything you need." To emphasize his claim, he pulled a piece of foolscap out from a drawer and set it in the middle of the blotter.

Dara sat and composed her letter. She promised she would be home in the morning and that all was fine. She could only imagine what Gwendolyn and Tweedie must have been thinking when she took off with Michael after Sir Duncan was murdered.

Teddy and Michael left her in privacy while she wrote.

When she was done, Michael gave the letter to his valet. "Please deliver this to Number 7 Willow Street." Teddy left.

And she was alone with Michael.

She was also exhausted. She couldn't stifle a yawn.

He offered his hand to help her from the chair. "Come, the bedroom is this way."

Dara balked. "I will not—"

He held up his hands to stave off her protest. "I already know how you think. You may have the bedroom. I shall sleep on the settee, and Teddy will soon return to be our noble chaperone. I promise."

She scoffed at the idea. "No one would believe he is a decent chaperone."

"Oh, he's not." Then, seeing her eyes widen in surprise, he hurried to add, "I'm teasing, Dara. Besides, if I tried anything, you would strangle me with my neckcloth. I understand the rules."

"If you did, I wouldn't be here." Realizing how priggish she sounded, she sought to ameliorate her position by saying, "These are your rooms. I shall take the settee. Besides, I could probably fit to lie on it, and you can't. You are too big." On those words, she marched right into the sitting room and plunked herself down on the leather.

She leaned back and felt herself relax—until he sat next to her. "Dara, I insist. You take the bed."

"I will not. I will stay out here."

"In your gown? Wouldn't you be more comfortable in a bed?"

"I would be wearing my gown in the bed," she replied sensibly.

"No, while you were writing, I had Teddy lay out one of my shirts for you. It will make a decent, and actually rather fetching, nightdress. Please, use my room."

Dara balled her still-gloved hands into fists. "I am reaching the point when boxing your ears sounds like a very good idea."

"Careful, Miss Lanscarr. Ladies should never threaten violence. Or isn't that one of the rules your sisters complain about?"

Slowly she turned her head. With a glare, she said, "I thought once one started using a name, they couldn't go backward."

He tilted back his head and laughed. The sound of life. It echoed through the room, and she could lose herself in it. She started laughing with him. After all of the events of the night, this was a release she needed. Tension drained from her. In its place was exhaustion.

They had spent a very difficult couple of hours in each other's company. If anything, she trusted him more now than before. She had a better sense of his character.

No, she was not afraid of being ravished. What she feared was ravishing him. And that was the problem, wasn't it? She could understand Elise's feelings.

Michael removed his jacket. He offered it to her. "Here. If we are going to sit side by side on this damned settee, we might as well make ourselves comfortable."

"You don't need to sit up with me," Dara said. "And I don't need your jacket. I'm fine."

"Always fine," he echoed. He dropped the jacket on her. "Will you do me the honor of letting me be a little gallant?"

The weight of the expensive wool settled around her. It felt good. It also made her feel protected, just as it had the day she'd jumped into the Serpentine. Considering the evening they'd had, offering his jacket was the least he could do.

Dara snuggled down inside it and let herself relax. Safe. She was safe, and not just from murderers but also from opinions and responsibilities and all the little ways she believed she had failed.

MICHAEL RECOGNIZED THE moment she fell asleep. Her body slumped into his coat—while he was very much awake, aware of her every movement.

This was not how he had imagined he would fall in love.

He'd assumed that he would go through the usual pattern of noticing a woman, having her capture his interest, courting her, and then making an offer of marriage. Of course, she would say yes because, after all, he was a gentleman of substance. He'd also pictured that whatever woman he chose would actually have been like Lady Henrietta or Elise Lanscarr. Both beautiful. One with excellent connections and a fortune. The other lauded and celebrated.

So, how had his heart become wrapped around this headstrong, independent, penniless little Irish gentlewoman? One who was an admitted schemer?

He'd fallen in love because she was the sort of woman who hadn't gone off into vapors over murder and the resulting dead bodies. She had courage. And she hadn't hesitated in giving a newly widowed woman an embrace and much-needed empathy. How could a man not love such a woman?

Michael knew she felt likewise toward him. She just didn't know it yet. But it was there in the way she'd blush slightly when he complimented her, in how she never held back her opinion, in the tightness of her breasts whenever she came near to him.

If only she wasn't so stubborn.

Except she was asleep now, hunched in his jacket.

Michael reached for her. Dara did not wake as he gently stretched out and leaned her into the crook of his arm. She felt good there, right. He smiled when, after a few moments, she sighed and nestled in against him. *She loves me.* He was certain of it.

Tomorrow morning, she would wake and argue with him. She would give all the reasons she must not marry him while knowing she had no choice.

He would tease her, cajole her, and make her his wife.

Then he would deal with the embezzlers. Because Michael knew who the leader was now. The knowledge was devastating. He'd only told one man about Ferrell. One man sworn to secrecy. One man he had trusted because he was so rich, so why would he steal?

Holsworthy. His great-uncle.

Ferrell had believed the stealing had been going on for close to twenty years, perhaps more. Holsworthy had been involved with the War Office back then. He could have set up the scheme at that time. Meanwhile, the world assumed he was shrewd at investments. Actually, was it simple theft?

The question was, why did Holsworthy have Sir Duncan murdered? Why now?

The only answer Michael could imagine was that, just as the lackey had said, Holsworthy had decided to bring everything to an end. He didn't want anyone alive who could testify to his guilt.

And Michael had to wonder at the horrid actions that had been set in motion. Holsworthy had not been himself when he'd started shouting at Michael in his club. He'd been incensed about the news of Dara—

No, he had been furious that Michael was not falling into line. His heir had rebelled, something Michael had never done. Then again, he'd not had cause to challenge his great-uncle. However, Holsworthy's shouting, his demands, had been completely out of character. Usually he was more circumspect.

Michael didn't understand all the whys; however, he was certain of the who. He just couldn't prove it. Not without Ferrell's help. He'd even wager that Ferrell's superior—what was his name? Plummer?—might have come to an untimely end tonight as well. Three murders, of men involved in the same plot, had to appear suspicious to the law. Might there be a chance a judge would listen to Michael's suspicions?

Otherwise, who would believe Michael against the word of the mighty Holsworthy?

It was also important that Michael keep Dara close. If his uncle had become deranged, he might strike out at her. Certainly there was only one way he could truly deny Michael the title—death.

Whatever Holsworthy's plans, he was giving Michael a reason to never let Dara go. Not when she was snuggled so sweetly against him.

He dared to brush his lips against her hair, enjoying the wild clover scent that reminded him so much of his home. "Do you believe you could love me?" he asked. "Even just a little?"

Her answer was a soft, sleepy sound. Neither yes nor no.

However, having her in his arms was enough.

CHAPTER SEVENTEEN

Marry only for the right reasons.
THE RULES (ACCORDING TO DARA)

Make yourself happy.
TWEEDIE'S ADVICE

Dara woke the next morning when Gwendolyn burst into the room holding a valise in one hand and two dresses over her arm.

"Awake, awake, awake!" her sister said gaily.

Rolling over, Dara yawned. She was usually an early riser, except for today. Today she wanted to be a lazybones and hug her pillow—

She lurched up in alarm, suddenly remembering the night before. She was in a bed. She distinctly remembered sitting on the settee. She had fallen asleep there . . . and then he had moved her.

Fortunately, she was still wearing her muslin gown, which was hopelessly wrinkled, almost beyond repair. Not that she thought Michael would lewdly take advantage of her. Still, he had not listened to her, and his gentlemanly high-handedness was vastly annoying. "I wished to sleep on the settee. I told him he could have the bed."

Gwendolyn had opened the wardrobe with the gowns in hand. Dara noticed that one of the dresses was Gwendolyn's yellow muslin. Her sister frowned at all the male clothing before turning to Dara and saying, "Why would you wish to sleep on a settee instead of a comfortable bed?"

"Because this is *his* bed." The bed was huge, as it would need to be for a man Michael's size. The headboard and footboard were cherry, as were the other furnishings in the room. She was glad to see that he, like herself, did not like painted furniture or dainty chairs. The drapes and bedcover were a rich wine color.

Gwendolyn laid the dresses on the bed and started to make room for them among Michael's clothes. "Well, *his* bed looks far better to sleep in than a settee. However, what is important is that you need to climb out of it. You are marrying in a few hours."

Dara stared at her blankly. She was. The thought was shocking, and a touch horrifying. She was marrying Michael Brogan. *All* the implications of that statement roared through her. She was going to be his wife. This couldn't be happening to her. He was too—*too.*

And as was so often the case when she found herself in the center of things, fear took hold. This could not be happening to her, even if, secretly, she was elated. She pushed back the mess and snarls that were her hair, embarrassed as pins fell from the tangles.

Gwendolyn bounced down on the bed beside her. Her sister appeared well rested and lovely with her dark hair perfectly coiffed and the gold in the deep brown of her eyes giving them a sparkle. She looked so beautiful, Dara covered her own sleep-wrinkled face with her hands as if to hide from everything she was not. She heard herself mutter, "I can't marry him. It's not right."

Gwendolyn pulled down Dara's hands from her face and looked her in the eye. "Stop this. You are marrying him, and you deserve to marry him. Besides, I'm not the one who knows *all* the rules in the family. If Elise or I had taken off with a gentleman, especially one we were betrothed to—"

"I never said yes to him."

Gwendolyn ignored the protest. Instead, she held Dara's hands in hers and said, "—*you* would insist we marry the man. Especially if we liked him."

"I don't like him," Dara said stubbornly.

Her sister countered with a soft "Liar."

"Why do you say that?" Dara challenged her.

"Because I realize Tweedie was right. You and Mr. Brogan—well, he's asked me to call him

Michael. A very good name, Michael. I like it. You and Michael had been conducting a flirtation from the beginning. I actually believe the two of you will suit each other very well. That is, if you don't play martyr."

Dara took offense. "I am not a martyr."

"Oh, please." Gwendolyn let go of her hands and rose from the bed. "You take pride in thinking of everyone else before yourself. Why, I wouldn't have put it past you to marry that one duke who called on us—what was his name? I blocked it from my mind. The old one with the short sparrow-like legs and bad breath."

The Duke of Minton. Dara kept silent. She'd danced with him, often out of pity. But would she have accepted an offer from him?

Gwendolyn returned to her original point. "You would have sacrificed yourself if it meant helping Elise and me. At the same time, the whole reason we are in London is that you wouldn't let *me* marry Squire Davies. I was not to sacrifice for you. Well, I believe we should both be done with settling. Be happy, Dara. You are marrying a remarkable man who I suspect might love you. He certainly acts as if he understands you very well. He warned me that you would not be a willing bride this morning once you found yourself in his bed. And do not be fussy. He informed Tweedie and me that he slept on the settee."

But Dara was only half listening. Her mind had caught on the word *love*.

Michael might love her? Such as in romantic novels?

Or as in the heartbreaking sobs of Mrs. Ferrell last night? That type of love? Where one feels as if one's soul had been attached to another?

Dara had not thought a great deal about love. She'd been too busy managing everyone's life save her own. She ran her hand along the crisp, clean sheets and remembered tucking herself in next to Michael on the settee last night. It had felt good to burrow into his warmth, and that was not like her. She usually kept a bit of distance between herself and other people, but not with him. He upended all of the barriers she placed between herself and others. He acted as if he understood her, and still liked her.

What woman would not wish to marry such a man?

She looked up at Gwendolyn. "Is Elise here?"

Her sister's smile faded. "No." There was a pause, and then Gwendolyn said, "But Tweedie and I are. In fact, Tweedie is out in the sitting room, trying to cajole Teddy into fixing her a little nip. I warned him he must not. However, she can be persuasive."

Gwendolyn was trying to distract her. "Does Elise *know* about the ceremony?"

Her sister picked up the valise and set it on a

chair by the bed. She opened it to pull out Dara's hairbrush before saying, "I sent a note to Lady Whitby. And now we must prepare. Teddy is very efficient. He has everything planned, and the minister will expect you at eleven o'clock."

"Do I have anything to say about all of this?" Dara usually was the one making the plans, although she'd never really thought of her own wedding. Her musings had always centered on her sisters. Was that martyrish?

"Not today," Gwendolyn answered. She began pulling errant pins from Dara's hair. "Let me take care of you today."

Dara allowed her to do what she wished without complaint. "A first!" Gwendolyn murmured.

As Gwendolyn attacked the snarls in Dara's hair, she talked about what had happened after word of Sir Duncan's murder spread at the ball. Apparently many women, and one man, had swooned.

"There were so many reacting to the news in that manner that the servants couldn't catch them all. It made crossing the ballroom difficult," Gwendolyn said. "Tweedie and I were worried, but when we were informed you were with Michael, we knew you were safe."

Dara didn't share the information about Mr. Ferrell. Then Gwendolyn *would* worry.

Gwendolyn left to fetch a pitcher of hot water and to give Dara a moment of privacy. Dara noticed his jacket, the one he'd given her last night as a blanket, was hung over a chair next to a small desk. She had to touch it, to feel the wool beneath her fingers.

This *was* happening.

And in spite of Elise's bitter disappointment, Dara wanted it. She wanted him.

At that moment, Gwendolyn returned to the room with the pitcher and Tweedie.

"Come, come," Tweedie said, clapping her hands like a dance master. "We must prepare you for a wedding. We want you to be a beautiful bride."

THE CEREMONY WAS swift.

Dara did not know Reverend Lucas and would have been hard-pressed to tell anyone what he looked like even after meeting him. No, her focus was on the man standing in front of her.

She didn't know when or where Michael had changed, but he was freshly shaved. He wore a jacket of evergreen wool. She liked green on him. It brought out his coloring. His buff breeches seemed molded to him, and his boots shone as if they were newly made. She recognized his gold brocade waistcoat from the Royston ball when Dara had taken him aside and told him to leave her sister alone.

Every square inch of him was a Corinthian, a man of his world . . . and a man who acted as if he was pleased to be marrying her.

He waited for her at the altar alongside the Reverend Lucas. Apparently, it had been up to Teddy to see her and her family to the church.

As Dara walked into the stone sanctuary and saw Michael's eyes light up at the sight of her, she felt almost beautiful.

Teddy had helped with the styling of her hair. He had shown a true skill, one that rivaled Molly's. It was piled on her head with some daisies Gwendolyn had purchased from a flower girl tucked in the curls. The daisies went with Gwendolyn's yellow gown, which she and Molly had quickly shortened for Dara that morning. There were even matching yellow gloves.

The ensemble was one Gwendolyn had been saving for a special occasion and Dara was touched that her sister had given it to her.

Around her neck was a pendant that Gwendolyn had insisted she borrow. It was a small gold heart threaded onto an emerald ribbon that had belonged to Gwendolyn's mother. Dara didn't have anything from her own mother, Lydia. She'd brought Wiltham to the marriage, and if there was anything else, then either Captain Sir John had gambled it away or Gram had sold it to pay for tutors or to keep food on the table.

Dara was a knot of nerves. It didn't help that,

when it was time for her to repeat her vows, she sensed a presence in the back of the church. She glanced in that direction and saw Elise. Her sister had taken a seat by the door. She was accompanied by a woman who appeared to be a servant.

Their gazes did not meet. Elise seemed inwardly focused.

But she was *here*.

To Dara's surprise, Michael had a ring for her. It was a thin gold band with a single ruby in the center. She had to remove her glove to put it on. Her hands were shaking as he slipped it on her finger.

This marriage, the words, the ring—it all made the marriage seem real. When Michael had repeated his vows, he'd sounded sincere. His voice had been strong and clear.

Everything would be perfect if only Dara didn't feel uncomfortable about Elise's feelings.

Directing the couple to face the few witnesses in the church, Reverend Lucas said in sonorous tones, "I pronounce you man and wife."

The only person Dara saw was Elise. Elise frowning, looking away. Elise not forgiving her.

Michael had tucked her hand in the crook of his arm. He smiled down at Dara, a look that made her knees weak, and scattered the grief of disappointing her sister.

Then she noticed Elise rise and practically race out of the church. The sight hurt.

Amid the congratulations, if Gwendolyn or Tweedie had noticed Elise wasn't there, they didn't say.

Michael took them to the Clarendon Hotel for the wedding breakfast. Reverend Lucas happily joined them, and they all rode in the open barouche Michael had hired for the occasion.

"I never miss a chance of eating at the Clarendon," Reverend Lucas informed them on the drive. "Jacquiers is the best cook in London. It is the only place you can find a genuine French dinner."

Since the Lanscarrs had never eaten anything remotely French, they didn't understand what he meant. They soon found out.

They dined on squabs and champagne. Food had never tasted so grand. Even Tweedie was impressed, and she was not one for praising anything French. She even forwent her sherry.

Most important of all, Dara sat by Michael's side. He touched her often. His presence served as a bulwark of sorts between her former habit of worrying and accommodating others and this new, slightly unnerving attitude of doing as she pleased.

After dinner, they drove Gwendolyn and Tweedie home. The reverend did not live far from the Clarendon, so he chose to walk.

Once the goodbyes to her family were said, Michael asked, "Do you mind if we pay a visit to Mrs. Ferrell? It will only take a moment."

"I believe we should."

He gave the address to the driver. As they rode over, he said, "If we were marrying in Carlow, we would have a celebration that included everyone in the village. They would all turn out for the wedding feast."

"The same in Wicklow."

"We can't do that here. We can't invite everyone in London, but it does seem we need to do something to honor the vows we have just taken."

"What do you propose?"

He reached into a pocket of his jacket and pulled out a small leather purse. He poured the contents into Dara's hand—five gold coins.

She raised her eyes to his in amazement. He smiled. "For Mrs. Ferrell?"

"I believe this is an excellent way to celebrate this day."

His smile widened, and he gave her the leather pouch. "You can present our gift to her."

Our gift. And he was letting her give it.

The words, his sharing an act of kindness, touched Dara. He treated her as if she mattered. And she wasn't even a duchess.

The Ferrell house was in mourning. Dara hesitated to enter in a yellow dress with daisies in her hair. When she expressed her doubts about entering in her attire, Michael had a word with a woman who had just exited. She took the dark brown shawl she had been wearing and gave it to him. He carried it over to the carriage, and Dara threw it around her shoulders and over her hair.

They entered the house. Mr. Ferrell was still wrapped in the canvas from last night, although the room had been draped in black as per custom. Mrs. Ferrell sat in a chair beside the table holding her husband's body. She was surrounded by people who cared for her, although she looked as if she hadn't slept all night.

However, when Dara and Michael gave her the bag of coins, she almost collapsed. Reaching for their hands, she repeated "thank you" over and over. Then she confided that she was with child. It was still early, but at least her husband had known.

"He was so proud. He liked children." She drew a deep breath and said softly, looking down at the leather bag, "I didn't know what I was going to do."

"Come to me whenever you need help," Michael answered. "Your husband was a brave and honest man."

A gent sitting close by overheard him. "It's not safe to walk the streets," he complained, a verdict seconded by many of the other mourners. "Not right what happened to him."

Mrs. Ferrell leaned close to Michael. "I haven't told anyone about what Thomas was doing. He'd wanted me to keep it secret."

"For your own safety, continue to say nothing," Michael answered.

"But will those who murdered him receive what they should?" she asked.

Dara wanted Michael to assure Mrs. Ferrell they would avenge her husband. Instead, he looked away a moment before saying, "You take care of yourself and your child."

Mrs. Ferrell did not find his words satisfactory or reassuring. "I want justice. Thomas wanted it as well."

"We all do," Dara agreed. She glanced at Michael for confirmation. He was making no promises.

They took their leave then. The ride was somber on the way home. Michael seemed lost in his thoughts.

Finally, Dara had to ask, "There is no hope you will find who murdered him?"

He looked to her, his gray eyes bleak, as if the matter weighed on him. "We need proof. Otherwise . . ." He let his voice drift off.

"No justice," she finished with a whisper. Dara's heart hurt for him. She took his hand. "You did all you could."

"A good man died." He didn't look at her. Then he added, "He'll never know his child."

"Did you expect the danger?"

His jaw tightened. "I should have anticipated it."

"Why? Because you are the axis of the world?"

That statement caught his attention. He turned to her, the concern in his eyes belying the lightness of his tone. "Is this the Dara Lanscarr I know? The one who believes she is in charge of everything?"

She leaned one shoulder against the seat, facing him. "Michael, you are being too hard on yourself. I understand because I, too, hold myself to a high standard, and it is bitter when I try to do what is right and I fail. I have a sister who refuses to speak to me, and all I ever wanted was to take care of her."

His response was bitter. "Have you ever cost a man his life?"

"Because you didn't take action? You followed Sir Duncan. Did you anticipate murder?"

There was a long silence, and then he said, "No."

"And once you knew there was danger, you tried to reach Mr. Ferrell. Let us hold the murderers accountable. Not ourselves."

He took a deep breath. "I also regret that this may be the end of it. Ferrell had the proof, including documentation. It is all gone now."

"Then we will find another way," she promised. "There is always another way."

His lips twisted wryly. "You never cry quarter, do you?"

"May I?" she wondered. "Is it possible—?"

A new thought struck her, a suspicion. "Wait, do you know more than you are telling me? Or suspect who is behind these murders?"

"Dara, if I did, I would not say. This is on me."

"Except I stand beside you now."

"The woman who didn't wish to be married to me?"

"Oh, I wished," she allowed herself to confess. "I was just afraid that wishes like that never come true."

It was the closest she'd come to making a declaration of love, of allowing herself to be vulnerable. And honest. He was too fine for her. She was unimportant—

He drew her hand to his lips. He pressed a fervent kiss on the back of her fingers. And where his lips touched, her skin burned, even through the thin material of her glove.

And then he said the most amazing words. "I need you. Especially now. The weight of this . . . ?"

"I'm here," she whispered. "You are not alone."

His response was to kiss her. Right there, in an open carriage where everyone could see them . . . and Dara was not going to argue. She was more than ready for his kiss—although this one was different from the past ones. Those had been about passion, about a meeting of wills.

This kiss seemed to expose *his* vulnerability. His need for her trust, her faith. What woman could resist such a kiss?

The driver cleared his throat. The carriage had rolled to a stop in front of the brick house, and they hadn't realized it.

Michael broke the kiss, but he didn't move away from her. They were so close, she could see every line of his face. His gaze held hers. "I have a new rule for your list—a man can kiss his wife wherever he pleases."

"Is that all he can do as he pleases?" she heard herself ask, her voice whispery and low.

"In public," he answered, and then he smiled. It was a strange expression, both self-deprecating and wistful. He jumped out of the carriage to settle with the driver before offering his hand to help her out.

Dara watched his every move, even the tiniest details—and when he reached his hand out for her, she finally accepted that, at last, she had what she truly wanted.

She wanted him.

Chapter Eighteen

A husband has the right to a wife's body.
THE RULES (ACCORDING TO DARA)

Actually, it is a privilege *if she gives herself to him, and a blessing if he knows how to make her happy.*
TWEEDIE'S CORRECTION

Michael knew neither Teddy nor his secretary, Elliot, was in his rooms upstairs.

In fact, earlier, while he'd been helping Michael dress for the wedding, Teddy had taken it upon himself to list all the changes he believed needed to be made now that there was a mistress among them. On the list were the rental of a decent house, one befitting a man of Michael's station and, of course, more servants.

"You should also consider hiring a coach for your needs while in town," Teddy had said.

"Holsworthy is cutting off all funds," Michael had pointed out. "There is Ian's education, Mother's living, and my soon-to-be wife's family to care for. A coach might be too much."

"You haven't spent a shilling of the money Lord Holsworthy has given you over the years," Teddy countered. "I discussed this with Elliot. You can manage a coach."

Michael knew when he was outvoted. "I shall leave that to you."

"Very well, sir. Also, just for your knowledge, I shall make myself scarce this evening."

"Thank you, Teddy," Michael had answered, copying the servant's clipped approval—and had earned one of Teddy's rare smiles.

"Good luck on your marriage, sir."

Now, as Michael led Dara up the stairs to his rooms, he was glad they were going to be alone. Because suddenly, he had doubts.

What if she truly didn't have feelings for him?

Her kisses hinted at her passion, but she'd also protested this marriage. He had noticed her reaction to Elise's presence. Her sister's anger, as childish as he found it, disturbed Dara.

He also wondered if she understood he wanted *her* for his wife. No other. Yes, the circumstances had made for quick decisions, except he was pleased with how things had transpired. And he believed his respect, his devotion, and, yes, his love for Dara would only grow over time—*if* she returned his feelings.

Michael opened the door to his apartments,

determined to give the most persuasive speech of his life. One that would convince his petite wife, a woman who had the mind of a barrister, that his commitment to her was real, in spite of the short time of their acquaintance. He planned to confess that he didn't know what she wanted from this marriage, but his mind was quite clear. He wanted everything. A lover, a partner, a confidante . . . a conscience. Oh, yes, he was pleased with his choice of wife.

He turned the key in the lock and opened the door. He stepped aside to let her enter first. She moved past him. The late-afternoon sun filling the front room caught the strands of gold in her brown hair and gilded the yellow in her dress.

Michael shut the door and set his hat on a side table. Dear God, he prayed he didn't botch this—

"I grew up in the country, Michael." She removed her gloves. "I know what is expected . . . although I'm not quite clear on some details. I assume you will show me."

For a blink, he was speechless, and he almost laughed, because was there anyone like her? She'd take charge of even this. She went right to the heart of the matter. So could he. "Then you are fine with this marriage?"

She tilted her head. "Are you suggesting that—" She paused, frowned. "We do *not* consummate our marriage?"

That suggestion stopped him. Is that what she was thinking? He prayed not and yet decided to take on the subject. "You've had your doubts."

"It has happened quickly." She didn't shy away.

"True."

"And Elise is very angry." Her hands closed into fists around the yellow leather gloves, as if she was anxious.

"She has no reason to be—"

"Oh, please. You can be honest, Michael. Any man would prefer her over me—"

"Not me."

Dara's lips parted in surprise at his swift, emphatic response. He moved toward her, reaching to cup her face in his hands. "I prefer you even when you are soaking wet and smelling of the lake."

He meant his words as a declaration, of how much he cared for her. Instead, she countered, "It isn't fair that you have gone to such lengths to rescue me from my own rash behavior."

"Maybe I'm not rescuing you." She was so perfect for him. "Maybe I'm rescuing myself."

"Oh, Michael—"

"Dara, will you stop debating and kiss me?"

And she did.

She lifted on her tiptoes, curled her fingers in his neckcloth, and pulled him down to her. Their lips met and she kissed him, fully, completely, and, blessedly, without reservations.

Michael wrapped his arms around her, making their kiss long and deep. When his tongue brushed hers, she responded, catching him, savoring him, and it was almost his undoing.

Doubts evaporated.

He swung her up in his arms and carried her down the hall to his room. The door was open. That clever Teddy had even turned down the covers. Michael stood her on the mattress. For once, she was taller than him.

She placed her arms around his neck and kissed him, leaning her body against him. She held nothing back, because she was Dara. She met life with everything she had to offer.

He untied the laces of her dress, enjoying the feel of her curves beneath the material.

After tugging at his neckcloth, Dara tossed it to the ground. She bent her knees so that she could unbutton his waistcoat. This gave Michael the opportunity he wanted to remove the sweet daisies attached to pins and let her hair tumble around her shoulders.

Her hair was glorious to him—a blend of gold, deep molasses brown, and light toffee. It was longer than he imagined, falling midway down her back. The strands felt like silk as he combed his fingers through them.

Her lips found his. Her kiss became eager as she shoved his jacket and vest down over his shoulders. She let the clothing fall to the floor as she turned her attention to his shirt. She freed it from his breeches. "Help," she whispered against his mouth.

It was his pleasure to obey. He stepped back and lifted his shirt over his head. With a low hum, she wrapped her arms about his neck and flattened her breasts against him. He could feel hard nipples beneath the layers of her dress, and he was done with being patient. He wanted her, in a way he'd never desired a woman before.

He lifted her skirts and sent her dress to join his clothing on the floor around them.

Dara was a vision in her thin chemise and petticoats. She was perfection. He kissed her neck, tasted the sensitive skin under her chin, and worked his way to one of her delicate ears. Dara all but melted into his arms.

He sat on the mattress, pulling her down into his lap.

She had to feel the strength of his erection, to realize how aroused he was, but she did not balk. Instead, while he started untying the tapes holding her petticoats to her chemise, her fingers slipped under the edge of his breeches. They twisted the first button free. And then another.

And that was it.

They became serious now, shedding clothes and helping each other until they were both gloriously naked. She was more beautiful than he could have ever imagined. His wife. His perfect, lovely wife.

He leaned her back against the pillows, his desire for her more than evident. He settled himself beside her and kissed her ear, her neck, working his way to her breasts.

She was so responsive. She gasped when his teeth caught her earlobe between them. When his mouth covered her nipple, she cried out. Her legs opened to him as if with a will of their own.

So he had to touch her. What he wanted was to taste her. He held back. They would play again later. In fact, he promised himself he was going to make love to her every day of their lives together.

She gave as good as she received, and there was something bewitching about a woman who wasn't afraid to touch and explore his body. It took all his skill to maintain his control.

Her hand smoothed over and cupped his buttocks. She arched and moved with a sensuous grace, her skin against his creating a delicious fiction.

It took little to please her—the heat of his mouth on her breast, the slide of fingers as he tested her tight wetness, the play of their tongues. Her skin tasted like the sweetest cream.

At last, Michael knew he could not hold himself in check any longer. The time had come.

There would be pain. He wanted to do this right, to protect her as much as he could.

Settling himself over her heat, battling a drive as old as time, he kissed her fully, deeply. Then, his mouth close to her ear, he said, "This will hurt. I'm here. I'll stop at any moment."

If he could.

Her lips curved into a dreamy smile. "I want you, Michael. *I want—*"

Anything else she might have said ended on a gasp of shock as he thrust hard and deep. He felt her give, felt the tear. If she'd ordered him to stop, he didn't know if he could.

She cried out. Her body stiffened. He held her close. "I'm sorry. I'm so sorry," he repeated over and over. A tear rolled down her cheek. He tasted it. Hated himself for hurting her. Hated that his every instinct was to drive into her. Instead, he kept himself in check.

Ever so slowly, she relaxed. Her gaze met his. She appeared uncertain. He dared to move. He could not help himself. She felt so good. So right.

The breath she had been holding released. Her hips curved to cradle him.

Michael tried to keep it slow. But with each thrust, he wanted to go deeper. He could feel the tension building, the need. It goaded him, demanded he find satisfaction, that he release—

The quickening, the tightening in her body almost shattered what little control he had. Her muscles quivered, and what seemed to be waves of sensation took hold of her, carrying him with them.

Michael could hold himself back no longer. He buried himself in her, feeling the contractions all around him until he all but burst with the joy of his release. It poured out of him, and for the first time, he understood what it meant for two people to become one.

He gathered her in his arms, holding her as if he would never let her go.

Because he wouldn't. Ever.

And if her feelings weren't as intense as his? Well, then, he'd love her enough for them both.

DARA WAS THANKFUL Michael's arms were around her. Otherwise, she feared she would have flown straight through the roof and ascended to the heavens. Or perhaps she was already there.

She had been warned the wedding bed could be painful. Other women talked, other brides back in Wicklow. She'd not been unprepared. Although she hadn't anticipated how sharp the pain was. It had felt like a knife.

And yet she knew that Michael had been as kind and gentle as he could be. Then, he had shown her the joy of this act between a man and a woman. At last, she fully understood. This closeness, the bond of it, was what life was truly about.

Before she was ready to let go of his body heat, he rose from the bed. He crossed the room without bothering to dress. Dara's curiosity made her look. His appendage didn't appear so wondrous now, but the rest of him did. He was a marvel of strong and graceful muscle in the late-afternoon light. He poured water into the basin and carried it over to her along with several linen towels.

Dara was surprised at how comfortable she felt with their nakedness. She rather liked it.

However, when he dipped the cloth in water, wrung it out, and started to reach for that intimate part of her, she balked.

"What are you doing?"

"Taking care of you," he said calmly. He held up the cloth. "Do you trust me?"

"Such a question after what we've just done."

Laughter lit his gray eyes. "True. And now, I'm going to do something more intimate."

She didn't understand what that could be until he began washing her. Cleaning her as if she was a babe, or an object of great value. The wet cloth felt good against her overheated skin and the stickiness of blood and him.

When he returned to bed, he took her in his arms. The day's fading sun burnished the room with gold. He fitted his body against hers, letting her head rest on his shoulder.

She reached for his hand. An ungloved hand. Finally. At last. Never again would they have gloves between them. Or anything else.

"That was very good," Dara whispered.

He smiled. "Only very good?"

Of course he would challenge her. She smiled and suggested, "Perhaps we can practice more."

He immediately hardened against her leg. She grinned and gave him a nudge with her hip. "You are ready for practice."

His laugh was deep. He rolled on his back, bringing her up and over to rest on his chest, her hair a curtain around them. He pushed it back, letting his fingers play with it, curling one strand around his finger. "It's too soon. We need to let you heal."

"You can wait?" She'd always heard that men were very demanding in bed. But he was right. There was a bit of discomfort.

"Of course I can. The first time is a little difficult but after that . . ." He shifted his weight beneath her so she could feel the length and hardness of him. "We may play all we like."

"How long must we wait?" She wiggled her hips, letting him know that she was not going to be patient.

"You will have to tell me. But once you say the word—" He kissed her, a promise that he was as anxious to couple again as she was.

He was so handsome, so perfectly formed, so

engaging and intelligent, she had trouble accepting that he was her husband. "You don't mind being married to me?" She had to ask. She felt childish and yet, he could have done so much better—

"I've never wanted to marry anyone else but you. Ever."

Tears welled in her eyes. She closed them, feeling silly. Of all the things she had *not* cried over, why would his declaration touch her in a way she'd never experienced before? However, doubt came easy for her. It was comfortable.

She needed to be sophisticated about the matter. "The circumstances—" she started, but he cut her off with a kiss, one that curled her toes.

"Do you believe me now?" he asked when he was done.

Dara nodded.

"So, we won't have any more discussions where you compare yourself to your sister or other women?"

She was honest enough to admit, "You may have to remind me, perhaps every day. You don't have to use words. I think kisses work very well."

He laughed with such a beautiful, full-bodied sound, her heart seemed to dance with it. And then he rolled so that now she was the one with her back on the mattress. She liked the feel of his weight upon her.

Balancing himself on his arms, he looked

down at her and said, "I will remind you *several times* every day. However, there is more than one way to pleasure. Would you trust me to show you?"

"But you told me you wanted me to heal?"

"This won't hurt," he promised. Then he kissed her lips, her chin, a line down her neck. He spent a good deal of time with her breasts. He nibbled the skin of her abdomen—his whiskers ticked—before he went lower. And then lower still. He kissed her intimately.

Dara was stunned. She forgot to breathe.

He was also right. There was more than one way to pleasure.

Nor was she afraid to return the favor.

Because she was just that bold.

DARA WAS THE first to wake the next morning.

She lay in the circle of Michael's arms and realized she'd never felt so well used and content. Turning in his arms, she faced him. He sensed her movement and started to wake. His long legs brushed hers, and then he hooked one over her hips. His eyes opened. She marveled at that black ring around the gray.

He brushed some loose strands of her hair back from her face. After all the energy they had expended the night before, she was amazed it wasn't a mass of knots. For once, her curls were behaving.

"Good morning," he said quietly.

She answered by kissing his nose. It was silly thing to do.

His hand cupped her face as he gave her a searching look. She waited, curious, and then he stretched, his toes going all the way to the end of the mattress. "I smell toast," he said. Her stomach growled as if agreeing. She brought an embarrassed hand to it, but he sat up.

"The landlady makes our meals. Teddy may be back, and he sets breakfast up in the sitting room. Here, I'll let you have a moment of privacy while I fetch warm water."

He rose from the bed, looked down, and shook his head over the piles of clothes and shoes there. With an amused glance in her direction, he said, "It was a good night."

"Very good," she echoed.

He made his way to the wardrobe and took out a dressing gown. Picking up the pitcher from the washstand, he left the room.

Dara sat, and realized that Michael's warning about needing to heal was a good one. She experienced uncomfortable tugs in muscles that she'd never known she had.

But she wouldn't have traded one moment of last night. Even the pain. Because what she had liked best was the knowledge that he'd *wanted* to marry her. This was a miracle that defied her belief. Except, she was beginning to allow herself to believe.

Her stomach protested again. She got up and started to see to her toilette.

Michael returned with hot water. He took some clothes from the wardrobe and told her she could have the room to herself.

"I will make space for you in the wardrobe," he said.

"You already have. I only have two dresses. Gwendolyn took my muslin one with her yesterday to see if it can be salvaged."

"Then we need to change that," Michael answered. "You should go shopping."

Dara considered that for a moment. "I am fine. My sisters and I are very good with a needle."

"You should go shopping," he repeated.

"You need to see to your mother and your brother," she answered, more direct this time. "You are being cut off. And while the Earl of Holsworthy can't stop you from receiving his title, he doesn't have to share his money."

Michael's expression turned so grim, Dara immediately wished to call the words back. "I didn't mean it as an insult. I'm accustomed to economy."

His grimness vanished into a smile. "I have money, Dara. Go shopping."

She nodded dutifully, uncertain if she would.

He shook his head. "I have the only wife in the

city who argues when I tell her to purchase a few dresses." With that, he left.

A half hour later, she made her way to the sitting room, having bathed and dressed for the day. She had loosely braided her hair and wrapped it around her head. She was wearing her sprigged day dress. He was right. She did need more dresses.

Michael was already enjoying his breakfast at the room's table. He had several papers and offered her one. He was shaved and ready for the day.

She took a seat across from him while Teddy asked if she would like cider, tea, or "perhaps something else?"

"Tea is perfect and just some toast."

"The announcement of our marriage is in *The Morning Post*," Michael said. "My secretary, Elliot, managed to change the betrothal notice."

"It is official then," Dara murmured.

Michael understood her dry comment. He grinned. "Ah, so the announcement is what makes the marriage official, right?"

She thought of the night before and her face burst into flames. Oh, yes, she was truly married. He laughed with delight.

"While I have you here, ma'am," Teddy said, "we should discuss growing our household. These rooms are barely large enough for you and Mr. Brogan. I don't know what will happen when there are at least two, maybe three added?"

"Two or three?" Dara repeated.

"We need room for Lady Eleanor and Gwendolyn," Michael said—and that is when Dara fell in love.

She'd been leaning in that direction. She'd always been attracted to him. She'd certainly *wanted* him. But *love*? She'd read novels where people who loved made declarations, very stilted ones to her way of thinking.

Nothing had been stilted about what she and Michael had shared last night.

She'd *loved* that. She was also humbled to her knees that he would offer to see to the care of her family.

But what she felt right now, over toast and tea, was that there wasn't another soul in this world she'd wish to share toast and tea with.

No one she admired more. Or *trusted*, another dangerous word.

What else could love be save this feeling that she'd found the person who made her feel as if she belonged with him?

Michael gave her a look, and she realized she was staring at him like some infatuated milkmaid, and that, too, must be love.

Right now, in this moment, he was the person who meant the most to her in the world. Perhaps even more than her sisters. The realization was both startling and liberating.

Of course, he hadn't said anything about loving her. He wanted her, which was very nice. But was *she* the only one he wished to share tea and toast with?

After all, Dara had studied London Society. Men had mistresses. Except, it would devastate her if Michael kept one. She wanted his lips and his body for her, and her alone.

A knock sounded on the door. Teddy crossed to open it. A lad was standing there, breathing heavily as if he'd run hard. "I'm here for Mr. Brogan."

"I'm he," Michael said, folding his paper and crossing the room.

"Mrs. Ferrell asked if you'd come. She said she found something you will want to see. They are burying her husband today, sir. However, she says she should be home by the evening. She says it is important."

"We'll be there," Michael answered, giving the lad a coin.

"We?" Dara questioned hopefully after the door was closed.

"Are you saying you aren't curious?"

"What time do you suggest we plan to leave?"

Chapter Nineteen

A wife may do what she wishes,
provided she is discreet.
The Rules (according to Dara)

At last, a sensible rule.
Tweedie's opinion

Wishing to be respectful of Mrs. Ferrell on the day she buried her husband, Dara knew she must wear black. That meant she needed to borrow Gwendolyn's dress.

Michael asked if she would like him to accompany her to Willow Street. If not, he had some business to see to.

"See to your business. It shouldn't take me very long."

"Don't walk there," he advised. "Teddy, go with her."

Dara shook her head. "The advantage to marriage is that I can go where I please."

Michael raised a hand to brush her cheek with

the back of his fingers, one corner of his mouth lifting. "The only advantage?"

Everything inside of her reacted to his touch, to being close enough to see the texture of his skin, his whiskers . . .

"There are other advantages." She sounded breathless and had a strong desire to drag him back into their bed.

Their bed.

His smile said he knew what she was thinking.

Teddy interrupted them. "I would be happy to escort you, ma'am," he said enthusiastically. "Then we can drive by a few of the houses I believe are suitable." He had used every opportunity this morning to expound on what sort of house he felt she and Michael should consider.

He would have gone on, except for Michael taking Dara's arm and directing her to the bedroom. "Oh, yes, sir. I see," he said, busying himself with the dishes.

"We shouldn't upset him," Dara whispered.

Michael's response was to close the door and kiss her so thoroughly she couldn't remember her name.

Dara leaned against him. They stood only steps from the bed. "We could—" she started to suggest.

He kissed her nose. "We can later, and you will feel better for it."

"I feel fine now."

His smile said he doubted her. "No pain? Not even a twinge?"

"A twinge," she had to admit.

In response, he pressed his lips against her forehead. "Later," he promised. "I'm willing to wait because I want the next time to be as pleasurable for you as it was for me last night."

"But I like some of the things we did. Very much."

"We will do them, too," he promised. He opened the door. "I should be back before the afternoon."

"Where are you going?"

"I have a meeting. An important one." He held up a hand. "No questions, Dara. The less you know, the safer you are," he reminded her.

"I'm not certain if I can live that way," she answered honestly.

"Only on this matter," he assured her, and she knew he referred to Mr. Ferrell's case.

Before she could ask more questions, he was out the door. She sank down on the bed. How quickly her life had changed. How happy she was it had.

Within the hour, she and Teddy set off in a hired conveyance for Willow Street and to look at the outside of a few of the houses he thought she should consider. "You have been thinking about this for a while," she said.

"Elliot and I believe Mr. Brogan should be entertaining. He has a growing reputation. A wife is a wise addition."

"Why, Teddy, how you go on," she teased.

"I'm not codding you," he said, reverting to a very Irish word that meant he wasn't teasing. "I've never seen him look so content."

Dara had to ask, because she wouldn't be who she was if she didn't pry a bit. "Do you know all that is going on?" She left the question open, because if Michael's man didn't know about the embezzlement—well, that meant she was in his inner circle.

"I don't, ma'am," he answered. Then with a glint in his eye, he asked, "Do you?"

She didn't hide her smile. "You are a good man, Teddy. Also, a good friend to my husband."

"I try to be, ma'am."

They turned onto Willow Street. All looked exactly as she had left it, and yet everything had changed.

When the driver stopped, Teddy helped her out. "Do you wish me to go in with you, ma'am?"

"Please stay with the driver." She went up to the door and then paused, struck by a new dilemma. Should she knock? Walk right in?

Fortunately, Herald solved the issue for her. He opened the door, greeting her warmly. "Mrs. Brogan, how fine you look." This was the first time someone had addressed her as a married lady.

"Good morning, Herald. You look fine, too. It is good to see you. Is everyone home?"

"They are—"

Before he could finish, she heard Gwendolyn's voice coming down the hall. *"Dara."* Her sister gave her a welcoming hug.

Tweedie followed. Her eyes were crinkled half-moons of delight. She kissed Dara's cheek. "Was it a *good* night?"

"It was," Dara confided happily.

"Come in," Gwendolyn said, urging her toward the sitting room. "How do you like married life?"

"It is wonderful," Dara confessed. "He's been thoughtful and caring, everything I could have imagined and more."

"Well, that is a lovely thing to hear," Elise's voice said.

Dara gave a start. She looked over Tweedie's head, and there was her loveliest sister. Elise stood down the hall, almost ten feet from them. Her back was straight, her chin lifted. There was no happiness in her eyes.

"Of course," Elise continued with the tone of an inquisitor, "*I* knew he was all those things. I knew it back when you were telling me to leave him be. You know, back when you were ordering us to speak only to dukes. Pot-bellied, sour-breathed, almost ancient dukes."

"Shush now, Elise," Tweedie said. She was using her walking stick today. She didn't like using it, but here she was, leaning on it. "This is no way to treat your sister."

"I'm all right," Dara demurred before forcing a smile and saying, "It is good to see you, Elise. Are you home again?"

Elise gave a cold, hard stare, and Gwendolyn stepped between them. "Let us all move to the sitting room instead of filling the hallway. Shall we?"

"*We* shall not," Elise answered. She shot Dara a bitter look. "Do you have something you should say to me?"

Dara studied her sister. The late-morning sun streaming in the hall window made her hair shine like the gold coins Michael had given Mrs. Ferrell.

"I know what you want me to say," she told Elise. "There was once a time—not that long ago—when, without prodding, I would have been offering apologies. I always wished peace between the two of us. I often gave in because then you were happy." Dara drew a deep breath, weighing what she was about to say. "But I can't do that now. Not over Michael. I've done nothing wrong."

Elise stiffened. "I claimed him."

"Michael is not a yard of ribbon we can argue over," Dara protested. "He has the right to decide his own mind."

That brought Elise charging forward. "And he was paying attention to me," she said. "Then you had to make a fool of yourself—"

"Elise," Gwendolyn warned. "We are done with this conversation."

"*She* is the one with all the rules," Elise argued. "She probably broke a half dozen of them stealing him from me. Certainly, *she broke my heart*."

Her argument was old; however, her last few words gutted Dara. She leaned back, thankful to have a wall behind her or else she might have fallen to the floor—

Tweedie pounded her walking stick on the floor several times. "Elise, your heart hurts, but it will heal. He was not the man for you. If he was, he would *not* have married Dara. You saw him yesterday. He did not appear as if he was being coerced. But don't you worry, lass. There will be a man for you. And when he finds you, nothing will deter him from claiming your love. Do you hear me? He'll want only you. I, for one, praise the Almighty that you haven't thrown yourself at one of those—" She paused, looked to Elise. "How did you say it? Pot-bellied, sour-breathed dukes. Each of you is finer than that."

"Dara is the one who wanted a duke," Elise muttered. She crossed her arms, almost as if she was trying to hold herself together.

"Life rarely gives us what we want, or expect," Tweedie said, quite pleased with herself. "Please come into the sitting room, Dara." Tweedie led the way in.

Instead of following, Elise stood her ground in the hall.

Gwendolyn touched Dara's back, a silent urge to ignore Elise's poor manners.

In the sitting room, Dara said to Gwendolyn, "May I borrow your mourning gown?"

"Of course. Do you wish the veil as well?"

Considering the funeral was this day and many in Mrs. Ferrell's house had been dressed for mourning yesterday, Dara nodded. "That would be nice. And may I borrow a needle and thread?" She didn't know if Michael had sewing things and she would need to tack up the hem.

"I'll fetch it for you." Gwendolyn started to leave.

"Thank you," Dara said. And then, because she was so rattled with Elise standing like a stone statue in the hall, she shared her other news, the news that would affect all of them. "Michael has asked if you would do us the honor of coming to live with us."

Gwendolyn stopped midstep. Even Tweedie acted surprised. Dara knew Elise overheard her.

"He's—*we* are going to move to a house," Dara continued. "There will be room for everyone, including Herald, Molly, and Cook. It would be lovely to have you all with us. Then we wouldn't have to continue to rent this house. That is good, isn't it?"

Gwendolyn gathered herself first. "That is a lovely offer."

"Absolutely, and generous," Tweedie said. "When would he do this?"

"He told Teddy to take me around to look at suitable homes. Teddy is his man—Michael's valet and, really, whatever he wishes to be."

"Thank you," Gwendolyn said, meaning the words. "We could only afford this house for maybe a month more and, to be honest, I wasn't ready to go back to Wicklow. I haven't had my fill of London yet."

"Nor have I," Tweedie agreed. "I'm having fun seeing my nieces make their mark in the world. Your father would be as pleased as punch to know his daughters were spinning Society on their fashionable ears."

There was one person who hadn't spoken. Elise's face had gone pale.

"Elise, please come live with us," Dara said. "Please." She took a step toward her. "I know losing him was a terrible blow. Still, you are my sister, and I love you."

There was a long moment of quiet, and then words burst out of Elise. *"I wish we'd never come to London."* She ran up the stairs.

Dara stared after her, her heart hurting for her sister, but she didn't chase her as she would have in the past.

"What should we do?" Gwendolyn asked Tweedie. "Elise is so angry."

"Let her be. Each of us must work out some matters for ourselves, especially when we are wrong."

"*Is* she wrong?" Dara had to ask. "Don't I bear a responsibility for the way she is feeling?"

Tweedie shook her head. "You know in your heart the answer to that. Whether you do or you don't, is she seeing reason?"

"But what if she holds this against me forever?" Dara wondered.

"Then she'll pay a very dear cost. No man should ever come between sisters. Your bond was formed at birth. She knows you didn't trick her. That's not your nature, Dara. Although I believe you've been surprised to realize how human you are. You now know that *you* are like the rest of us." Tweedie looked to Gwendolyn. "Fetch the dress."

Gwendolyn acted almost relieved to have something to do.

Dara walked over to her great-aunt. "Thank you."

"For what?"

"For understanding. Events seemed to have just swept me along."

Tweedie lowered herself to the settee, her hands resting on her walking stick. She appeared wise, an oracle. "Sometimes, life gives you a gift, and your best choice is to value it, not rationalize it. I've had three husbands, each a good man, and I have no idea how I fell in love with any of them. I just did. One day you are alone, and then the next, your life has expanded to include this other person—and it is a *good* thing. Because now your existence isn't about what someone can give you, but what you bring to them. And," she hastened to add, holding up a bony finger, "I'm not talking about a dowry or a title. Those things mean nothing compared to having someone who understands you. Someone who sees you as you really are, and accepts you nonetheless." Her smile turned bittersweet. "Live your life and let Elise find hers. Mr. Brogan has been yours from the beginning. If you can't see that, I pity you."

Dara leaned over and gave her aunt's cheek a kiss. "Thank you."

Tweedie waved her off. "If you truly want to thank me, you could convince Gwendolyn to restock the sherry. She has been economizing because she worries over the money. The two of you are very alike. However, your husband's offer arrived just in time."

A beat later, Gwendolyn came down the stairs with the black mourning gown and veil over her arm and the needle and thread. She stopped in the doorway and looked from Tweedie to Dara. "Did I miss something?"

"We've been waiting for you," Tweedie replied before adding innocently, "Dara, what is it you wanted to say to your sister?"

Gwendolyn laughed. "You don't have to tell me. I will send Herald out for sherry. I believe I could use some as well. Here's the dress."

With the dress over one arm, Dara gave them all hugs, including Herald, and left the house determined that she and Teddy would find the perfect home for her family. She wanted them close. All of them, including Elise, although she understood why her younger sister would not wish to live under the same roof as Michael and Dara.

If their roles had been reversed, Dara would have found the situation difficult as well.

However, perhaps, if Elise could unbend a bit from her hurt, then in time, she *would* find a love of her own. Then all would be forgiven . . . Dara hoped.

THE ROYAL ARMS was a public house located next to docks. It was not fashionable.

However, one could usually find Steele someplace close if he was in town. Or, at the least, send a message to him.

Fortunately for Michael, Steele was nursing an ale at a corner table. He appeared lost in thought.

But nothing got past Steele. When Michael approached the table, he looked up. "I've been expecting you."

"Sir Duncan is dead."

"I know." Steele traced a circle on the table in front of him with one finger. "As well as one Andrew Plummer. He's gone missing."

Michael was not surprised by the news. He had feared for Plummer's life.

"You also lost your man, didn't you? Ferrell was his name."

Michael sat at the table. "How did you know?"

Steele shrugged and picked up his drink. "The Runners. There was a report of a stabbing."

"And they offered that information to you?"

"Everyone offers me information," Steele remarked. He smiled, the expression curiously without conceit. He'd stated a fact. Nothing more; nothing less. "The watch gave them the name of a man who identified the body—Michael Brogan, MP."

Michael had given it to them, exactly like that.

"Now what?" Steele asked.

"We have lost."

Steele sat up. "What do you mean?"

"Ferrell had the proof, the knowledge. Without it, we have the suppositions of a dead man. We don't even have Sir Duncan to badger."

"I wanted to," Steele reminded him.

"My fault. I called you off. I insisted we do this

the right way. One that no judge could deny. We needed that, considering who set this scheme up."

Now he had Steele's interest. Leaning forward, Steele asked, "Do you know who our thief is?"

"I believe I do. Except I have no proof, and this one will need to be proven," Michael said. "Ferrell was the man who knew what was going on. He could trace the accounts and the monies stolen. Now we have nothing."

"And you are giving up?"

Michael thought of Holsworthy sitting in his private court at Brooks's, living off of money that had been marked for soldiers fighting Britain's wars. He was the worst villain the world had ever known. "I will find a way. In the meantime, here is a description of the man who killed Sir Duncan, and perhaps all the others." He gave Steele what he knew. "It isn't much."

"I don't always need much. I will share with my friends. Someone will know him." Steele sat back in his chair. "Who we really want is your person. If you have an inkling, share his name. There are ways of handling the matter beyond the courts."

That didn't sit well with Michael. "Not yet. I want to see this done right. We must in order to make a case so clear, no one ever attempts such thievery again."

"You are naive. Especially if you think you aren't a target like Ferrell. But don't worry, I'll keep my eye on your back," Steele muttered. He drained his tankard and held it up to show the serving girl he wished a refill. She ran over, smiling at him.

Michael shook his head. "You make people nervous."

"Do I?"

"Yes, everyone but the serving girls."

Steele gave him his almost feral grin. "They like me. Which reminds me, I hear congratulations are in order."

"Thank you."

"And now for the favor you owe me . . ."

Michael sat up. "I didn't think I was paying a favor. School lads, and or the sake of the country, and all that."

His companion grunted his response and then leaned forward. "My favor—don't let Gwendolyn Lanscarr leave London."

"Because she owes you a favor?"

He knocked on the table, a sign the guess was correct.

Michael shook his head as he came to his feet. "Steele, do you honestly believe I can tell a Lanscarr what to do?"

"You succeeded in corralling one. What is another?" Steele pushed a few coins across the table as his ale was delivered.

"Now that is a jest. Because, actually," and Michael almost took great pride in admitting this, "*she* has me, my friend." He thought about last night and about how fresh and lovely she'd been across the table from him at breakfast. "As to Gwendolyn, she is my sister-in-marriage. I will allow no harm to come to her."

"You wound me, Brogan." Steele touched his chest in a mocking gesture.

"Leave her be."

Steele pursed his lips for a minute as if taking Michael's measure. The man had the coldest eyes. Another reason to keep him away from Gwendolyn.

"We will see," Steele said at last.

Michael's response was to walk toward the door. The matter was closed as far as he was concerned. Steele called after him, "When you are ready to share the name, I will be right here."

Pausing by the door, Michael asked, "And expect another favor?"

"No, I just hate traitors."

On that they were agreed. Michael left.

IT WAS LATE in the afternoon when Dara returned with Teddy.

The ugliness of her confrontation with Elise had been balanced with a truly good time looking at the houses Teddy recommended. He had been considering this matter for some time and had done his research. They saw three houses that Teddy knew would soon be offered to let. All were in good neighborhoods and, according to the estate agents' notes, had enough room for their needs. The question was, which would Michael prefer?

Dara entered the apartment ready to discuss the matter with him. Teddy had some errands to run. He left her at the door. Michael's hat was on the table. He was here, but not in his office.

She untied her bonnet and removed her gloves, placing them beside his hat before moving toward the bedroom. The door was partially open. She pushed it, and there was Michael. He sat in a wooden chair by the open window. His expression was pensive, resigned.

Now was not the time to talk to him about properties. She understood that instinctively.

Dara moved into the room to lay the black dress over the wardrobe door. Michael appeared so lost in thought, he hadn't registered her presence, and she realized he was somewhat like her. She could be despondent when a plan didn't go the way she wished after she'd plotted, worried, and nurtured.

She crossed to him and knelt.

This caught his attention. He looked down at her. "I'm sorry. I was thinking."

"It is a bitter pill to lose Mr. Ferrell."

"He was everything to this case."

There was more here. She could feel it. "Is it me?"

"You? No, oh God no." He reached for her hands, raised them to his lips. "This isn't about you."

Then she understood. "You know more about the embezzlers than you wish to let on. Have they threatened you?" She didn't know what she'd do if he was in danger. She didn't want him to end up like Sir Duncan or Mr. Ferrell.

"Why do you suspect I know more?"

She'd perceived it, almost as if she could read his mind. What had Tweedie said? One day she'd been alone, and now there was *him*.

Her answer was to kiss him, her hand hooking around his neck and bringing him down to her. She savored the taste of him, and yet she also experienced sadness. At some point, truly without conscious consideration, she'd decided she must confess her feelings. She was too honest not to. She prayed the intensity of her emotions didn't upset him.

"Dara?"

She pressed her fingers against his lips. "I'm in love with you." There, she'd said it. "And don't feel you must return the feelings. I understand we are not a love match, and I do find you sometimes infuriating. You are also always interesting, undeniably handsome, and you are mine. For always. Whether you wish to be or not—" She was saying inane things and she couldn't stop until his lips on hers shut her up.

He enveloped her in his arms, easily pulling her up to him, and the kiss didn't stop until they were ready.

Then he looked down at her. "I'm glad I'm yours." Then he added, "I find you sometimes infuriating, always interesting, and undeniably beautiful—"

His use of her own words startled a laugh out of her. His claim that she was beautiful made her doubt him. "Michael—"

"Hush. Don't deny it, Dara. You will always be the most beautiful woman in the room to me. Perfectly beautiful in every way," he insisted, leaning to kiss her again. And then, right as his lips met hers, he whispered, "I'm madly in love with you. Out of all that has gone on, what we have is right."

He loves me.

Her—Dara, the middle sister, the one most overlooked. "Madly in love"—that's what he'd said. This remarkable man *loved* her.

His words sang through her. She reached for him. This time, their kiss was a pledge, a troth. He rose from the chair, lifting her with him. He carried her to the bed.

They undressed each other. They couldn't help themselves. He kissed her neck as he undid her laces. She lifted his shirt, breathing on his skin right where his chest met his collarbone. He found her breast, covered it with his hand, the palm against a tight nipple.

She pressed herself against the length of his manhood. "Please," she whispered. A need was building inside her, a need only he could release—

And then he stopped as if coming to his senses. "Dara, it is too soon."

Her answer was to stroke the long, thick shaft. He groaned. "Keep doing that."

Except she wanted more. She pushed him down on the bed and stretched out beside him. "It is frightening how quickly you have caught on to the way of things," he whispered. "Except, we shouldn't."

"Say it again. Say you love me."

"Oh, Dara, I adore you." She lightly circled the tip of his erection with one finger. "I can't imagine my life without you." She kissed his neck. "Dear God, I love you." Her hand tightened around his shaft and she fell back on the mattress, gently bringing him to her.

He rose up over her. "It might hurt."

"Nothing could hurt more than not having you inside me again," she answered, "because I love you."

He rested his full weight upon her. His hardness was exactly where she wanted it. She opened to him, receptive. Their lips met, and he slid into her like a key into a well-oiled lock. They fit together that well.

Furthermore, he'd been wrong. There was no pain or at least nothing that bothered her. And this time was better than the last—because he loved her.

UNFORTUNATELY, THE WORLD wouldn't let them stay in bed. They had promised to call on Mrs. Ferrell. Dara quickly tacked up the hem and donned the mourning gown.

There were still mourners present when they arrived. Dara wrapped the black veil around her as a shawl and scarf. As she and Michael stepped into the house, she was struck by how empty the front room seemed with Mr. Ferrell's body gone. His presence no longer dominated the house, and it felt empty.

Mrs. Ferrell came up to them. Her face showed the stress of the last few days. "I'm glad you came. Please, come with me." She informed one of the other women that she needed a moment alone with these visitors.

Dara and Michael followed her down a narrow hall and up the stairs. She led them to a bedroom with simple furnishings. The room she had shared with her husband.

She closed the door. "Last night, my sister and

I prepared Thomas for burial. I'd put it off. I was having a hard time seeing him the way he was. You know, the marks of his murder. However, it had to be done and I'd not let anyone else touch him. He was mine."

Dara could empathize with the woman. Tears stung her own eyes. She now understood what it meant to love someone so completely as to feel bonded to them even after death.

Mrs. Ferrell knelt on the floor and pulled up a board. It was a hiding spot.

"We found these papers on Thomas." There were three pages folded in half. She held them up to Michael. "He had them hidden in his jacket. He'd pulled a seam open in the lining to create a secret pocket. And then I remembered I'd caught him replacing this board one day and had sensed he was hiding something he hadn't wanted me to know about. We wives have a canny sense about these matters."

She reached down again and pulled out a thick packet of the same sort of paper. This, too, she offered to Michael. She replaced the floorboard.

He looked at what she'd given him, at the writing, the column of numbers, and then he said in amazement, "Oh, Ferrell, you brilliant man."

"What are they?" Dara asked.

"These are copies of the requisitions and ledger entries Ferrell had been tracking." He helped Mrs. Ferrell up. "It is all here. He laboriously copied the documents we needed and put explanations for how these accounts were compromised."

"Will this help you catch whoever did this to my husband? Will it give me justice?"

"Most certainly," Michael promised.

Chapter Twenty

While wives should try to be obedient,
their husbands should treat them as
their dearest friends.

The Rules (according to Dara)

An obedient wife is a dull one.

Tweedie's belief

I agree with you.

Michael's response

Michael found Holsworthy at his usual post, the side room at Brooks's. The hour was eleven in the morning. The club was not busy other than a few tables in the Subscription Room.

At Michael's entrance, his great-uncle scowled, an expression that gave him the appearance of a dissatisfied toad. His gouty foot was again propped on a stool. His jacket coat was open and his wig slightly askew. He held a full glass of port.

"Have you come crawling to beg my forgiveness?" he asked Michael. "You won't receive it. I told you not to marry the Lanscarr chit. You did it. You have cast your own fate."

"You don't look well, my lord," Michael replied in greeting.

"I'm healthy enough, *and* I should tell you that I no longer consider myself your uncle. You are *no* kin to me. Now turn yourself around and go." He circled a finger in the air to demonstrate his instruction—except the circle was more like a zigzag.

Michael took the chair opposite his. "No one has ever credited me for being obedient."

"The bankers have been instructed to cut you off. Your family will not have one shilling of my *wealth.*"

"My family doesn't want a shilling from you. However, there is something we should discuss."

"I have nothing to say to you. If I could withhold the title from you, I would. I tried. There is no way around it."

"It isn't that good a title," Michael pointed out pleasantly.

Holsworthy reacted as if he had slapped him. "I should call you out."

"Possibly," Michael agreed, "but if you do, let's make it for something important." He leaned forward. "Ferrell left notes."

His great-uncle was practiced in the art of deception, or else he was well into his port. His face didn't even show a flicker of interest. "Ferrell?"

"Come, my lord. You and I have discussed him. You brought his name up the last time we spoke."

Holsworthy shrugged. "I may have. I don't have any recollection. Now, begone. I don't want you here. I'll have them toss you out like a commoner."

"Back in your salad days, before you came into the title, as a young lawyer, you served in the office of the Chancellor of the Exchequer. You were in charge of Accounts and Audits—"

"Rogers," Holsworthy called for the servant who usually waited upon him. "I need you to remove this *scoundrel."*

"He's not coming," Michael said.

"Why? What did you do to him?"

"Rogers understood I needed a moment alone with you."

"So you can talk about my past?"

"Exactly. You were there when you came into the title and discovered it an empty one with no land, no money." This was family lore. Michael had never questioned it until now.

"And I built it into what it is today." He took a gulp of his port. "Good investments."

"You have always been ambitious, my lord."

"I didn't waste myself on a woman with no dowry or connections."

"It is unfortunate your son died. A true tragedy."

The corners of Holsworthy's mouth turned down as if the memory saddened him. But then he straightened. Lifted his chin. "Life is what it is. However, there are few as rich as I am. Riches you will never see."

"You are quite right about that, because I don't want them."

"Ha!"

"You see, Ferrell put together a trail of requisitions that go to accounts connected to you from years ago. The government saves everything."

"What are you going on about?" Holsworthy gripped his half-full glass as if it were a shield in front of him.

"Ferrell studied the history. He was a very good accountant. He actually found some of the original requisitions, but they didn't match the vouchers. These were so long ago, you personally signed for them, something you managed to avoid later. However, your connection to these fraudulent claims isn't hard to prove."

Holsworthy puffed up. "Are you calling me a thief?"

"Yes. You have been stealing from the military accounts for decades. Few have questioned your actions. After all, military disbursements are numerous and ofttimes quite large. You would only take a hundred here, fifty there, or a thousand. However, over time, the amount has added up."

"And what did I do with all this money I *supposedly* took?"

"You invested it. As you said, you are good with investments, and you became the wealthy man you are today. You even handpicked Andrew Plummer to fill your position when you left and used Sir Duncan as an accomplice. I don't understand why. Sir Duncan was not very bright. However, the two of you had once been in that same office. Was he on to you?"

"This is *preposterous*. Complete conjecture. *Rogers, come here.*"

Rogers didn't come running.

"Ferrell was so resourceful," Michael continued, "he even ferreted out some of the different investments you made. He compared the investment with the amount of money that had been falsely requisitioned. Now, I agree that is conjecture, but very damning, don't you think?"

Holsworthy leaned forward, so angry spittle shot from his mouth. *"You can't come here and say these things to me.* I will not be slandered by the likes of you. 'A person's name ought to be more precious to him than his life.' Eh? You consider yourself a skilled lawyer, and you come in here with this swill? Don't expect any mercy from me. 'Tis a pity your accountant isn't alive, because I'd gladly see him in court, too. *Ro-gerrrrs.*"

Michael waited for the echo of his uncle to fade before he said, "I never said Ferrell was dead."

Holsworthy had been busy glaring around the room as if Rogers was hiding behind a chair or a table. At Michael's calm words, he snapped his head around. "I didn't say he was dead."

"You said it was a pity he wasn't alive. I'm, as you say, a skilled lawyer. We are devilish on details. Also, we have the man who killed Ferrell. And Sir Duncan. We don't know where Ferrell's supervisor is. Or if he is alive. He might have wisely up and vanished, leaving behind a confused wife. If that is the case, Steele will find him."

"Steele?"

"Beckett Steele. He's the one who found Jedidiah Watkins, the murderer. I had told Steele I didn't think it possible to trace the actual killer, but he likes a challenge. You've heard of Steele, haven't you?"

Holsworthy wasn't looking so certain now. "I don't know him," he answered.

"He is an enigma. No one claims to know him, and yet everyone does. He manages to accomplish whatever he sets his mind on and he set his mind on you."

"How does he know me?"

"He and I are friends. I find Steele an odd character, albeit a persuasive one. Watkins has confessed to him in return for transport instead of a noose. He told Steele, and presumably the magistrate, that your man Charles contacted him."

"Charles would never give out my name. This blighter is making false accusations."

"Actually, Watkins followed Charles to your home early on in your association. Apparently he didn't trust someone who would hire him to kill not one but three men. Sir Duncan, Ferrell—and myself."

Michael leaned forward. "You can imagine how surprised, and actually honored, I was that I had made a list of your enemies. Although I am thankful you only recently included me on the list of tasks for Watkins."

The glass fell from Holsworthy's hand, splashing port onto his breeches. He didn't move.

"The most damning evidence of your connection," Michael said, "was that you sent a message to Sir Duncan to meet Watkins in Lord Reeve's garden the other night. Now, that was careless. The note was found on Sir Duncan's body. He hadn't obeyed instructions to burn it. Sir Duncan's servant recognized the messenger as your man Charles. If you are starting to wonder where Charles is, I assure you, he is with Steele."

Instead of acting panicked, Holsworthy pulled his gouty leg off the stool so that he sat up straighter. With the arrogance of the very wealthy, he calmly said, "Well, this is a conundrum. No matter what I've done, your accusations will come to naught."

His comment surprised Michael. "Why do you say that?"

"Because if you bring all this information before the magistrate, you will be destroying yourself. Your actions will taint the title. You don't want to do that. You've just married. You'll have children, a son. You will want him to be proud of the name Holsworthy."

"I would rather he knew that when justice had to be served, his father didn't flinch."

At that moment, several Runners and Sir Percy Dingby, the local magistrate, came out from behind closed doors on the opposite side of the room. Michael had decided Ferrell's papers had given him more than enough proof of Holsworthy's involvement that he hadn't bothered with Gammon and the War Office. He'd gone straight to Sir Percy, who had agreed with him.

The magistrate spoke. "The time for worrying about your reputation is past, my lord. You bring dishonor to your name all by yourself."

"What are you doing here?" Holsworthy asked.

"Listening. I had to hear your responses with my own ears," Sir Percy answered before saying to the Runners, "Take him."

The two Runners moved forward, helping a sputtering Holsworthy from his chair. His wig fell off his head; however, the Runners had him by each arm. He couldn't reclaim it. Instead, he protested, "You can't take me away. I'm no common criminal. I shall wait in my home."

"You shall wait wherever I put you, Lord Holsworthy," Sir Percy answered. "Treason is a serious matter, and there isn't a lord in the realm who can't be tried for it."

His answer appeared to shock Holsworthy, and just like that, he was escorted, bald-pated, from the room. Sir Percy looked to Michael. "Excellent work, sir."

"Don't let him wiggle out of anything."

"I won't," Sir Percy promised. As Michael went to leave, Sir Percy stopped him. "You spoke about Steele."

Michael paused.

"Does anyone know anything about him?" Sir Percy asked. "He shows up in the most damning places. More than once, I've received instructions from higher up to do as he asked."

Michael wasn't going to give away their school connection. Besides, Steele enjoyed being mysterious. "I know nothing—other than he seems to appear whenever someone has done what they shouldn't, and he always exacts a price."

Sir Percy nodded. "The Runners talk about him as if he has supernatural powers."

"He might," Michael agreed. It was possible.

On those words, Michael took his leave and

he didn't stop until he walked out of Brooks's—and there, across the busy street, standing by the hired carriage that had brought them, was his wife.

She wore her straw bonnet, the one she'd left at Lord Reeve's. His lordship had had a servant deliver it. Her dress was the yellow one she'd worn to their wedding.

Michael wanted to fill her wardrobe full of dresses, each of that same creamy yellow.

Most of all, he wanted to be in her arms.

He crossed the road.

Dara smiled, and all the ugliness of Holsworthy vanished. A man could bask forever in such a smile.

"Is it over?" she asked. "I saw them lead him away."

"He'll be the talk of Brooks's for generations to come." And then he leaned down and kissed her, right there on the street where anyone could see them—and he hoped they did. After all, they were newly married . . . His desire for her would never dim.

He loved his wife.

"Shall we go home?" she asked, slightly breathless when he was finished. She leaned closer to whisper, "I have something to show you in the bedroom."

Her manner was so coy, he laughed and helped

her into the carriage—blessed to have such a willful, bold, and adorable wife.

And once home, he couldn't remember ever having spent a more engaging and delightful afternoon.

After all, knowing what she wanted, and asking for it, was Dara's charm.

And so . . .

July 1817, The Road to Liverpool

Rain wracked the mail coach, slapping against it, making it hard for the horses to pull. That didn't stop the driver from pushing them.

His driving was madness as far as Elise was concerned. The angry weather had turned the road to mud, causing the coach to weave back and forth. The fast-approaching darkness didn't help.

Elise wasn't the only one worried about the driver. At the last coaching inn, most of the travelers had disembarked and had not returned in time to leave. Apparently, they thought their lives were worth more than reaching Liverpool.

Not Elise. She was going home. She was running away to County Wicklow, where everything made sense. She couldn't put enough miles between herself and London.

She knew that her disappearance would upset her sisters and Aunt Tweedie. When Elise had slipped the money for her trip from the carved wood box where Gwendolyn kept the family funds, she had left a note. She'd promised she would pay the money back—some way. She wasn't certain how yet. She'd also asked them not to worry. She would be fine . . . she hoped.

What she didn't tell them were her plans. And, no, she hadn't formulated a complete strategy for her future beyond going home. She just knew she must leave London before they expected her to swallow her pride and live under her sister Dara and her husband Michael's roof. One huge happy family.

Except they weren't.

Elise loved Michael. She had from the moment she'd laid eyes on him. Out of *all* the gentlemen in London, of *all* the gentlemen in Wicklow, she'd wanted *him*. And no gentleman of her acquaintance had ever favored Dara over her.

Having him offer for Dara and, worse, act as happy as he was with her, crushed Elise.

Nor could Elise live under their roof and pretend her heart wasn't broken. She also didn't like feeling so mean and spiteful. The only solution was to return to where she had once felt as if she belonged, a place where she would never run into Michael—Wicklow. Of course, this also meant she would be living with her miserly cousin Richard and his wife, Caroline, but so be it.

A clap of thunder startled the horses. The

coach swerved, almost sending Elise tumbling over to the opposite side of the coach and against the body of the only other passenger.

Originally, he had been one of those sitting in the cheapest seats, those on the roof, which must have been a miserable experience, especially with the way the coach had been swaying *before* the storm. His clothes were soaked through. The smell of wet wool burned her nose.

When the other passengers hadn't returned, he had climbed into the coach and hunkered down in one corner. He was a big man in dark clothing. A proper Ruffian. And he reminded Elise why women were cautioned against traveling alone. Her sister Dara must have a dozen rules on just this topic, and Elise had broken all of them. Unfortunately, one couldn't run away with a chaperone in tow.

Besides, Elise hadn't been worried in the beginning of her trip. She wore a shawl over her bonnet to hide her hair and a cloak to disguise her body. She hadn't bothered with a valise but wore several dresses, one on top of the other under the cloak and two shawls. The bulk made her appear quite plump and that was good.

She'd also been surrounded by people. Before they'd all run for the coaching inn, there had been a rector and his wife, a governess, and several businessmen. She'd felt perfectly safe.

Now she hoped she was showing some sense

by sitting as far away from the Ruffian as possible. She also had a small knife tucked in her walking shoe. She'd use it if necessary.

To be honest, he hadn't bothered her. He'd stayed in his corner, his collar up, his hat pulled down. He appeared to be sleeping. His legs took up more space than they should, but there was no one else but the two of them—

The coach hit a bump, and Elise flew up off the seat like some rag doll. She would have landed on the floor—except the Ruffian reached out a gloved hand—a very wet one—and caught her arm. He helped settle her to the seat before he released his hold. He'd barely even looked at her.

"Thank you," she murmured, her words drowned out by the fierce storm and the fiercer-sounding curses the driver hurled at the horses.

The man didn't answer.

She wasn't accustomed to men ignoring her. Granted, she was a bit of a fright in her rumpled clothes. She also hid her looks under a battered straw bonnet that was not managing the trip well.

Between Michael choosing her sister and then this silent passenger ignoring her, Elise was beginning to feel a bit depressed. Perhaps no one paid attention to her because the cloak she had purloined from Tweedie covered her figure? That is what she'd intended for the cloak to do, but still—most men were a little curious about her.

Or maybe, she was just not attractive to anyone anymore. That thought drove her to huddle miserably on her own side of the coach.

The rain lessened, but that didn't make the travel smoother. She didn't care. What did it matter where she went or what happened to her . . . ?

A cracking sound was the only warning they had. The coach lurched to one side, then heeled over as if a wheel had come off.

Elise was rolled across the seat, right against the Ruffian. Once again, his strong arms saved her, but this time he didn't let go, even as the coach hit the ground.

Wood splintered all around her. Horses screamed. The driver and guard shouted their swears.

Rain beat in. The coach was dragged through the mud on its side, and then—silence . . . save for what sounded like the horses running off into the night.

Paradoxically, one of the coach lamps still burned.

Her heart was in her throat, her pulse racing madly. Elise waited to feel pain. After such a frightening accident, she must have broken something. Why, she should probably be dead. She wiggled the toes of one foot experimentally, then the other. All good. Even her fingers moved.

The Ruffian had protected her fall, but he had paid the price. He was still, deadly still. A nasty cut marred his forehead.

Elise slid off his body. Her skirts were tangled with the cloak, making movement difficult. Her straw bonnet was destroyed but still tied to her head. She pushed it and the hood back from her face and moved gingerly to avoid the splintered wood.

"Are you all right?" she asked her rough companion. "Sir?"

He didn't answer.

"Let me fetch the driver," she said as if he had. She didn't want to be here with a dead man.

The door for her side of the coach was over her head. She reached up and turned the handle. Then, bracing her weight with her arms, she lifted her body out of the coach. The rain made every movement more challenging than it should have been. She sat on the edge of the door, close to the coach lamp.

Almost as if offering an apology, the rain slowed and then stopped as she surveyed the scene.

The road was lined with the dark shadows of trees. There was no movement. Or sound.

Her suspicion that the pole attaching the horses to the coach had broken appeared correct. The horses had indeed run off. She saw no sign of them and assumed they still wore harnesses. Poor beasts. She prayed they didn't become tripped up in them.

She did not see the driver or guard. "Driver?

Sir? Can you help us?" She waited for an answer. The wet air deadened sound. "We need help."

In the darkness, just beyond the circle of coach light, she saw a pair of boots attached to legs bent at an unusual angle. This was not good.

From her perch, Elise looked over the other side of the coach and saw the guard. He was on the ground, his eyes open in death.

And her first thought was—the rules were right about women traveling alone. Bad things did happen.

At that moment, a hand from the inside of the coach grabbed her ankle, and Elise knew she wasn't alone—the Ruffian was alive.